A WALKING SHADOW

A WALKING SHADOW

CATHERINE MOLONEY

ROBERT HALE

First published in 2018 by Robert Hale, an imprint
of The Crowood Press Ltd, Ramsbury, Marlborough
Wiltshire SN8 2HR

www.crowood.com

British Library Cataloguing-in-Publication Data
A catalogue record for this book is available from the
British Library.

ISBN 978 0 7198 2742 6

Typeset by Jean Cussons Typesetting, Diss, Norfolk

Printed and bound in India by Replika Press Pvt Ltd

Contents

Prologue

Bromgrove Municipal Cemetery on the eve of the millennium. An appropriately miserable day for a teenager's funeral. Cold, sodden and overcast. The dregs of winter, with dripping boughs scoring the sky like snapped guitar strings.

Though not a fanciful man, it seemed to Detective Inspector Mike Bamber that the blackened walls of the little disused cemetery chapel on the south side – long abandoned in favour of the modern facilities on Bromgrove Avenue – bulged dropsically in the gloom as though from the accumulated damp of centuries.

God, it was a dismal scene, with all those dark stone slabs glistening wetly and weathered headstones pressing in like a ghostly army.

The sonorous words from the burial service echoed in his head.

Sown in corruption... Man born of woman cometh up and is cut down like a flower.

He swallowed hard as he thought of that picture on the coffin – the happy, laughing boy flushed with pride at a sporting triumph – and remembered the pitiful skeleton they had dragged from the slurry.

They might bury the poor lad facing the east, Bamber said to himself, but he hadn't really had a shot of life at all and his parents would never see the sun shining on their son's bright golden head again.

He took a long drag on his cigarette, looking across at the grave, denuded of its sheets of fake grass, a mound of sludgy earth waiting to be shovelled on top. It would be six months before it had a headstone. What would the grieving parents inscribe on it? *Jonathan 'Jonny' Warr. Treasured memories...*

Now that everyone had left, the gravediggers too were seizing the chance to have a crafty fag. Nobody bothered him.

Three boys gone missing together in the summer of 1997. Now they'd got one of them back, albeit in a coffin.

Bamber shivered. He had a bad feeling about this case. The trail had gone cold long ago. Three ordinary lads. There one day and gone the next. As if a black hole had opened and sucked them in. A hole like the one where Jonny Warr lay mouldering.

No good getting morbid. He'd be no use to the families like that. The ravaged face of Jonny's mother was seared on his retina. The fancy send-off – all the great and good of Bromgrove out in force – wouldn't comfort her when the night horrors struck.

He took another fierce drag, wondering if the boy's parents would stay together, whether their marriage could survive the spotlight that would be shone into every corner of it. Something about the way that they had looked at the graveside – as if they were seeing each other from a long way off – made him doubt it.

It was getting colder. Bamber flicked his cigarette butt away and hunched his shoulders inside the heavy trench coat. Ducking his head to the grave in an embarrassed little gesture of respect, he began trudging towards the cemetery's main entrance off Bromgrove High Street.

The cusp of a new century, yet everything around him seemed shrunken, hard and dry, without hope.

That's my job, he chided himself. *To bring hope where there is none.*

Passing through the gates, he turned towards the lights and hum of the town.

1

The Summons

Twenty years later. Another cemetery.

Mrs Georgina Hamilton, pillar of St Mary's Cathedral, eased herself stiffly upright to contemplate the fruits of her labours. *Much* better! No more straggly weeds, and the tasteful cellophaned bouquet struck just the right note. Nobody would be able to accuse Geoffrey Hamilton's widow of failing to show appropriate respect. She ran a critical eye along the line of graves in the south-eastern corner of the cathedral graveyard. Yes – it was far and away the best tended plot, she reflected smugly, slipping the miniature trowel into her coat pocket.

Complacently, she cast a proprietorial eye around her. To her left, dominating the graveyard, rose the great cathedral. Just beyond that, on the other side of a low wall, was St Mary's Choir School, its outlines dimly visible through the gathering twilight. The proximity of the celebrated St Mary's Grottoes, that ancient religious shrine which lay behind the school, made these precincts doubly blessed.

Somehow, she had lost track of time and it was nearly dark. Shivering in the December twilight, she was uncomfortably conscious of the silence which lapped the precincts of the cathedral. Mist was coming down, wreathing the ancient memorials in clammy vapours. She peered apprehensively through the gloom. For all her sturdy unimaginativeness, she had an uneasy sense that the *memento mori* and gargoyles were leering at her in the knowledge of some private joke.

With a shake of her head, as though to dispel the fog from

her mind, Georgina squared her shoulders and, clutching her capacious handbag like a shield, picked her way along the muddy gravel path between the rows of graves, resolutely ignoring the pale obelisks which beckoned with spectral fingers and the ranks of crooked headstones coated in slippery moss.

There was no avoiding the squat, lichen-stained mausoleum which brooded at the side of the path, affording the nearest exit from the graveyard. In normal circumstances Georgina felt an almost proprietorial pride in the proximity of the Soames Vault – as though the mouldering relicts of Bromgrove's first family shed a ghostly lustre on those who slept near them. On this occasion, however, as she looked up at the tomb's rusting iron railings guarded by two angels, curved wings swooping high above their disdainful marble heads, she felt an urge to run. Don't be ridiculous, she told herself. Long-forgotten lines from some school play came unbidden to her mind. *The sleeping and the dead are but as pictures. It is the eye of childhood that fears a painted devil.* Quite right too!

At that moment, she heard a harsh scraping noise coming from the rear of the mausoleum. Scarcely daring to breathe and somewhat amazed at her own daring, she tip-toed round the side of the monument to ascertain the source of the disturbance.

Blinking myopically through the murk, a strange sight met her eyes. An odd time to be digging graves was her first thought. Two men, their backs to her, were standing in a trench shovelling vigorously by the light of a heavy-duty lantern. Grunting and panting from their exertions, they were oblivious to everything but the task at hand. A couple of mud-stained headstones and some cracked granite plaques leaned drunkenly against a wheelbarrow piled high with earth.

She vaguely recalled Geoffrey saying something about 'sensitive' operations occasionally needing to be carried out at night-time. As verger and local councillor, he was in a position to know. It had been tacitly understood, however, that subjects such as burial law and policy were not suitable to be aired around the tea table. With the cathedral graves being Church of England property, Geoffrey would no doubt have liaised with the archdeacon in the event of any irregular activity in the cathedral environs...

With a sharp pang, Georgina wished she had taken more of an interest in her husband's municipal responsibilities. Perhaps he would have liked it. Perhaps it was only her own hidebound obsession with gentility that had kept her from being a true helpmeet. And now it was too late...

She was jerked back to the present by a low growl. The taller man was berating his fellow labourer.

'Get a move on, won't you! What's the matter? They can't hurt you. They can't hurt anyone.'

The other merely spat on the ground and bent to his work once more.

Even though these words merely echoed her self-admonition of a few seconds earlier, a creeping sense of unease descended on Georgina. Watching the two men in the eerie half-light – presumably cathedral labourers (yes, that looked like the logo of a local contractor on their overalls) – she felt an overpowering urge to get far away from the cemetery and its ghoulish secrets.

Shuddering and slick with perspiration, she caught her breath before inching her way back around the mausoleum. There was nothing for it but to take the long way around. She could hardly interrupt the grave reclamation – or whatever it was – going on at the back of the Soames Vault. It would be almost like gate-crashing a funeral, she told herself firmly. She willed her heart to stop its unnatural pounding before retracing her steps.

Like a sleep-walker, Georgina Hamilton slowly made a circuit of the graveyard and left by the main gates. Once safely clear, she felt herself begin to revive. It would do no harm, she thought, to drop by the town hall on Bromgrove Avenue tomorrow. Just to reassure herself. The police station was round the corner in Bromgrove Drive, so she would call there after her visit to the council offices. Obscurely she felt she owed it to Geoffrey to see that everything was as it should be. That comforting resolution made, she wended her way home.

The following morning, DS George Noakes, lurking hopefully in the back office behind the desk sergeant's counter at Bromgrove Police Station with a view to picking up stray gossip, listened with half an ear as a distinctly bored constable endeavoured to fend off an importunate visitor. God, that dreadfully insistent voice was giving him a headache.

'St Mary's … husband sub-treasurer … council … graveyard … irregular activities … desecration … duty to investigate…' On and on it went. *Put a sock in it, luv,* he thought.

Eventually the woman, whoever she was, ran out of steam and he could hear her storm off, presumably in a cloud of self-righteous indignation. Noakes sauntered out and grinned at the young officer who was staring at the visitor's departing form with no very benign expression.

'What was all that about?'

'Your guess is as good as mine, Noakesy. Old biddy, name of Hamilton. Seemed to think folk have been up to no good at St Mary's. Saw something peculiar when she visited her husband's grave apparently.'

'Fancies herself Miss Marple, does she?'

'Sounded like it. Probably been at the sherry too.'

Noakes was thoughtful. 'Best get it checked out, son. Dot the Is and cross the Ts. The DI's a man on a mission when it comes to detail. It's all "back to basics" now. No detail too unimportant, if you get my drift.'

The other grimaced. 'Wilco, mate.'

Noakes riffled through his mental rolodex. Hmmm. St Mary's Cathedral. With choir school attached. All perfectly respectable to the best of his recollection. Quite ordinary for a cathedral he'd thought, though the chairwoman of the Police Liaison Committee was always wittering on about it being 'the jewel in Bromgrove's crown'. Still, might be worth doing a quick recce. Call it a field trip. And if he just happened to take in the Bromgrove Arms on his travels, that was surely all to the good. Publicans, in Noakes's humble opinion, were the force's secret weapon!

Standing at the window of his top floor office in Bromgrove Police Station, Detective Inspector Gilbert Markham watched Noakes's furtive departure with resigned amusement. What was the old devil up to now? His sergeant was hardly an advertisement for cutting edge policing, dressed as he was in an old-fashioned two-piece suit of indeterminate age and colour, his shirt adorned with a tie that appeared to be knotted somewhere under his left ear, and the whole ensemble topped off with a shabby beige mac. Bromgrove's answer to Columbo. Whatever the nature of his mission, Markham was willing to bet it involved a pit stop at some hostelry or other. All in the interest of community relations!

But Noakes's role as his wingman was non-negotiable. No amount of pressure from the gold braid mob would induce him to part with the stolid and plain-spoken veteran who always 'had his back'. Whenever evil stalked his dreams, it was invariably to George Noakes that he turned. As though, by some unfathomable scientific principle, there was something in Noakes's blessedly normal pH which neutralized the demon and forced the genie back into the bottle.

Superintendent Collier was bemused by the nature of their bond. 'For God's sake, Markham,' he had barked in his usual aggressive semaphore, 'the man's a throwback. A complete bloody neanderthal. Professional Standards has a file an inch thick. Beats me why he wasn't booted out long ago.'

But Markham knew better. He had a high regard for Noakes's native guile and wisdom, and a sneaking sympathy with the DS's notorious disregard for the fashionable tenets of political correctness. Oddly enough, Markham's teacher girlfriend Olivia Mullen had taken to Noakes in a big way despite the fact he clearly regarded her as some sort of seductress who had ensnared Markham by means of sexually suspect, if not necromantic, practices. 'He's a great big teddy bear,' Olivia had laughed when Markham apologized for his DS's latest gaffe. 'Doesn't know what to make of arty-farty leftie types like me. I bet that wife of his, the redoubtable Muriel, crosses her fingers whenever she claps eyes on me. Isn't that how you're supposed to ward off witches!'

Olivia.

Perhaps it wasn't so surprising that Noakes persisted in regarding Olivia as some sort of *belle dame sans merci*. She had certainly cast a spell over Markham despite being, at thirty-seven, five years his senior.

He recalled the moment he had caught sight of her from the window of his third floor flat in The Sweepstakes – a complex of upmarket apartments and townhouses at the end of Bromgrove Park, off Bromgrove Avenue – as she moved into one of the ground floor studios in the block opposite his own on a windy Saturday afternoon in November.

To be more accurate, Markham had *heard* Olivia before he saw her, a full-throated, joyous peal of laughter breaking through his frowning perusal of local authority crime statistics and drawing him across to the French window.

At first all he could see was that she was tall, with a mass of unruly copper hair whipping across her face. A girlfriend was with her, helping to empty the contents of what looked to be a hired van. The boxes of books which gradually covered the pavement, and which appeared to constitute the bulk of his new neighbour's possessions, were greeted like old friends, the two women pulling out volumes at random and exclaiming happily over each new discovery.

All rather touching and unworldly, reflected Markham. He wondered idly what line of work they were in. Certainly didn't look the corporate executive type. The shorter woman was wearing some sort of floaty ethnic get-up topped by a *Doctor Who* style scarf, while her willowy companion sported a voluminous sloppy joe jumper and leggings.

Social workers, perhaps. Or no, more like teachers, he

decided, spotting a couple of sturdy laundry bags piled high with exercise books.

At that moment, as though she sensed Markham's scrutiny, the tall woman looked up and met his gaze head on.

He caught his breath.

It was an instant attraction, the most perturbing that he had ever experienced. Not reducible simply to the stranger's pre-Raphaelite allure – flame-red hair, graceful physique and ethereal colouring, it resided in something else ... an immediate sense of psychic affinity. As though the remarkable grey-green eyes had seen beyond his iceberg cold exterior to the passionate man beneath.

Not at all put out by being spied on, the new arrival smiled. A look of mischievous amusement as if they were partners in a shared complicity. To Markham, it felt like the sun had suddenly come out. And then, with a rueful quirk of her lips, she was gone.

Discreet enquiries established that she was a supply teacher at a local comprehensive school, a job she apparently combined with freelance writing. Longing, but at the same time fearing, to meet the woman who had affected him so deeply, he finally encountered her at The Sweepstakes monthly residents' meeting.

Markham's colleagues would have been amazed to see how their legendarily chilly boss unbent to the newcomer, with her teasing irreverence and gentle, unaffected charm. His habitual proud reserve melted, all barriers were swept away, and the social part of the evening flew by on wings, the two of them trading anecdotes about their daily skirmishes with officialdom. By the time they parted, he was surprised by the strength of his desire to see her again.

That was the start of it.

As time went by, the cord of communion between them became stronger. Quick-witted and with an endearingly roguish sense of humour, there was an innocence about Olivia's underlying character which had somehow survived unscathed through all the sordid politics, back-stabbing and petty treacheries of school life. When he was with her, Markham felt himself to be sustained by an endless spring of solace and refreshment. Apart from her, he was like a man dying of thirst. When it came to the grim realities of his job, she never pushed or probed, just listened with a grave-eyed earnestness and generous sympathy that was all her own.

She loved me for the dangers I had passed, And I loved her that she did pity them.

One summer evening, around eight months after their first meeting, as they strolled in Bromgrove Woods, drinking in the beauty of bosky, sun-dappled coppices, Markham asked Olivia to move in with him. With the open-hearted tenderness, lack of self-regard and entire absence of affectation which set her apart from other women, her complexion glowing with exercise and happiness, she agreed without hesitation.

Since then, their mutual affection and regard had only deepened.

Markham knew that Olivia had been badly hurt by men. With characteristic frankness and child-like candour, she withheld nothing, gamely laughing as she described the shattering of her romantic ideals. And yet, he frequently reflected, there was something oddly chaste about her. Like those classical goddesses he remembered from rainy days in art galleries as a child.

He did not lift the veil on his own past, waiting for her to ask about the emotional scars that he so clearly bore. Every other woman he had ever known tried to poke around in his psyche, but not Olivia. She remained silent, confident that he would admit her to that inner sanctum when the time was ripe, letting their dialogue develop at its own pace. For that he loved her even more.

Every morning as he looked down at Olivia lying next to him, her auburn tresses spilling across the pillows as though she was floating underwater, Markham was surprised anew by a fierce rush of protectiveness. He feared for her even as he loved her, and the fear intensified the love. Currently working at Hope Academy (popularly known as 'Hopeless'),

Olivia insisted that she relished the challenges posed by a gritty comprehensive, but Markham sensed she was ready for a change and suspected that she missed being part of a regular school community.

His thoughts turned to their conversation over dinner the previous evening when Olivia told him she had been contacted by an old friend, Cynthia Gibson, who currently taught at St Mary's Choir School.

'That beautiful house next to the cathedral?' Markham vaguely recalled a crocodile of startlingly shiny and well-scrubbed boys glimpsed goose-stepping purposefully across a forecourt towards a gracious building in honey-coloured stone.

'That's the one. An oasis of peace compared to—'

'What you've been used to,' interposed Markham smoothly.

She smiled at him gratefully. Such an incandescently trusting look, that it took his breath away. He vowed to himself that nothing and no-one would ever hurt her again.

'So, what does Cynthia want then?' he asked curiously.

'She was rather cagey over the phone.' Olivia was thoughtful. 'We were very close at one time, then lost touch. You know how it is.'

Markham smiled rather sadly. 'Only too well.'

'Anyway, she'd heard on the grapevine that I was doing supply at Hope and wondered if I might be interested in a permanent role at St Mary's.' Olivia strove to sound casual, but Markham detected the underlying note of interest.

Equally nonchalant, he replied, 'How do you feel about that?'

'Might give it a shot. We're going to meet up tomorrow for a chat. Their principal – Roderick Strange, the one everyone called the Brylcreemed Dracula – has been poached by King's. Cyn likes the new man, so presumably he's on-side.'

Playing it very low key, Markham refrained from pressing further, but he was pleased to detect the resurgence of energy and optimism in Olivia's voice. Perhaps this was the fresh start that she needed…

Recalling himself with a jolt to the present, Markham reluctantly abandoned his daydreams of Olivia and moved away from the office window to his cluttered desk. Contemplating the towering piles of paperwork which covered every inch, he experienced a fierce impulse to sweep the whole lot onto the floor. Only the thought of the alarm this would cause Miss Purcell, his timid mouse of a PA, stayed his hand.

He liked to think of himself as a 'copper's copper' – despite his meteoric rise through the ranks and what Noakes regarded as the disadvantage of a degree in psychology – and shuddered at the thought of becoming a careerist technocrat. Slowly but surely, however, he felt himself being sucked into a quagmire of unction and smarm.

Oh God, as luck would have it, tonight was the buffet supper for Bromgrove's Police and Church Partnership Committee. That meant Collier and assorted local worthies. The unspeakable in pursuit of the inedible. Markham exhaled sharply in frustration.

Raking his unruly mop of thick black hair, he shuffled through a sheaf of correspondence until he located the agenda. All the usual suspects would be there. His eye fell upon a name. *Dr Desmond O'Keefe, Principal, St Mary's Choir School*. Well, well. Perhaps the evening wouldn't be entirely a waste of time. He brightened at the thought that he might even be able to do some networking on Olivia's behalf.

Did he dare risk taking his DS? Mrs Noakes was a prominent member of St Mary's Women's Guild, which seemed almost a guarantee for Noakes's good behaviour. On the other hand, there was always a chance that his fierce Anti-Ecumenism (no quarter given to anyone outside the Anglican Communion) might ruffle feathers. Hastily, Markham scanned the list of attendees. It looked like a C of E affair, so there were no Rabbis or Mullahs to be outraged. Yes, on balance, he thought the old war horse could join the party. If nothing else, it would be diverting to watch his reactions to the proposals for a civic prayer event to be hosted by Bromgrove Police Station.

Markham sighed. Before the evening's schmoozing, there were acres of statistics and data to be digested. Better get to it. He hoped that Olivia's meeting with Cynthia would be productive. With any luck, he would have some useful information for her before the night was over.

While Markham grappled with the contents of his in-tray, Olivia sat savouring the conventual peace of the visitors' parlour at St Mary's Choir School.

The aroma of beeswax from the highly polished wooden flooring mingled pleasingly with the heady scent of lilies displayed on a mahogany sideboard. A fire blazed cheerfully in the hearth, and the only sound was the steady ticking of a grandfather clock in the corner of the room. The December morning sun streamed onto the room's linenfold panelling through recessed mullioned windows which gave onto an inner cloister garth.

Altogether it was a cosy room. The only discordant note was struck by various gargoyles ornamenting the window reveals: it seemed to Olivia that the snub-nosed little creatures smirked as though they knew something to her disadvantage.

The parlour featured two paintings. In the first, a lugubrious Madonna hovered over a whey-faced child, his right hand extended in benediction. The second was familiar to her. It depicted the English and Welsh Catholic martyrs in a sort of 'group portrait' – all looking incongruously joyful, with tonsured priests celebrating an open-air service next to Tyburn gallows; presumably the jollity being meant to underscore the power of the church triumphant. As a piece of propaganda, Olivia had to concede that it was remarkably effective. She had heard that St Mary's was not merely a choir school of some renown but also a shrine with custody of various holy relics. Well screened from prying eyes, if the relics were ever to be removed from the school – so superstition had it – the school and its inhabitants would fall under an eternal curse.

Shuddering pleasurably at thoughts of heroic witness, romantic intrigue and mystery, Olivia gave herself up to enjoyment of the excellent coffee that had been brought to her. Finally, with a sigh of satisfaction, she set down her cup on the antique reproduction side table with *deuil blanc* napkin, closed her eyes and drifted off into a reverie.

'Liv!' Her nickname.

Olivia opened her eyes to find Cynthia Gibson regarding her quizzically.

'Same old Liv. Away with the fairies.'

Olivia jumped up and the two women embraced before drawing their high-backed tartan armchairs into a conspiratorial huddle.

Looking more closely, Olivia was struck by the alteration in her friend's appearance. The Cynthia Gibson of remembrance possessed the perky irrepressibility, crisp curls and curviness of a Fragonard heroine. The woman opposite her, however, looked hollowed-out and somehow withered, almost as though a secret canker was eating her up from inside, while the trademark chestnut curls were scraped into a witchy plait which snaked halfway down her back. She gazed at Olivia with a greedy intensity which the latter found faintly unnerving.

Blimey, they must be slave-drivers in the independent sector, Olivia told herself. Cynthia looks completely done in. Easy does it, she checked herself, repressing her initial impulse to come straight out and ask what was wrong.

'How's tricks then, Cyn? Impressive set up you have here. All very *Tom Brown's Schooldays*.'

Her light tone did the trick. Cynthia's wary expression lightened and she rolled her eyes playfully.

'Might have guessed you'd like the manicured lawns with the hint of smells 'n' bells! Bit of a far cry from Hopeless!'

There was a pause. Olivia noticed the way her friend kept glancing furtively around the room. Almost as though she expected there might be a bogeyman hiding in the walls. A vein pulsed at the corner of her mouth. Olivia waited patiently. The ticking of the clock sounded abnormally pronounced.

'I've got a class shortly, so I need to be quick. Liv, there's an English job coming up here very shortly and I think you should apply for it.' She gave a swift indrawn hiss of breath. 'I know you've done wonders at Hope for one thing.' She had clearly done some research. 'And for another,' Cynthia's eyes locked onto Olivia in unashamed appeal, 'I could do with a friend. This place is such a goldfish bowl...' She gestured impatiently at their imposing surroundings. 'You'd be like a breath of fresh air!' Leaning closer, she urged, 'Seriously Liv, you'd be a shoo-in. And you'd be able to get stuck into the pastoral side too. Responsibility galore if you want it.' Her tone was almost wheedling now. That was what discomfited Olivia most of all – confident, self-possessed Cynthia Gibson pleading like a supplicant.

Gently, Olivia laid a slender palm on her friend's clenched fist.

'We had good times back in the day, Cyn. And you need all the allies you can get in our line of work!'

It seemed as though her friend's whole frame tingled with hope.

With a spasmodic movement, Cynthia snatched away her hand and jumped to her feet.

'So, you'll think about it then?' she asked eagerly.

'I guess I'm ready for a change, and a permanent position would be good.' Olivia smiled wryly. 'But aren't you in a bit of an interregnum right now, what with Voldemort moving on? What's the new principal like?'

Cynthia's strained expression softened.

'Oh, Dr O'Keefe's a *huge* improvement. No more *Sturm und Drang*, thank God!' More soberly, she added, 'I think you'd fit in really well here, Liv. Obviously this is on the QT, but if you're interested in going ahead I can fix up a meeting with Dr O'Keefe and Dick Woodcourt. He's one of the residentiary canons at the cathedral and our Chair of Governors.'

A bell rang somewhere in the distance.

Cynthia pulled a face. 'God, the tyranny of the school timetable! I'd better get off.'

She thrust a card at Olivia. 'It's got all the school contact details. We must catch up properly, Liv.'

'When the two of us get time to draw breath.' Olivia laughed, rising to her feet.

Suddenly Cynthia stiffened and fell silent. Following her gaze, Olivia noticed that the rectangular bar of sunlight at the bottom of the parlour door had disappeared. Cut off.

The goldfish bowl. *A neighbourhood of voluntary spies.*

Cynthia squeezed Olivia's hand and walked her to the door. There was no-one in the corridor outside.

Striding across the forecourt of St Mary's Choir School, Olivia looked back at its elegant neo-Italianate façade. It might just have been her fancy, but she could have sworn she saw a bloodless face pass from window to window like a wandering light until it fixed itself in one and watched her.

2

St Mary's

It was some time before Olivia could dispel the troubling impressions left by her interview with Cynthia.

After their conversation, she wandered through Bromgrove Park, lost in thought. Despite the brilliant sunshine striking fire out of the spindly birches to create a winter canopy of spun gold, she felt cold inside.

For a moment, walking across the forecourt at St Mary's, she had felt her neck prickle, as though a pair of hostile eyes was boring into the back of her head. And she could have sworn there was something else too. The sound of a sly, malicious snicker.

Come off it, she chided herself. Next thing, I'll be imagining one of those funny little gargoyles is after me. St Mary's is church property, not an outpost of middle-earth!

She must have voiced her thoughts aloud. A tweedy gentleman coming the opposite way shot her a disapproving look before giving her the widest possible berth as he scuttled past.

Paradoxically, this made Olivia feel much better. Chuckling to herself, she quickened her pace. Matthew Sullivan, her friend and colleague from the English department at Hope, was calling later and she looked forward to hearing what he had to say about the choir school.

Later that afternoon, back at Markham's flat in The Sweepstakes, Olivia felt her earlier misgivings melt away under the influence of her friend's robust common sense.

Tall, lean, and bespectacled, Matthew Sullivan's owlish appearance belied a penetrating intelligence and sardonic personality. Lounging in a battered but comfortable recliner, nursing a restorative whisky, he smiled across at Olivia, pleased to see the sparkle in her eyes. She's got some sort of project, he thought to himself.

Looking round, he took in the piles of books, knick-knacks and scented candles which covered almost every visible surface.

'Well, you've certainly put your own stamp on this place, Liv.' He grinned. 'I bet it was all tasteful Scandinavian minimalism when you arrived.'

Olivia laughed. 'Oh, there's no clutter allowed in Gil's study, Matt. Everything so ship-shape, it's downright nautical!'

Pouring herself a generous G&T, Olivia took up her favourite position, cross-legged in front of the ruddy wood-fire.

'Be sure to give my regards to Cynthia when you next see her. She certainly landed on her feet, didn't she?' Sullivan gave a short bark. 'But then she paid her dues to the huddled masses when she was at Hope, so I reckon she's earned it.' He smiled wistfully. 'They were good times with the three of us together in the English department, Liv. And now here you are wanting to jump ship too...'

'What can you tell me about St Mary's?' Olivia spoke eagerly. 'I figured you'd be sure to know about any skeletons in the closet.'

Her friend raised his eyebrows, steepling his fingers as he considered the question.

'Very High Church of course. Ancestors of the school's patron Sir Philip Soames founded the original school back in medieval times when it was attached to a nunnery, but the current building and cathedral are mid-Victorian. The cathedral ended up Byzantine revival with gothic twiddles – totally OTT, but impressive enough if you like that sort of thing. Personally, I prefer the school ... lovely Cotswold stone, sort of neo-Palladian frontage—'

'Don't go all *Restoration Man* on me, Matt!' Olivia groaned. 'Forget the bricks and mortar, what about the *moral* fabric?'

Not at all put out, Sullivan spread his hands wide.

'Nothing scandalous to the best of my knowledge. No defrockings or anything like that. The outgoing principal Dr Strange ruffled a few feathers locally.'

'Yes, I remember seeing him at that inter-school competition we did a couple of years back,' Olivia said reminiscently. 'Very mean and moody – Heathcliff in a cummerbund – if not borderline psycho ... barking orders left, right and centre and generally throwing his weight around. All those poor little lads with their ears pinned back in terror. Musically top-notch, but something really sinister about him.'

'Only a bruiser like Strange could cope with Sir Philip Soames,' commented Sullivan ruminatively. 'Sir Philip's family founded St Mary's and he's the school patron, though I believe he's a semi-recluse now. Lives in that dilapidated hulk of a house at the bottom of Bromgrove Crescent—'

'The one with the great wilderness of a garden, backing onto the cathedral graveyard?'

'That's it. Thurston Lodge, named after a distant ancestor. Beautiful place in its heyday apparently, but pretty much gone to wrack and ruin since then.'

Sullivan burst out laughing at Olivia's doleful expression. 'Sorry to disappoint you, Liv. You were hoping for something a little more Edgar Allan Poe, am I right?'

Olivia looked shamefaced. 'Cynthia was like someone trapped in a gothic horror story...You should have seen her, Matt. A bundle of nerves. Something's not right at St Mary's.'

'Hmmm.' Sullivan was thoughtful. 'There was a story a few years back about the school matron, or housekeeper, whatever you like to call her.'

'Yes?' Olivia was suddenly alert.

'The woman suffered from major depression, apparently – took to the bottle in a big way. A couple of pupils had absconded from St Mary's on her watch and she took it personally. Did a bunk. No-one's seen hide nor hair of her since.'

'Strange,' said Olivia slowly. 'What about the boys who ran away – did they manage to trace them?'

'Come to think of it, I don't believe they did. But Liv,' Sullivan's voice held a warning note, 'it wouldn't do to read too much into it. Musicians are always highly strung, you know. From what I remember, these were teenagers. One was worried about his voice breaking while the other came from a broken home. There was a feature about them in the *Gazette* – lots of publicity too – but the newshounds didn't manage to dig up anything suggesting dodgy doings at the school.'

'I'm sure you're right, Matt,' Olivia said reluctantly. 'What with Gil's job, I'm a bit paranoid … jump at my own shadow, you know.'

Sullivan could imagine only too well, though from what he'd seen of Markham it was likely that Olivia received only the most tightly edited feedback from the police front line.

'Hey, no reason you shouldn't put in for a job at St Mary's if Cynthia wants some support and you feel up to it,' he declared reassuringly. 'Far more satisfying than all the supply malarkey. To be honest, you're wasted at Hope.'

Olivia gurgled. 'I certainly don't speak the head's language.'

'As in fluent bullshit?'

'*Precisely*! Now, how about a refill?'

By mutual consent the subject of St Mary's was dropped, the two friends launching into a highly enjoyable round of gossip and mildly scabrous character assassination.

When Markham returned later that night, he was secretly thrilled to note that Olivia was looking more animated than he had seen her for some time. Breathing a silent prayer of thanks to Matthew Sullivan, he sank into his own especial armchair and enquired, 'Well, I'm all ears. How did the intel-gathering go?'

'Matt couldn't offer me much in the way of dirt unfortunately.'

Was it Olivia's imagination, or did Markham look relieved?

'There was some case he told me about – something about a female member of staff disappearing a while ago. And there were a couple of boys who absconded too.'

'Umm, yep. Rings a bell. Think it was before I transferred here.' He shot her a keen glance. 'You want me to check it out?'

Olivia flushed. 'I know you'll think I've got some mad idea about sleuthing with Cynthia, sweetheart, but honestly it's not that.' She shifted uncomfortably. 'I just want to be there for her – help her with whatever's wrong.'

Markham kept his tone deliberately light. 'Bet you wouldn't mind having a peep at those relics too, my little amateur historian?'

His reward was a look of deep gratitude. 'It'd certainly be an interesting place to work,' Olivia agreed. 'And lashings of glorious music into the bargain – perk of the job!'

'Plus a free pass to the St Mary Grottoes.'

'Grottoes! Matt didn't say anything about them!'

'Don't know all that much about them myself, to be honest. They featured on the agenda at tonight's meeting.' He yawned. 'Long story short, there used to be a pagan ossuary in the caves and tunnels under land at the back of the school.'

'Like a catacomb?'

Olivia's voice was eager.

'Yes, something like that. Anyway, over the centuries this boneyard was replaced by votive altars to the Virgin Mary. The place became a site of pilgrimage apparently, then fell into disuse when restoration work was halted for lack of funds. Thanks to Sir Philip Soames, the renovations are back on, but the earthworks are dangerous so the place isn't open to the public.'

'How romantic!' Olivia breathed, her eyes like stars.

Suppressing a sigh, Markham smiled at his rapt girlfriend. 'I guess that just about clinches it for you. When will you be signing on the dotted line at St Mary's?'

Olivia had the grace to look embarrassed. 'After Cyn told me about the vacancy, I sent a quick e-mail to the principal's office – an on-spec enquiry so to speak. They've asked me to come in for an interview tomorrow.'

'I might have known!'

But Markham sounded resigned and Olivia knew then that she had won the day. Diplomatically, she turned the conversation.

'How was the meeting? Did Noakes behave himself?'

'He was so busy hoovering up the sarnies and vol-au-vents, that opportunities for causing mortal offence were mercifully limited. Actually, Noakesy mentioned something to do with St Mary's. Now what was it? Oh yes, something about a reported desecration in the cathedral graveyard. From the sound of it, just an elderly parishioner frightening herself over nothing. He went down there to have a look – spoke to the cemetery staff – but everything seemed to be in order.'

'*Shame.*' Olivia spoke teasingly. 'I was waiting for something blood-curdling!'

'Sorry to disappoint! Come on, dearest, let's call it a night. You'll need to be bright-eyed and bushy-tailed for that interview tomorrow.'

They were heading for the stairs when Markham stopped and laid his hand on her arm.

'Just one thing, Liv. I'm sure everything's above board at St Mary's. But if the place does hold any secrets, then for God's sake tread carefully. You don't want to stir up old troubles.'

It felt like a premonition.

As she turned into the forecourt of St Mary's Choir School the following morning, Olivia ruefully told herself that late-night discussion of ossuaries, boneyards and the like was not the best prescription for a sound night's sleep. She felt heavy-eyed and sluggish, her downcast mood a perfect match for thin drizzle and leaden skies. The brilliant sunshine and perfect winter crispness of the previous day had vanished along with her earlier optimism. Suddenly she felt rather foolish. Did she really imagine she could waltz into this sedate little enclave like some latter-day Lara Croft and begin ferreting out its mysteries? Wasn't it sometimes better to let sleeping dogs lie?

Then Olivia thought of Cynthia. The alteration in her friend's looks was disturbing. What on earth could have wrought such a dramatic change?

Olivia looked up at the glorious honeyed frontage of St Mary's. Not even the murk of a dreary December day could wholly muffle its radiance. The yellow Cotswold stone glowed softly like yellow jessamine.

'Beautiful but deadly.' The words were out of her mouth almost without her being aware of uttering them. As though triggered by something in her subconscious. As though to warn her of a worm in the bud.

At that moment, other details forced their way through Olivia's preoccupation and she noticed the large number of cars parked in front of the school. One vehicle was a Bromgrove police car.

Some sort of trouble, she asked herself with a flicker of curiosity.

A tall, thick-set man lumbered down the elegant front steps.

Distracted by her anxiety about Cynthia, Olivia nearly cannoned into him. Close-set eyes regarded her with unmistakable hostility and his jaw shot out pugnaciously. Surely this couldn't be the charismatic new principal?

She became aware that a voice was barking at her. 'I asked if you have an appointment.'

The voice was as unattractively abrasive as the man's appearance.

'I'm here to see Miss Gibson,' she answered politely but with a hint of frost.

'It's all right, Alex.' Cynthia suddenly appeared behind him, out of breath and uncharacteristically flustered. 'This is Miss Mullen. She's here for a meeting with Dr O'Keefe about the English position. Liv, this is Alex Sharpe, our Director of Music.'

The Director of Music did not appear mollified. 'Unfortunate timing to say the least.'

Olivia looked from one to the other in confusion.

'I'll take it from here,' Cynthia said swiftly. 'Come on, Liv, I'll explain in the parlour.'

As she meekly trotted along behind Cynthia, Olivia felt Alex Sharpe's gaze hot on her back.

In the visitors' parlour, tranquillity reigned. The English and Welsh martyrs in their gilt frame continued to gaze at some vision of celestial bliss beyond the reach of mere mortals. Olivia would have given much to share that serenity. But she sensed a shift in the atmosphere of St Mary's.

'What's with the police car, Cyn? Has something happened?'

Cynthia looked uneasy and her eyes slid away from Olivia. 'I don't really know, to be honest,' she said hesitatingly. 'It's something to do with the renovations. You'll have heard of the St Mary Grottoes—'

'Yes, Gil filled me in.'

'Gil?'

'My partner.' There was an awkward pause. 'He's a DI with Bromgrove CID. Not many people know. We're happier to keep it under the radar.'

Cynthia looked startled.

'A policeman,' she said slowly. 'I had no idea.'

'Anyway,' Olivia continued brightly as though oblivious to the other's obvious discomposure, 'he said you've got some sort of necropolis or temple down there – pagan and Christian artefacts, that kind of thing.'

Cynthia recovered herself. 'That's right. The site has archaeological significance, hence the excavations and preservation work.'

She fell silent then resumed.

'Well, it looks like the workmen have found human remains.'

The words dropped into the silence of the parlour like pebbles into a deep well.

Olivia was puzzled by her friend's visible constraint.

'Isn't that to be expected? Presumably they're bound to disturb the odd set of bones.'

There was a pregnant pause.

'It's not quite as simple as that, Liv. Actually, there was a bit of a mistake...'

'How do you mean, a mistake?' Olivia did her best to keep impatience out of her voice.

Cynthia spoke slowly, cautiously, as if the words were being dragged out of her.

'Well, the workmen weren't supposed to be excavating that particular area. The architect and Local Heritage Committee had decided it was out of bounds for redevelopment. I don't know the ins and outs,' a slight flush rose to her cheek, 'but the cathedral architect Edward Preston says it was something to do with the protocols for disturbing human remains. There's a little Christian cemetery backing onto the old pagan burial ground, so any exhumations would mean a big headache for St Mary's, what with all the regulations on safeguarding decency and privacy, not to mention the expense.'

'Can't they just rebury the remains? Or does the council have to OK it? Is that why the police are here?' The questions tumbled out of Olivia.

Noticing her friend's ashy complexion and haunted expression, she pulled herself up short. 'Sorry, Cyn, I'm being a pain. Tell me to shut up if you like!'

Cynthia smiled wanly. 'The whole thing's been a bit of a shock. You see—'

Olivia waited. Her friend's face twisted and she suddenly looked much older than her years, her forehead furrowed by lines which seemed to have sprung up overnight.

'The workmen uncovered two bodies about five feet down, one on top of the other. Apparently, the skeletons were instantly recognizable as modern-day from what was left of their clothing. But,' she took a deep breath, 'there was evidence of foul play. There was a garrotte around the neck of the body underneath, with dried blood on it and the remnants of a tourniquet. But most horrible of all...'

The parlour seemed to have darkened and a shade fell across the faces of the holy martyrs – hung, drawn and quartered centuries before – as though they recalled their own agonized earthly sufferings.

'...the uppermost skeleton was lying over the other, facing it – as though they were locked in an embrace. Its arms and hands were stretched out like claws ... like a strangler...'

Cynthia visibly struggled for composure. 'I heard one of the guys saying it was sick. As though the skeletons were posed. From the look of it, one had murdered the other before somehow ending up in the slime and sludge with him.'

' "The wages of Sin is Death," ' said Olivia sombrely. 'A murderer killing to order, then disposed of in his turn. Dead men tell no tales...'

'It's *horrible*.' Cynthia spoke with surprising passion. 'A desecration. It's as if St Mary's has been polluted.'

'Maybe these victims wanted to be found – were ready to be found – and drew the workmen to the grave. So that what was hidden could be brought into the light.'

Olivia sounded strangely detached, dreamy, like a somnambulist. She started in surprise. Now where had those words come from? It was as though they had risen ready-formed to her lips.

At that moment, a tempest broke outside, hail rattling like shot against the mullioned windows. Shouts indicated that people were rushing for cover. Inside the parlour, however, all was still.

Olivia felt oddly disconnected, with an eerie sense of déjà vu. She badly wanted to go away, to make sense of it all. More than anything, she wanted to speak to Markham, to hear his deep gentle tones making light of her fearful imaginings.

The parlour door opened softly. A slight bespectacled figure, with dark close-shorn hair and keenly observant brown eyes, came towards Olivia with a hand outstretched. She wondered who he was and how much of their conversation he might have caught.

'My apologies for keeping you waiting, Miss Mullen. I'm Desmond O'Keefe, the new principal.'

The cultured, musical voice held a hint of Irish brogue which was like balm to Olivia's disordered senses. She understood instantly why Cynthia had warmed to this man. He was dressed formally in a rather crumpled charcoal grey suit, over which he wore an academic gown, which went well with his quaintly fogeyish courtliness. She wondered how he and the man Alex Sharpe would manage to work in harness. O'Keefe the diplomat no doubt spreading sweetness and light where Sharpe sowed discord!

Disconcertingly, as though he had read her thoughts, O'Keefe commented mildly, 'I'm on a steep learning curve just now, Miss Mullen. And, to cap it all, as Miss Gibson has no doubt explained, my arrival has coincided with a criminal investigation!'

Olivia, who had risen to greet the new arrival, spoke hurriedly. 'I'm not going to get under your feet. In the circumstances, it was very good of you to see me. I was interested in the English vacancy but—'

'When can you start?'

Wrongfooted, she stared at him. He smiled back at her.

'I know your academic credentials are rock solid, Miss Mullen, and Miss Gibson has spoken very highly of you. That's good enough for me. I need a strong team round me and have a feeling we'll suit very well. The job's yours if you want it. Have a think and let me know later today if possible.' He grimaced at the sound of a commotion in the corridor.

'The Visigoths are at the gates! Speak to you later, Miss Gibson. Good to meet you, Miss Mullen. Once the downpour has cleared, why don't you have a recce … get the feel of the place. There are some maps at reception.'

And with that, he glided from the room.

Olivia realized that the die was cast. For better or for worse, St Mary's was her destiny.

Half an hour later, under pewter-coloured skies, Olivia stood in the forecourt feeling better acquainted with the layout of her new domain.

To the right of the forecourt as she came out of the school was a low wall with a simple arch which gave access to St Mary's neo-Byzantine cathedral. Olivia felt some of Matt Sullivan's distaste for the edifice whose stumpy blue slate cupola clashed rather garishly with the red and white geometric pattern of its striped buttresses. Certainly, the cathedral had none of the subdued grace of the choir school with its mellow rendered stonework.

On the other side of the forecourt, an alley of chestnut trees, barren in the December murk, ran the full length of the school. Wandering through a trellised arch, Olivia passed two blocks of weathered cloisters with checker-block black and white tiled floors; each garth surrounded a courtyard with neat squares of lawn and circular flower beds. The inner walls of the cloisters connected with a glassed-in corridor giving onto studios and classrooms.

Olivia had found the overall effect pleasing. There was something conventual about the place, in keeping with its ancient monastic origins she supposed.

Behind the cloister blocks was an uncultivated sedge meadow. Its dun-coloured dreariness and the mournful cry of curlews made Olivia shiver. In keeping with its bleak aspect, a narrow path led to a little cemetery with a row of blackened crosses atop coarse gravel tumuli bearing tarnished brass plaques. From the various inscriptions, it appeared that this was the final resting place of former principals. A straggling hedge separated the strip from the signposted grottoes behind. Presumably this was what Cynthia had meant when she spoke of the complicated position regarding exhumations. It was a desolate place to end up, Olivia reflected, all jumbled up with the accumulated detritus of centuries.

The famous grottoes themselves were something of a disappointment, though they hardly wore their most promising aspect, looking more like a swampy, churned-up demolition site than a renowned heritage attraction. Three terraced caves, their lichen-encrusted bony sockets open to the sullen sky, formed a natural boundary to the rear of the site, brooding over the sea of peaty sludge like sightless prophets of doom. Olivia pictured the famous catacombs radiating out from beneath their depths.

More pagan than Christian, she thought with a shudder as she retraced her steps back to the front of the school, speculating that a cordoned-off section of mud guarded by two miserable-looking young policemen likely marked the place where those pitiful, unhallowed remains had been found. All in all, she almost preferred the poky, fussy little school chapel – all pilasters, cherubs and baroque mouldings – situated immediately behind the visitors' parlour and into which she had peeped before commencing her external tour.

It began to rain once more, as though the elements wished to signal to Olivia that she should take her leave.

With one long, lingering look behind her, she headed for her car.

3

A Mystery

'So, there you have it, Gil. The *Curse of Olivia Mullen*. No sooner do I renew 'Auld Lang Syne' with Cynthia than they find a couple of skeletons on site! Victims of homicide to boot!'

There was a manic edge to Olivia's mirth, thought Markham as he watched his girlfriend downing her G&T like lemonade. And no wonder. After what she had recounted, he had been unable to stop picturing the gruesome bedding consummated beneath St Mary's Grottoes. Victim and murderer entwined in that horrible parody of a lovers' embrace; locked together in their putrid underworld for eternity. The notion of some demonic intelligence gloating over the tableau brought Markham out in goosebumps, though he strove to hide his shock and revulsion from Olivia.

Making short work of his own whisky and soda, he spoke matter-of-factly. 'Well, the SOCO boys should be able to shed some light in due course. Meantime, I'll get Noakes started on research. Whoever buried those poor souls must have been able to come and go, so we need to work out who had access. Archaeologists. Contractors. Council staff.'

'You're taking over the investigation then?' The note of relief was unmistakable.

'I asked to be assigned to this one, Liv. By virtue of my new-minted status as police *wunderkind*.'

Markham said nothing about abasing himself before 'Slimy Sid', as DCI Sidney was popularly known, to ensure he bagged the St Mary's investigation. He dreaded to think of the DCI's likely response to the news that Olivia was working at the choir school. He'd have to make sure that Noakes and the rest of the team preserved *omertá* about her employment there.

Olivia's agitated tones interrupted Markham's private monologue.

'Terrible to think that two human beings were tossed into the slurry like so much worthless garbage.' Her eyes were wide with horror. Then she corrected herself. 'Though Cynthia said that the burial was *staged*. A sick joke. Some sort of propitiatory ritual – you know, a sacrifice to appease the deities of the grottoes.'

Markham repressed a shudder as he recalled the crime scene photos: the skeletons exposed like braille for experts to decipher; the pitiful wet nest of dark hair on the skull which bore the garrotte; the bleached cavities of stomach and sockets, where the bodies had been slowly digested; the carious piano work of ribs. The uppermost skeleton had the awful gaping mouth of death. The head of the other rested at an acute angle, looking as though he had nodded off to sleep in the grave.

Unexpectedly, tears rose to his eyes.

'"The snares of the wicked surround me. My life is poured out like water,"' he murmured softly. '"I can count all my bones."'

Olivia reached across and sympathetically squeezed Markham's hand, comforted by the words of the funeral psalms, as though their utterance had somehow cast a protective mantle around the wretched inhabitants of that dank grave. The fact that her lover never lost sight of victims' individuality – never regarded them merely as serial numbers on case files – struck her anew. Somehow, he had resisted the coarsening effects of daily contact with Bromgrove's underbelly, and he was known to react savagely when subordinates treated human remains with any want of decorum. Members of his team knew better than to exhibit gallows humour at homicide crime scenes and generally retreated to a respectful distance while their guvnor communed with the dead.

Markham cleared his throat.

'I suppose it's too much to hope that these sinister goings-on at St Mary's have given you second thoughts about accepting the job?'

A part of him fervently wished that he could wrap his girlfriend in bubble wrap and keep her well away from those sinister grottoes. He knew all too well, however, that the scent of a mystery, together with concern for her friend, was catnip for Olivia.

'I called Desmond O'Keefe earlier to say I'd take the position,' she said sheepishly.

'Well,' replied Markham, resolving to make the best of it, 'from what I saw of him the other night, he seems a pleasant fellow. More like a churchman than a layman, though... Reminded me of school and the Jesuits...'

Markham rarely spoke of his upbringing and described himself as a lapsed Catholic, but Olivia – herself a practising Anglican – had early detected the undertow of a deeply felt religiosity.

She spoke lightly. 'Yes, I know what you mean. Moves as though he's on castors, very suave and discreet. I kept looking round for the cassock and surplice! Quite attractive in an understated sort of way.'

'Hmmm. Hugh Grant of the grottoes then?'

'Hardly!' Olivia's giggle was so infectious that it elicited an answering grin from Markham.

'Forgive my dog-in-the-manger instincts, love. It's good to know I've nothing to fear from any clerical smoothies.'

For answer, he received a further squeeze of the hand and a tender look. It was enough.

'When do you start?' he enquired.

'I asked for a couple of days just to get ready – go through some schemes of work with Cyn, find out the lie of the land, that kind of thing. I start officially next week. They're breaking up for Christmas in another fortnight anyway, so it'll be an easy run-in.'

'Excellent. Perhaps you might be interested in coming with me when I pay Sir Philip Soames a visit tomorrow morning. This discovery at the grottoes means he'll have to be consulted, though I can't imagine he'll have anything much to contribute to the investigation.'

'Matt said he's more or less a recluse.'

Markham was amused to note Olivia's whippet-like air of alert interest. Maybe this business at St Mary's wasn't such a bad thing, he told himself. She'd become jaded and run-down at Hope, and this was the first real flare of animation he had seen in a long time. He decided to fan the spark.

'I reckon Sir Philip will agree to see a representative from Bromgrove CID,' he commented drily, 'if only to keep himself in the loop. He's supposed to be suffering from *myasthenia gravis* – some sort of neuromuscular condition. Lives alone in that mouldering pile with just a manservant for company. So, gird yourself for a trip to Castle Doom. We can pass you off as teacher liaison or some such, but for God's sake *no PDAs!*'

Olivia threw her arms around his neck. 'I'll be like your number two,' she exclaimed happily.

'But no unnecessary risks, eh, Sherlock!'

'You're the boss!' Olivia was ready to promise anything.

Markham hugged her close with fierce intensity. 'Yes, and don't you forget it!' An image of the honeycombed trenches of St Mary's Grottoes – stretchers borne away to waiting hearses – rose unbidden to his mind, but he ruthlessly beat it down and the conversation shifted to other subjects.

Gazing around the neglected garden of Sir Philip Soames's residence the following morning, Olivia reflected that the square unsheltered house in Bromgrove Crescent, a sedate cul de sac at the bottom of St Mary's Lane leading from the cathedral, seemed almost to shun its neighbours. A low Georgian structure, Thurston Lodge stood behind high iron gates swinging drunkenly on their hinges. Two turrets reared up at either end of the property, with dead-eyed shuttered windows which repelled scrutiny. The frontage was stained with damp, rising up the stark grey stone like a defilement, and a couple of cracked slates hung crookedly from the eaves. There was a blankness about the place, unrelieved by a sparse shrubbery with its straggling bushes of elder and lilac. Altogether an unwelcoming aspect.

Markham stepped up to the oak door and tugged at its massive bell pull. From deep inside the recesses of the shadowy building came an answering echo.

The door was finally opened by a beefy sallow-skinned man whose hangdog features gave him the look of a dyspeptic bulldog. His right leg exhibited a distinct peculiarity of gait – or foot drop – so that, as he walked, it seemed that he was attempting to genuflect to everything in front of him. Perfectly correct in manner, however, he escorted them through various gloomy reception rooms – hecatombs of furniture muffled up in great winding-sheets – to a small sitting room-cum-library. Compared to the ungarnished appearance of the rest of the house, this was a thickly carpeted room, lined with quaint cabinets full of morocco-bound books, coins and oriental curios. There was a certain odour of cigar smoke, overlaid by the mustiness of a church vault, which seemed to emanate from the chimney breast. Over all hung a pall of silence and mystery. The retainer waved them to two dreary button backed chairs and departed to fetch his master.

The visitors sat for some minutes, drinking in Sir Philip's sanctum before Olivia moved across to the vast mahogany desk which dominated the centre of the room and picked up the leather gilt-tooled volume which lay face down on its cluttered surface.

'*The Secret Doctrine*,' she said wonderingly. 'Sounds mystical.'

'Indeed it is, young lady,' came the sardonic response from somewhere in the shadows. 'No need to be embarrassed,' the gravelly voice continued, brushing away Olivia's flustered apologies as its owner emerged from the shadow of the doorway and advanced into the room. 'Your curiosity is natural. It's a text about the universal essence and the self-denial that leads to enlightenment.'

Which leaves us none the wiser, thought Markham in amusement, though a renunciation of material comforts might go some way to accounting for the dilapidated state of the house.

Time to make the introductions. 'Miss Mullen is a new member of staff at St Mary's,' said Markham, 'and I am—'

'The rising star of Bromgrove's CID. Your reputation has preceded you, Inspector Markham. How may I be of assistance?'

The words were perfectly polite, but the expression of the great hooded eyes was watchful.

Despite age and infirmity, the man opposite Markham radiated considerable power. Squat and barrel-chested, his massive head – broad forehead made squarer by the horizontal sweep of white hair, hooked nose, surprisingly sensual mouth and glittering coal-black eyes – spoke eloquently of a forceful character. He took Olivia's hand and kissed it in the continental fashion, raking her with a keen glance before returning his attention to Markham.

Careful, Markham told himself, *this is a man to be reckoned with*.

'No doubt you've heard about the discovery in St Mary's Grottoes, Sir Philip. Given that you are St Mary's patron, I wished to say that you will of course be notified of any developments.'

'Most courteous, Inspector.' Sir Philip paused. 'I suppose nothing is known of the victims' antecedents?'

'Nothing yet, sir, but if you can think of any incident from the school's past...' Markham looked interrogatively at the other who returned his gaze with calm equanimity.

'Alas, nothing comes to mind, Inspector. It is some time since I last visited St Mary's.' He grimaced. 'I regret that I did not find the previous principal temperamentally congenial.'

Markham decided this was an avenue best left unexplored. Hastily, he added, 'There was also the reported interference recently with graves adjacent to the Soames Vault.'

Something flickered at the back of Sir Philip's eyes and

was gone. For an instant, his gaze was empty, devoid of all expression.

Markham felt a spasm of self-reproach. *God, this is too much for him. Local grandee or not, he's a sick man.*

'Nothing for you to worry about, sir. An over-zealous parishioner, recently bereaved, with too much time on her hands.'

'An occupational hazard for the elderly, Inspector.'

Sir Philip's tones of ironic detachment reassured Markham that he had not delivered the *coup de grâce* to St Mary's patron. Nonetheless, aware of the manservant hovering protectively, he decided to bring the meeting to a close.

'We won't take up any more of your time, Sir Philip. It was good of you to see us.'

'Please feel free to consult me at any time, Inspector Markham.' He turned his penetrating gaze on Olivia. 'You too of course, Miss Mullen.'

Olivia was looking at an engraved plaque on Sir Philip's desk. It bore the inscription: *When the pupil is ready, the teacher will be found waiting. Time and space are no barriers between the Master and his aspirant.*

'Bequeathed to me by my father, Miss Mullen. He was a theosophist.'

Theosophy! That was throwing them a curveball, thought Markham wryly, taken aback by this allusion to the pseudo-religion of occult mysticism. Sir Philip hardly looked like a man out there on the nuttier edges of the fringe, but his conventional appearance clearly belied more exotic interests.

With this, the taciturn domestic ushered them courteously but firmly to the door.

As Markham and Olivia walked down the driveway, a gust of wind blew up out of nowhere.

The elder and lilac bushes writhed and twisted as though to give a warning.

Then all was still once more and the mansion resumed its vacant Gorgon stare.

* * *

Later that day, Olivia was back at St Mary's at the behest of Dr O'Keefe, having agreed to meet two of the students – Nathaniel Barton (Nat for short) and Julian Forsythe, twelve and thirteen years old respectively – the plan being that they would show her the famous St Mary's relics and generally impart a flavour of school life.

'To be quite frank with you, Miss Mullen, I have an ulterior motive for arranging this meeting,' Desmond O'Keefe said to Olivia as they talked in the visitors' parlour before the arrival of the boys.

Olivia looked at him enquiringly.

'I'm concerned about these two youngsters.' O'Keefe's face was shadowed with anxiety. 'Nat has a sad family history. Both parents died in a road accident when he was very small, so he was adopted by an aunt. He's twelve and here on a scholarship. Voice of an angel with temperament to match … a sweet, sensitive boy. No issues to speak of. At least not until now.'

'What's changed?' asked Olivia.

O'Keefe appeared sensible and level-headed – not inclined to romanticize. If he thought there was cause for concern, then he was probably right.

'He's become increasingly tense and withdrawn. Very guarded too. As though he's hoarding a secret. I've tried to get him to confide, but the drawbridge comes down – he completely retreats into himself and I can't reach him…' His voice tailed off.

'You really care about this lad.' Olivia's voice was soft.

'Nat's very special. A bit of a loner, so I was really pleased when he chummed up with our head chorister Julian Forsythe. Julian's a little older than Nat – usually very frank and sociable, wonderful at drawing out the shyer boys. But something seems to have gone wrong between them…'

Olivia was matter-of-fact. 'Isn't falling out with friends normal at their age?'

'I suppose so...' O'Keefe hesitated before continuing. 'But the flare ups are out of character. It's as though some sort of silent distrust has sprung up between them and they're scared.'

Scared.

Something about O'Keefe's account was setting off all kinds of depth charges. Olivia badly wanted to consult Markham. She strove for a reassuring tone. 'Nothing like a pastoral challenge, Dr O'Keefe. Maybe the novelty factor will kick in and they'll open up to a newcomer.'

Later, as Dr O'Keefe performed the introduction, Olivia took a discreet inventory. Nat was a small, wiry boy, with nut-brown complexion, wedge-shaped face, Henry V pageboy haircut and lively hazel eyes set either side of an aquiline little nose which almost quivered with excitement. Olivia felt a surge of protectiveness as she observed the narrow torso, stooped shoulders and skinny pipe-cleaner legs – clad as they were in the billowing grey shorts which Olivia gathered was part of St Mary's games uniform. By contrast, Julian was tall, dark and coolly self-possessed. He looked in repose like a Florentine painting, contemplating her with an air of pensive abstraction.

'Right, boys, I'm leaving you to show Miss Mullen the relics,' O'Keefe announced briskly. 'Be sure to do them justice!' And with that he was gone.

Leaving the visitors' parlour, which was adjacent to the front door, the boys ushered Olivia through the entrance hall towards an alcove containing a stout oak door. On the other side of the door was a cobwebby flight of stone stairs whose mossy-smelling stillness recalled the interior of ancient village churches, vibrating with the histories of those who had worshipped in them down the ages.

Olivia was somewhat disappointed to find that the stairs led merely to a small plain room which had more the feel of a municipal records office than a holy place. The whitewashed walls and grey flagstone flooring gave it a distinctly clinical feel, relieved only by the dark pine of its pews and various framed mementoes of those martyred for their beliefs. The boys' attitude to this subterranean realm was touchingly proprietorial, however, and Olivia could tell that the hidden room and its relics exerted a powerful hold over their imaginations.

'In olden times the nuns at Bromgrove Priory hid some of the martyrs' remains in pincushions and sewing kits!'

Nat was flushed with pride at being assigned the task of initiating Olivia into the mysteries of St Mary's Shrine.

Personally, Olivia did not much care for what she regarded as backwoods superstition, but there was something beguiling about Nat's breathless enthusiasm for the treasures of the school's little museum.

Julian's dreamy, almost apathetic, detachment had vanished.

'One of the soldiers got suspicious,' he said animatedly. 'He knew how to find things cos his wife had told him. There was loads of stuff – fingernails, bits of bone and skin ... even rope from the hangings!'

Looking at the boys' eager faces, Olivia felt a sudden resolve so strong that it startled her. O'Keefe had said they were frightened. She vowed there and then that she would do everything possible to find whatever threatened them at St Mary's, the place above all others where they were entitled to feel safe.

Intertwined with this impulse was a certain wistfulness. She and Markham were blissfully happy despite the age difference, but she could not imagine children being part of the equation. Watching Nat and Julian, there came a stab of pain so fierce that it made her wince.

Much gratified by Olivia's sudden pallor and sharply in-drawn breath, Nat proceeded to cap Julian's ghoulish recital.

'And that's not all! We've got a priest's skull here, too. If people tried to move or bury it, there was thunder and lightning and all sorts of terrible things happened until they left it alone.'

'Don't worry, Miss Mullen.' Julian had observed Olivia's discomfort. 'The head's in a special chest. They only bring it out on important feast days.'

Nat delivered the *pièce de résistance*. 'Pilgrims kept cutting bits off it to keep as relics. Then one day when someone was cutting the neck, the head made a kind of whistling noise like a warning. After that, they kept the skull locked away.'

'Quite right too!' declared Olivia firmly. *'Blessed be the man that spares these stones, And cursed be he that moves my bones.'*

'That's what it says on Shakespeare's grave!' exclaimed Julian delightedly.

Olivia smiled at him. 'Indeed. *To dig or not to dig, that is the question!*' The sudden transformation in his appearance intrigued her, as the sad-eyed mask shivered and she detected a gleam of exuberant merriment.

Nat clearly didn't share their enthusiasm for the Bard. Tugging at Olivia's sleeve, he led her over to two wall-mounted rosewood reliquaries. Triptych-like, each had hinged shutters and an elaborate pediment, intricately engraved with what she took to be ecclesiastical insignia. The shutters were left open to display an interior luxuriously lined with crimson silk and studded with numerous little pouches, lockets, and pendants. Beneath each item was a tiny scroll inscribed with the most exquisite calligraphy. Olivia's mind flew to the painting in the visitors' parlour. Strange to connect those serene *Beati* with this lepidopterist's cache!

'There's a saint's tooth in that necklace, Miss Mullen. An' we've got heaps of holy hair!'

Nat scanned Olivia's face intently to see the effect produced by this revelation. Satisfied that she was suitably impressed, he embarked with lip-smacking relish on a catalogue of the tortures inflicted by authority on treasonous priests and their acolytes, interrupted by Julian only when his whistle-stop account occasionally strained the bounds of credulity.

Olivia was happy to indulge them. She sensed that this interlude in the stuffy little basement which housed St

Mary's relics was, as O'Keefe had no doubt intended, a useful distraction from whatever was preying on their minds; also, that it gave them a chance to scrutinize her before she joined the teaching staff.

It appeared that the boys' preliminary inspection of Olivia was satisfactory. Some invisible signal seemed to pass between them, for Nat suddenly asked, 'Have they found something bad down there in the grottoes, Miss Mullen?'

To Olivia's ears, his words seemed charged with a mysterious intensity – as though the apparently casual question held some vital import. She noticed uneasily that Julian's face had turned greenish-white and he looked as though he was about to faint.

Very gently, she put an arm round each of them and kept her voice light.

'Your guess is as good as mine, Nat. Archaeological digs often throw up weird and wonderful secrets from the past. We'll have to wait and see what the folk who deal with bones and fossils say about it. Hey, maybe you've got another Stonehenge here, with druids sacrificing to the Sun God!'

She had struck the right note. Tension seemed to flow out of the two figures at her words. She steered them across to the front row of pews which gave the room the air of a chapel. Sitting in a cosy huddle, she was relieved to see some colour slowly return to Julian's face.

'P'raps the Night Watchman got them.'

Julian stiffened at Nat's observation. He shot the younger boy a distinctly unfriendly look.

This was it.

Olivia waited. She felt an urgency in Nat that would not be repressed.

'He's the one who comes at night wearing a sort of hood. His shadow goes by on the wall, but we pretend to be asleep and don't move. He bends down to check.'

Looking nervously at Julian, who seemed almost turned to stone, Nat continued. 'Mr Woodcourt told us not to worry and just say a little prayer. So we wouldn't have nightmares.'

'Mr Woodcourt?' Olivia prompted.

'He's the chaplain,' Julian explained with quiet reserve. 'Takes us for divinity too.'

'He's *great*,' Nat piped up. 'Going to coach me for cricket next year. Thinks I can make the First Eleven. *An'* he said I've got a voice like a nightingale.'

The oppressive atmosphere lifted momentarily as Nat claimed top spot in Mr Woodcourt's good books. Then a shadow fell across his face.

'I don't think he believes it, though, Miss Mullen. He told us to stop bolting our food and not to eat cheese for supper...'

Nat's voice tailed away uncertainly. He sat silently, clenching and unclenching his fists as though nerving himself to take a step into the unknown. Meanwhile a tranquillity gathered round the little group, Olivia creating a stillness where Nat could feel safe.

Finally, Nat spoke.

'We didn't imagine the Night Watchman, Miss Mullen. *Honestly*, we didn't. He came so close one night, I could feel his breath hot on my face.'

Olivia felt the bottom drop out of her stomach.

A *predator* in the school. Prowling at night. Intent on God knows what.

Nat's voice was small but steady.

'There was scuffling sometimes. And a scream once which woke me up.' He looked to Julian for confirmation. The other boy was silent, but something in his expression gave Nat permission to continue.

'It was a high-pitched scream, as though someone was petrified. Then it just stopped and everything went quiet. It was really scary.'

Stuttering over the last word, Nat clutched Olivia's hand convulsively.

One thing was clear. He had been very badly frightened.

Julian shot Olivia a sidelong glance. It held such a desperate plea, that her heart turned over.

She tried to remember the background information O'Keefe had vouchsafed about the older boy. Julian Forsythe's parents were divorced. Mother re-married with step-children. Julian very much a cuckoo in the nest. *Not wanted on voyage.* Breaking through the assumed indifference was an ill-concealed hunger which went straight to her heart. Like Nat, it was obvious that he was labouring under a great weight of anxiety. More than anything else, Olivia wanted him to be able to set it down.

Anyone who tried to hurt these children, she told herself grimly, would do so over her dead body. Shivering as she recalled the grisly discovery in St Mary's Grottoes, she fervently prayed that it would not come to that.

'*You* believe us don't you, Miss Mullen?'

Nat's voice was timid.

The eyes of both boys were riveted to her face.

'Yes, I do,' Olivia answered simply.

Suddenly she badly wanted to be away from the stifling little chamber which seemed to be suffocating under the weight of centuries. A sense of ineffable sadness emanated from the relics in their wooden tabernacles: a poignant parade of death which made her think of the broken skeletons in St Mary's Grottoes. *Of your charity, pray for our souls.*

Olivia shook herself. It wouldn't do to be getting morbid. She needed her wits about her if she was to be of any use to these boys.

She was a new face, but with the reassurance which came from being a friend of Cynthia and trusted by Dr O'Keefe. This had helped to breach the floodgates and unlock their tongues.

But where to go from here?

Something was undoubtedly wrong at St Mary's. As yet, however, she couldn't make any sense of the jigsaw. There were too many pieces. Murder victims disinterred from the sludge of the grottoes. Pupils absconding. A missing matron. Desecration in the cemetery. Sir Philip's enigmatic orientalism.

It made her head spin.

Weirdly enough, both Nat and Julian seemed perfectly at home in St Mary's Shrine amidst the sinister paraphernalia of torture and death. Scraps of flesh and bone. Droplets of bodily fluids. Fragments of blood-stained linen. *The foul rag and bone shop of the heart.*

As though the patchwork of physical remains somehow symbolized the corruption lurking beneath St Mary's outwardly perfect exterior...

Heavy footsteps descending to the basement interrupted Olivia's reflections.

Alex Sharpe appeared in the doorway.

Both boys quailed before his evident exasperation.

'Sorry to break up the party,' he said sarcastically, 'but these two are late for piano practice.'

Nat and Julian scuttled away, waving shyly to Olivia when they reached the doorway. She gave them a thumbs-up and a cheery 'See you next week!'

'I do hope, Miss Mullen, you aren't going to encourage those two in any attention-seeking behaviour.'

Olivia assumed an expression of innocent surprise.

'They seem perfectly delightful and well-balanced to me. Very keen to tell me all about the history of the relics.'

For some reason, this answer disarmed the Director of Music. He was almost amiable as he shepherded her out of the basement, making politely inconsequential chat and proposing a visit to the cathedral. The boys would be free after that from tea until Prep and could show her round the school.

The shrine was left in darkness. One might have imagined the holy objects breathing softly from the reliquaries on the wall. If only they could have spoken, they would have whispered a warning. *Take care, Olivia. Take care!*

4

Brothers in Arms

'What's it like inside St Mary's, then?' asked Markham that night as he and Olivia lingered over supper. 'I'm taking Noakesy along for a recce tomorrow afternoon. We'll be out of our comfort zone tomorrow, but you can give me a flavour of the place. C'mon, Mata Hari, I just need some idea of what to expect.'

Seeing that he had won the day, he settled back into his chair expectantly.

'Well,' said Olivia thoughtfully, 'as you go in, there's the visitors' parlour on one side and the school chapel behind it with a little sacristy next door. The chapel's standard fare ... statues, cherubs, gilt communion rail, votive lamps, incense boats – very High Church, if you know what I mean.'

Markham nodded encouragingly.

'There's an unusual painting of "The Forty Martyrs" in the visitors' parlour. Strange but uplifting. It shows a *prie-dieu* beneath the gallows, with all the martyrs gathered round in full fig – doublets, ruffs, coifs ... one aristo even has his hunting dog with him.'

'I know the one you mean,' said Markham. 'Casts quite a spell, as I recall. Soft vernal tints, with the Tower of London in the background and all the saints wearing a sort of half-smile, as though they're sharing some private joke. Very appropriate for seditious Jesuits!'

Olivia smiled at her lover, always so perfectly attuned to her sensibilities.

'I couldn't tear my eyes away from it,' she admitted. 'There was another painting – one of those awful moon-faced Madonnas showing the whites of her eyes, complete with puffy baby – but the martyrs were in a different league. I found myself envying their untouchability. *Above and beyond us all...*'

Looking at Olivia's dreamy expression, Markham felt they were straying into dangerous waters.

'So, where's the school building?' he asked hastily.

'Two quadrangles with classrooms and refectory constructed round cloisters.' Observing the quizzical expression on Markham's face, Olivia gave a rueful laugh. 'I guess it is quite monastic in its way. The boys' dormitories are on the floors above, with a little infirmary tucked away at the end of the corridor. All pretty spartan. Wooden shutters, brown drugget, whitewashed walls with inscriptions in bold black letters over the doors. *Perfect Truth is in Silence Alone—*'

'Rather an odd motto for a choir school,' observed Markham.

'Yes, that's what I thought. *All Flesh is Grass* was another. Not very cheerful, but I suppose the boys are used to it.'

'And where do the famous grottoes fit in?'

'Oh, they're beyond the school and the outbuildings at the back. Before you get to the grottoes there's a meadow with a few hermitages round the side—'

'*Hermitages?*'

'Little stone altars. The boys told me they're dedicated to various saints.'

'Hmm. I wonder if we can fit in some catechesis for Noakes before tomorrow's visit,' opined Markham with a mock tragic expression. 'Otherwise we risk a virulent outbreak of No-Popery.'

Olivia chuckled. 'I'm sure Noakes will be fine. The worst High-Anglican flourishes are in the cathedral.'

'Ah yes, I'd forgotten about the jewel in Bromgrove's Crown,' sighed Markham.

'Actually, it's more restrained than you'd expect from the outside. Huge terracotta pieta and stations of the Cross.' Olivia grimaced. 'I'm not too keen on this modernist stuff, though there's an interesting side chapel to The Forty Martyrs and an amazing chandelier. The altar crucifix is gruesome. Christ looks like the Wicker Man. How that's meant to help worshippers "raise their hearts and minds to God" is beyond me.' She paused before adding, 'There are a few dark little alcoves dotted about – totally bare except for some weird inscriptions. *Seek the secret gateway that opens inward only and closes behind the searcher for evermore*, that was one. Then there was something about the Unnamed Power at the timeless centre of the earth.'

'The Marabar Caves come to Bromgrove! Methinks I detect the hand of Sir Philip.' Markham's voice was dry.

'Of course! I thought the orientalism was a bit odd, but it fits with the theosophy and he'd have the clout to commission something like that.'

'Did you get as far as the cathedral crypt?' Markham enquired.

'It had closed for the day.' Olivia sounded wistful. 'The Forty Martyrs Chapel connects with a glassed-in spiral staircase which leads down to what the guide book calls the Undercroft. It says this houses four small chapels dedicated to various martyrs – two each side of a central vestibule, with the bishops' chapel at the far end.'

'Ah yes,' said Markham ruminatively. 'The last resting place for former bishops of Bromgrove. It's got a sliding circular gate in limestone … to mimic the stone which sealed Christ's tomb. Out of bounds to the hoi polloi, I believe.' He grinned mischievously. 'Though I expect they'd make an exception for CID.'

Suddenly he was all business again, continuing with his mental footprint. 'Do you know if the school is linked to the cathedral?'

'There's a passageway which connects the room with the relics to the cathedral. Nat and Julian showed me the door. It's usually locked.'

'You were disappointed in the shrine.' Markham had detected that Olivia was underwhelmed by her tour.

'Well, you know me, I guess I'd built it up in my mind – a sort of gothic chamber of horrors.' Olivia sounded embarrassed. 'Mind you, according to local lore there are secret spaces and hiding places down there dating back to the dissolution of the monasteries and persecution in Tudor times.'

Markham regarded his girlfriend fondly. He never ceased to be amused by her soaring flights of fancy and regretted seeing her romantic preconceptions so rudely punctured.

'And yet,' Olivia added musingly, 'perhaps on reflection, the very *ordinariness* of that little room throws the heroism of the martyrs into sharper relief. Torture and death all in a day's work for the true believer, or something like that.'

Markham gave a melodramatic grimace. 'I hope not,' he snorted. 'Personally, I consider heroic virtue to be distinctly overrated.'

Olivia burst out laughing and the tension that had imperceptibly clouded their conversation lifted.

'Do the school staff live in?' enquired Markham, pouring himself a cup of coffee.

Olivia thought for a moment. 'One of the cathedral canons, Dick Woodcourt, has an apartment on the first floor of the main building, above the visitors' parlour. Alex Sharpe, the Director of Music, is on the other side. I think the second floor houses offices and the admin side of things. Above that, it's just attics.'

'What about the principal?'

'He lives in a cottage called the Chaplain's House. You can't see it from the front. It's tucked in behind the second quad just before you get to the meadow – very picturesque, with a pocket handkerchief lawn enclosed by a box hedge.'

Markham wondered about recreation. 'Where do the boys run about?'

'Well, each quad looks onto a little formal garden. But there are sports grounds on the far side of the grottoes.'

'Good to know they're not neglecting the more muscular pursuits,' commented Markham sardonically. 'Remember, "Waterloo was won on the playing fields of Eton" and all that.'

There was certainly nothing of the aesthete about Nat, Olivia thought, smiling as she recalled the way he had boasted about making the First Eleven.

Markham spoke with decision. 'After Noakes and I have given the place the once-over tomorrow, I'll find a way to have him meet those two boys without generating undue suspicion. Oddly enough, he's very good with youngsters – gets right down to their level and makes them open up ... leaves them feeling that he understands what they're going through.'

Olivia nodded her approval then added, 'Gil, it all looked pleasant enough. Just your typical minor public school with the cathedral as gilt on the gingerbread, but...'

'But what? You felt something wasn't right?' Markham scrutinized her closely.

'I couldn't put my finger on it. Call it something in the air ... something off key. Exorcists talk about a 'cold spot' in haunted buildings, don't they? Well, I felt like that at St Mary's in one of the dormitories. As if there was something evil alongside us. I could almost feel it breathing down the back of my neck.'

Markham's eyes never left her face. 'Go on,' he said.

'I could have sworn I saw a shadow move out of the corner of my eye. But then it whisked around a corner and disappeared. I didn't say anything to Nat and Julian because they were so excited about doing the honours of the school and I didn't want to scare them.' Her brow furrowed. 'But there was a moment in the cemetery when Julian became very quiet.'

'*Cemetery?*'

'Yes, there's a tiny cemetery at the back of the meadow, just next to the grottoes, by an old wash house. It's a forlorn little spot. There are eight or nine graves there, crosses in a little row – ex-teachers apparently. It was customary to bury them in the grounds until someone decided this contravened municipal regulations, leading to future interments taking place in the cathedral cemetery. Anyway, it was quite misty and dank down by the graves. Julian suddenly became very uneasy and subdued, jumping at the slightest cracking of twigs and looking around in such an odd, sly manner. Almost furtive.' She shivered.

'Go on, love.' Markham sensed that there was something else.

'A floodlight must have gone on in the grottoes, because one of the crosses was suddenly illuminated. I thought...' She stuttered slightly. 'I thought I saw a face just behind it. Well, a pair of eyes really. They were hate-filled, absolutely burning with loathing and contempt. It was just for an instant, and then they were gone. But I *felt* them, Gil. Like a brand scorching my skin.'

Markham's thoughts travelled uneasily to the report of suspicious activity in the cathedral graveyard. Desecration of a tomb, wasn't it? Could there be any connection with whoever had been lurking in the cemetery at St Mary's?

He reached across and took Olivia's hand in his.

'Don't let this prey on your mind, dearest. Easy enough for me to say, I know, but I promise I take everything you say very seriously. You concentrate on preparing for next week while Noakes and I pay St Mary's a visit. Is there a lepers' door for the likes of heathen like us?'

A tremulous smile greeted this sally.

'Oh, I think you can risk the front entrance! It'll all be thrilling for the boys.'

Markham's face was sombre.

'I don't believe in coincidences, Liv. St Mary's has thrown up too many mysteries for my liking. A report from Children's Services should be landing on my desk first thing tomorrow. We'll shine a searchlight into every nook and cranny, never fear.' He added softly, 'I know those two boys tugged at your heartstrings. Somehow St Mary's slipped under the radar, but we'll be keeping a close watch from now on. If some evil does threaten Nat and Julian, or any of those young lads, then believe me, we will root it out.'

A huge lump came to Olivia's throat and tears shimmered

in her eyes. 'Thanks, Gil,' she whispered. 'I was afraid that you might think I was losing my marbles.'

'*Never*,' came the emphatic reply.

Much later, nestled against Markham, Olivia did her best to banish the memory of that malevolent spectator. But, like a Hobyah from her childhood fairy tales, he came creeping through her dreams so that she tossed and turned restlessly through the night. Not until dawn streaked the sky did she finally fall into an uneasy slumber.

'Well, what do you make of it all?' asked Markham briskly the next morning as he and Noakes sat taking stock over coffee in the visitors' parlour.

'Glad we've got all the *Songs of Praise* malarkey out of the way, Guv,' replied his DS.

'That Cynthia's a bit nervy but nice enough,' he added, gesturing expansively at the tea trolley generously laden with elevenses. 'Mind, all the talk about a pile of old tat fair killed me. I mean, getting all misty-eyed over some old cups, *I ask you!*'

Markham sighed. 'Those old cups, as you call them, were a collection of priceless communion vessels, Noakes. Cynthia was giving us a glimpse of St Mary's ancient past. God, man, don't you have *any* sense of mystery and romance?'

'Can't really get excited 'bout stuff from before my time,' Noakes replied stolidly.

There we go, that's centuries of Judaeo-Christian culture consigned to the dustbin, thought Markham.

Noting that the DS's mouth was set in the stubborn line with which he was all too familiar, Markham moved on to safer ground. Notwithstanding his obdurate resistance to 'arty-farty nonsense', Noakes was sensitive to his surroundings and swift to detect subtle changes in atmosphere.

'What about the vibes then? Good or bad?' Markham abandoned his antiquarian by-ways for a more prosaic route.

'Kind of secretive,' was the unexpected reply.

'*Secretive*?' Markham stared at his subordinate.

'Yeah, it's chocolate box perfect from the outside, but...' Noakes groped for the right words. '...creepy and twisty-turny the further back you go, what with all those corners and cupboards and cubbyholes. An' those plaster saints all over the shop – there's no getting away from them.'

Markham smothered a smile. Noakes's anti-pietistic fervour was, as anticipated, at full flood.

'Like in that painting over there, Guv.' Noakes gestured at 'The Forty Martyrs', warming to his theme. 'They all look proper buttoned up and smug ... like they've pulled a clever stroke or summat.'

Intriguing, thought Markham, that Noakes too had detected the gleam of mysterious exultation.

'I suppose in a sense they *have*,' he replied slowly.

'Eh?'

'That painting depicts men and women who were cast out and turned into outlaws in their own land, just because they were true to the religion of their forefathers. All ignominiously executed as traitors, though they were loyal to the sovereign who persecuted them with their dying breath. Everything seemed lost. But look at them *now* – triumphant over thrones and dominations, raised to the altars, their relics reverenced and cherished. It's a powerful moral, Noakes. "Look on His works, ye Mighty, and despair!" '

'Well put,' said a voice behind them.

A lean man of medium height had slipped into the room just in time to hear Markham's tribute to a bygone age. Silver haired, of dignified bearing, he was immaculately dressed in a well-cut clerical suit and collar with discreet crucifix lapel pin. Behind spectacles, keen grey eyes regarded the police officers kindly.

Markham hastened to make the introductions. 'Good of you to see us, sir. I'm Inspector Gilbert Markham and this is DS George Noakes.'

'Glad to be of help, Inspector,' replied Canon Dick Woodcourt cordially. He gestured at 'The Forty Martyrs'. 'I like to think of that painting as St Mary's *genius loci*,' continued the gentle, cultured tones. 'It has a picturesque feel, doesn't it, and there's something very nostalgic about that vision of a lost Catholic England. I often think—'

'Who's the bloke at the front?' Noakes interrupted belligerently.

The newcomer did not appear at all put out. Motioning them closer to the painting, he looked enquiringly at the DS. 'Which figure do you mean?'

'The one kneeling on the ground with his back to us,' muttered Noakes gruffly. 'There's a little knife in his belt, and it looks like he's holding a chisel or some such. The rest of 'em look as if they're at a picnic, but he's got his wits about him, that one.'

'How astute of you, Officer! That's Saint Nicholas Owen. He was the master carpenter – master illusionist, really – who constructed priest holes where the gentry concealed their Catholic chaplains from Queen Elizabeth's priest-catchers. He was so good at his craft, that many of his secret rooms and hidey holes are probably still undiscovered. Rumour has it there may even be one here at St Mary's. The cathedral and choir school date from 1861, but parts of the site go back to Elizabethan times, you know.'

'What happened to this Owen then?'

The interlocutor's courtesy and benign warmth were working their magic on Noakes.

Markham was amused to observe that the bulldog had stopped baring his teeth and was practically wagging his tail.

'Oh, he eventually died a gruesome death in the Tower of London. They tortured him with fiendish ingenuity, but couldn't get him to talk.' Noakes nodded approvingly as though he would have expected nothing else from a working man. The other smiled warmly at him. 'They don't breed them like that anymore.'

Markham reluctantly cut short the history lesson.

'Cathedrals and choir schools aren't our usual beat, so please excuse any outspokenness.'

'It's not everyone's cup of tea,' was the mild acknowledgement. 'Certainly, our cabinet of relics and the more florid touches aren't much to my taste. But it's what Dean Buckmaster wants, so we must all suffer in silence.'

There was no attempt to winkle out their religious or churchgoing credentials. Markham's respect for the man increased tenfold.

Turning away from 'The Forty Martyrs', they shook hands and sat down.

Canon Woodcourt waved away Markham's apologies for the intrusion and canvassed the subject of the police investigation in a manner which reinforced the DI's impression of his intelligence and good sense.

Finally, he looked at his watch and declared, 'I'm sorry I haven't been able to shed any light, Inspector, but I can't imagine how those two poor souls ended up buried beneath the grottoes.' His face was sombre. 'Slung there like refuse on a dung-heap' – it was an echo of Olivia's words. 'Such *wicked* profanation!'

Woodcourt remained silent and reflective for some moments before rousing himself.

'I believe it's an away day for most of the lads, Inspector – some school trip or other – but there are one or two still rattling around the place who I'm sure would be glad to give you the guided tour, ghost stories and all.' He rolled his eyes melodramatically. 'That's assuming they can be enticed away from the enthralling spectacle of your forensic teams combing the grottoes!'

'An excellent suggestion, sir.'

Markham had scarcely dared hope that securing access to Nat and Julian would be so straightforward, but this eminently sensible and civilized clergyman clearly did not propose to put any obstacles in their way.

'Cynthia Gibson's on hand if you need her, Inspector. She's housemother as well as teacher – absolutely devoted to the boys – so feel free to give her a shout. Now I must be getting back to the cathedral.' He rose and flicked an imaginary speck of dust from his jacket. 'The widow of one of our vergers needs placating!'

'Of course. Canon, just before you go … there was a matron here, wasn't there, who went missing? Something to do with a couple of pupils absconding?'

A sudden stillness came over Woodcourt. His expression was unreadable but, in the shaft of sunlight which fell from the mullioned windows, Markham noticed that there were deep grooves on either side of the clergyman's decisive mouth while his face was laboured by myriad tiny fissures – like crackle glaze on porcelain. It made him wonder about the clergyman's age; early seventies, he guessed.

'Irene Hummles, Inspector.' The canon's voice was sad. 'One of my pastoral failures, I'm afraid. I didn't realize she was coming adrift and taking refuge in the bottle. She'd been very good at her job, but fell apart when two of our lads went over the side... I mean absconded... You must forgive me, Inspector. I have this habit of referring to the boys as though they were naval ratings!'

Markham found it more endearing than otherwise.

'I'm sorry to open old wounds, sir. You never had the impression there might be more to Ms Hummles's disappearance than that?' He paused, choosing his words with care. 'Something of a sinister nature perhaps?'

'Child abuse?'

Markham gave Woodcourt credit for the quiet, matter-of-fact nature of his response. No simulated indignation. No synthetic outrage.

'I don't see it, Inspector. Irene was just one of those women who poured everything into her job. Totally bound up with the boys to the exclusion of her own needs.' He paused. 'Unhealthily so, in hindsight.'

'Was there any sign that something was troubling her?'

Woodcourt's gaze dropped to his highly-polished shoes. It was obvious that an internal struggle was taking place.

'Forgive me, sir.' Markham's voice was gentle. 'I can see you don't want to speak ill of Ms Hummles and I respect your loyalty, but anything you can tell us may help solve her disappearance.'

The canon's head jerked up and he looked searchingly at Markham.

'You believe there may be a connection to the discovery in the grottoes, Inspector?'

Markham was circumspect. 'It's one possibility.'

Woodcourt looked troubled. 'I'd just assumed she didn't want to be found. She beat herself up endlessly over the runaways – couldn't accept that *all* of us had failed them...'

'Did she give any reason why she felt so guilty about them?'

'I believe Cynthia came across her a few times in tears saying she was having a very bad day and couldn't forgive herself.'

'Couldn't forgive herself.' Noakes sounded mystified. 'Wasn't that going over the top?'

'Absolutely, Detective. She was clearly on a hair-trigger, very unstable. Being treated for depression too, as it emerged. Looking back, we should have insisted on a sabbatical.'

'If you'd done that, she'd likely have thought you were kicking her out,' Noakes offered.

Woodcourt looked at him gratefully. 'Yes, that's true. Such a suggestion might have tipped her over the edge even sooner.' He sighed. 'It was difficult to know what to do for the best.'

At that moment, the door opened and the new principal appeared, trailed by Nat and Julian who hung back shyly while further introductions were made. Despite a certain self-deprecating Woosterishness, Dr O'Keefe exuded a quiet authority which suggested to Markham that he could be formidable. Certainly, Nat and Julian appeared somewhat intimidated, the former gazing up at his new headmaster with reverential awe.

Markham understood immediately why Olivia had yearned towards the two boys. Nat was clearly a doughty little character, with an expression of ingrained wariness, as though life had already dealt him a harsh hand and he was watchful for further blows. Julian was more difficult to read, but Markham sensed the lonely vulnerability lurking beneath a surface nonchalance. Evidently a unit, there was something infinitely touching about the boys' rapport – as though each had found in the other a whole family that had been lost.

'By way of a special privilege, Inspector, I am allowing two of our *more responsible students*' – Nat very solemn – 'to show you and DS Noakes around St Mary's.' The principal turned to Woodcourt. 'I wonder if I can walk over to the cathedral with you. Just a quick query.'

'Of course,' replied the canon affably. He smiled kindly, albeit somewhat absent-mindedly, at Nat and Julian, obviously preoccupied with thoughts of his next appointment.

Cynthia appeared at the door of the parlour with murmured injunctions as to lunch and tea. Their voices faded away down the corridor.

Noakes addressed Nat and Julian. 'It'll be good to see the grottoes through your eyes – have an *insider's* point of view.' With a little awkward gesture, he added, 'To be honest, I feel a bit out of my depth. More of a Church-at-Christmas-and-Easter kind of bloke, if you know what I mean.'

It was remarkable, Markham thought, how his colleague – so often crass and clumsy in his dealings with the public – had such a sure touch with children.

They visibly brightened at Noakes's respectful, man-to-man tones, and flushed with pleasure when the DS declared, 'Right, Guv. I'm off to have a recce with the lads. I'm in safe hands with these two.'

'Yes, we know all the secrets!' confirmed Nat.

The little party left the parlour.

There it was again. That word *secrets*!

Markham stood alone in the deserted room. The sun had gone in and a gust of wind whistled mournfully round the casement windows.

His eyes returned to 'The Forty Martyrs'. What was it the canon had called the carpenter-saint?

The *master illusionist.*

Was St Mary's shimmering golden radiance an illusion? And, if so, what lay beneath?

At that moment, Markham thought he heard a light rustle from the corridor, as though fingers had softly swept the panelling outside the door. Then silence.

Time to go.

Markham gathered up his papers and left the parlour. A fanciful observer might have imagined that the martyrs' eyes followed his departing form.

5

The Grottoes

Like Olivia the previous day, Noakes was distinctly underwhelmed by his first sight of St Mary's Grottoes. Nasty-looking place, he thought to himself, as he surveyed the caves. Like skulls they were, with all those gaps and hollows so many toothless bony gums.

Aware that Nat and Julian were looking at him expectantly, he did his best to look suitably impressed. And in fairness, he reflected, the place *had* been neglected over the years. Hardly a *Time Team* spectacular.

Fluorescent-jacketed officers waved cheerfully as he picked his way with Nat and Julian across the uneven muddy terrain to a narrow, sheer-sided little gully with crumbling sandstone steps projecting at right angles from the foot of the largest cave. A verdigris-encrusted rail formed a rickety balustrade which appeared more ornamental than useful.

'OK to go down, Mike?' he asked the paper-suited SOCO officer who was painstakingly bagging soil samples at the head of the stairs.

'Be my guest,' replied the other. 'The contractors were in earlier checking for earth-falls, shoring up and what have you. So it's safe. Have you got a torch? It's a bit murky down there.'

Quick as a flash, Nat whipped out a traveller-set with Maglite torch and Swiss army knife.

'Blimey, talk about coming prepared! Think we might have a candidate for the Cadet Corps here eh, Noakes!'

Seeing how Nat swelled with pride, the DS forbore to

produce his own police-issue flashlight. Gingerly, he led the way down the precipitous descent.

Once underground, it was cold, musty and perfectly still, as though hermetically sealed off from the everyday world above.

The three stood in a narrow passage at the bottom of the steps where the sandstone gave way to lime washed walls glistening with damp.

'*Yuck*, it smells like our bogs!' exclaimed Nat, wrinkling his nose in disgust.

Julian glanced apologetically at Noakes, visibly relaxing when the latter winked broadly and riposted, 'Nah, more like Bromgrove CID's!'

'There used to be a large marsh somewhere round here, next to the meadow,' Julian volunteered. 'That's most prob'ly why it smells so bad.'

'*And* it was used to store all those bones.' Nat was not to be outdone. 'You know the oss – oss—' he finally gave up, 'oss-thingy.'

'*Ossuary*,' Julian corrected patiently.

'What's one of them?' Noakes asked, seeking to draw out the quiet, serious boy.

'It's a place to keep the bones of dead people, when the graveyards are full and there isn't any more space,' Julian replied earnestly. 'In some countries, they even cover walls and ceilings with skulls and skeletons – like a sort of collage.'

'That's perfectly horrid!' Nat sounded outraged, but Noakes could tell he was enthralled by the notion of walls patterned with crania in a grinning cavalcade of death.

Unexpectedly, Julian grinned at the younger boy. 'It's meant to make you think about being good, Nat.' His voice dropped to a melodramatic whisper. '*What you are now, we once were. What we are now, you shall be.*' In response to Noakes's enquiring look, he explained, 'That's an inscription from one of the graves in the cathedral graveyard.'

Concentrates the mind right enough, thought Noakes, somewhat discomposed.

Aloud, he said, 'A bit spooky, that is. Reckon folk should stick with the Bible. Now, let's check out this corridor. C'mon, Nat, we're going to need that torch of yours!' As he spoke, with a prestidigitator's flourish, Noakes took a ball of string from his pocket and proceeded to loop it around the stair-rail.

'What's that for?' demanded Nat with lively curiosity.

'I'm going to spin out the string behind us so we can easily find our way back and don't have to wait for them above to come and rescue us.'

Noakes knew that the so-called catacombs were compact – a couple of hundred square feet at most – with no danger of the little group getting lost, but he figured Nat and Julian would respond to a touch of drama.

'It's just like in *Theseus and the Minotaur*. You remember that story, don't you, Nat?' Julian sounded keyed up. 'The one about the creature in ancient times with the head of a bull and body of a man. They built a labyrinth and the wicked king fed his enemies to the monster. Then Prince Theseus came and defeated the creature. He could get out of the maze cos the king's beautiful daughter had given him a ball of thread and told him to tie one end to the door post.'

'Oh yes! But he was really mean to the princess, wasn't he?' Nat was keen that Noakes should know of the princely perfidy. 'Left her behind when he sailed away!'

'Well, that was proper ungrateful,' agreed the DS.

Nat nodded with grim satisfaction. 'Theseus had lots of bad luck after that an' it served him right.'

The trio passed through several little corridors like the vestibule entrance. Each was lined with niches, some oval, some horizontal – desolate little bleached receptacles where bones had been left to moulder into a quintessence of dust.

The passages appeared to form an octagon, in the middle of which was a small claustrophobic space supported by squat pillars which seemed to strain under the weight of centuries. The ceiling at this point was so low that the top of Noakes's head almost brushed it.

The vault held four oblong shelves which looked to have been excavated more recently than the other alcoves, judging by the way their dark cement stood out against the neighbouring lime wash.

Noakes was not a man generally much troubled by his imagination, but something about the four narrow shafts – leprous blotches against the surrounding whiteness – made his skin crawl. While the other cubbyholes and crannies had inspired merely a quiet sadness, the sight of *these* ledges made his mind swim with charnel images of coffins, tombs and worms. At that moment, he felt a deadening numbness, even stronger than fear, which intensified the claustrophobia of the place. As perspiration rolled down his forehead and into his eyes, Noakes sensed that Julian felt it too. Their eyes locked for an instant like those of petrified rats trapped in a sewer. *What had been buried in that wall?*

The question hammered insistently inside Noakes's head.

The DS watched uncomfortably as Julian walked over to one of the burial niches and swept his fingers across its dank interior before slowly rejoining his companions.

Staring at the four narrow cavities, a half-remembered Sunday School image came into Noakes's mind of lost souls condemned to whirl like cinders down a bottomless shaft while a red-eyed devil gloated in the shadows. This impression was so vivid that he half expected to see his childhood bogeyman emerge from the gloom in a cloud of malignant ectoplasm.

'D'you think there could be any ghosts down here, Mr Noakes?'

Nat's voice sounded small and he looked pinched and wan, white face and arms specking the gloom and transforming him into a changeling.

Noakes became deliberately casual, almost gossipy.

'Well, I don't rightly know about this place, Nat. But they say there was a skeleton discovered down in the cellars out at Sir Philip Soames's property many years ago, long before my time, of course. Nobody could work out the cause of death or the identity of the poor wretch. Most mysterious of all, they found two iron staples, about two feet apart from each other, near the skeleton. One of these had a short chain hanging from it and the other had a padlock...'

'So, someone was kept chained up like a wild animal,' breathed Nat entranced. 'Is the skeleton still down there?'

'Sorry to disappoint, son,' replied Noakes lightly, 'They took it away for a decent burial in the cathedral graveyard.'

The DS's lips twitched at Nat's crestfallen expression as it dawned on the boy that his hopes of a further cache of macabre relics were doomed to disappointment.

At least the anecdote had served to distract him and lighten the oppressive atmosphere.

There's something wrong here, I can feel it, Noakes thought. *Best get moving.*

He shook himself, as though to slough off the pervasive taint of the place, noting uneasily that Julian was unable to tear his eyes away from the disfiguring stains which appeared to hold a fearful fascination for him. So much so, that it took two reminders and a firm prod to jolt him out of his trance.

'I think Julian's a bit freaked out, Mr Noakes.' Nat looked at his friend in concern.

'Mebbe he just doesn't like being underground,' the DS temporized.

Back on the surface once more, the little party gratefully gulped down lungfuls of cold fresh air. Noakes was surprised at how relieved he felt to have left the clammy little sepulchre and guessed that the two boys felt the same. Julian's face had turned the colour of putty, while Nat kept darting worried looks at him. Privately, the DS cursed himself for not having recced the place before bringing the two youngsters below ground. The *Boys' Own* detour had turned into something far more disturbing.

Nasty, Noakes thought again. Like that rank scrap of ground just over the hedge there, choked in long grass and weeds with its row of wonky crosses – the little teachers' cemetery or whatever it was. Bloody depressing place to end up.

Shrewdly taking in the situation at a glance, the SOCO officer who had admitted them to the lower levels engaged Nat and Julian in some sparky banter. Noakes meanwhile seized his chance to slip over to one of the uniforms.

'Anything?' he grunted.

'Nothing yet, Noakesy.'

'Where did they find the bodies?'

The young constable gestured to the perimeter of the excavation site which was criss-crossed in every direction by archaeological and police pegs, tapes and other boundary markers.

'That section backs onto the little private cemetery, right?' Noakes narrowed his eyes as he calculated the distance between the two plots.

'Yeah. *Ginormous* screw up. The diggers weren't supposed to be turning over that area. Site architect had said it was strictly off limits – smack on top of a burial ground, you see – but for some reason the message didn't get through. That's the architect over there, Edward Preston.'

As though conscious that he was under discussion, the object of their scrutiny waved a greeting and trudged across to Noakes. Tall, square-jawed, with wavy auburn hair and chiselled cheekbones, his startling good looks lent the unbecoming hi-vis waterproof and hard hat an air of distinction. *God, it's Richard Chamberlain in a donkey jacket*, the DS thought to himself as the piercing blue eyes met his own.

He cleared his throat and straightened up, inwardly cursing his lack of inches.

'DS George Noakes, Bromgrove CID. Mr Preston?'

'At your service.' A clear pleasant tenor to match the frank open features.

'Mr Preston! Mr Preston!'

Nat panted across to them. 'You haven't forgotten you're going to let me have a go on the digger?' he burst out.

The architect laughed. 'As if there was any chance of my forgetting!'

From the affectionate way he tousled the golden head, it was clear the architect was very fond of his would-be assistant.

Julian came up at a more sedate pace. 'Nat,' he said reprovingly, 'you *know* we're not supposed to pester Mr Preston.'

'It's no bother, Nat,' reassured the other. 'And you'll be welcome to have a go too.' He winked at Julian.

For all his resentment of Edward Preston's natural advantages, Noakes had to admit he had an easy way with the two boys.

'I'll be dropping into school later today, Detective. We could bring each other up to speed then.'

Noakes, having no great wish to conduct an interview while up to his hocks in mud, readily agreed to the architect's proposal and the little troop headed back to St Mary's.

On their return, Cynthia escorted Nat to clean off the mud with which he was mysteriously caked – 'as if you had *wallowed* in it!'

Noakes and Julian were left in the school kitchen toasting themselves in front of the Aga. A substantial high tea was laid out on the well scrubbed kitchen table but, with gentlemanly restraint, Julian clearly intended to wait for Cynthia and Nat before tucking in. With much inward sighing, Noakes followed his lead.

As they lounged in companionable silence, Noakes became aware that Julian held something in his hand.

'What have you got there, son?' he asked lazily.

Julian extended his hand.

A little plastic figurine. A *Star Wars* character, at a guess.

'It's Obi-Wan Kenobi, Mr Noakes.' Seeing the other's look of incomprehension, he added kindly, 'Luke Skywater's mentor and a Jedi Master.'

Noakes was none the wiser but nodded encouragement.

'You get them with children's magazines,' Julian continued, 'as free gifts. I found it inside one of those empty shelves at the grottoes.'

Noakes sat bolt upright, suddenly fully alert.

Careful, he told himself, *mustn't alarm the boy.*

'What, just now?' he asked with no alteration in tone.

'Yes, I put my hand down one of the holes when we were looking round.'

It was true. In his mind's eye, Noakes saw Julian gently caressing the inside of the tomb, almost as if he was communing with the spirts of the dead.

What was a child's toy doing in that miserable place?

As Noakes cradled the figurine wonderingly in his hand, it seemed to vibrate with a mysterious sadness. His mind teemed with questions. Who was its owner? How did it come to be down in the tunnels? Was there any connection with the bodies discovered in the grottoes?

The DS's hand closed upon the little plastic relic. Relic. He had the sudden sickening conviction that the owner of this little model was long dead.

'D'you mind if I hang onto this for a bit, Julian?' Nothing to show his heart was beating wildly.

'Could it be useful then, Mr Noakes?' There was something curiously intense about Julian's tone.

'Well, we've not much to go on right now, so I'd like to show this to Inspector Markham.' He hesitated then added, 'Can I ask you to keep this between the three of us for now – just you, me and the DI?'

'Not even Nat to know?'

'The fewer people in the loop the better, Julian.'

The warning that lives might depend on his discretion was never uttered.

Julian's eyes met his own with an oddly adult expression. 'You can rely on me, Mr Noakes.'

Footsteps were approaching along the corridor.

'Just one thing, sir.'

'What's that?'

'Would I be able to have it back later? You know, when you've finished the investigation.'

A lump rose in Noakes's throat. 'Never fear,' he said gently, 'I'll see you get it back.' Then, as though embarrassed by this momentary lapse into softness, he chivvied gruffly, 'Come on, lad, you could do with some flesh on those bones. Let's have our tea!'

With the arrival of Cynthia and Nat, conversation became general. The boys' affection for their teacher was obvious and any friend of Olivia had to be kosher, but Noakes found it hard to relax. These intense, highly-strung types were always heavy going and her eyes skittered everywhere. 'Course, folk were always uncomfortable when the police came calling, but Miss Gibson seemed unusually jumpy. Any fool could see she had a thumping great crush on the dishy architect. Dropped a whole plate of scones when he popped his head round the kitchen door, Noakes observed disapprovingly. The DS would never have pegged them for a couple, but there was no accounting for tastes, he opined sagaciously.

Throughout the meal, the little *Star Wars* toy burned a hole in Noakes's pocket. As though it was trying to communicate an urgent message.

As though it was a voice from the grave.

6

Widening Circles

Later that day, Markham sat at his desk in Bromgrove Police Station, contemplating the little *Star Wars* toy that Julian had given to Noakes.

'You're *positive* about it coming from the grottoes?' The DI looked hard at Noakes. 'Did you actually see Julian pick it up?'

'While we were down there, the lad ran his hand along one of the ledges. When we got back to the school, I saw he was holding something. I asked him what it was and that's when he showed me.'

Markham frowned, concerned to confirm an unbroken chain of evidence.

'You hadn't been separated from him at any point between when you were in the grottoes and when he gave you the toy?'

'No. Cynthia took Nat off to get him cleaned up.' Noakes grinned as he recalled the younger boy's begrimed state. 'Julian and I stayed in the kitchen. They'd left us a slap-up tea, Guv. Would have been rude not to stay for a bit.'

'A martyr to duty, that's you, Noakes,' Markham observed acidly. He picked up the figurine, turning it over and over with as much superstitious apprehension as if it was a primitive golem.

Outside, the day had darkened, sleety rain lashing the regiment of leylandii which screened the police station from Bromgrove High Street. It was very quiet in CID, with most of the detectives out on calls. The building seemed to be waiting. Holding its breath.

'You know what this could mean, Noakes?'

Markham's voice held a suppressed urgency that was almost painful. Restlessly, he pushed his chair back from the desk and paced in front of the window.

'Yeah, Guv. That toy didn't take itself down to the grottoes. Stands to reason a kid must've been there.' Noakes was phlegmatic.

'But the grottoes have been out of bounds to everyone for the last couple of years, haven't they, because of the restoration work? I know we were OK to take Nat and Julian down there, but previously it's been no-go.'

Noakes put his head on one side. 'That's not to say kids couldn't have poked around down there without anyone knowing.'

Markham pounced on this hypothesis. 'But is that really likely? I mean, wouldn't Preston and the principal between them have put a stop to any adventures like that? Anyway, from what you've told me, I think children would have been afraid of the place on account of it being a burial site.'

'Reckon you're right, Guv. It's a long shot, but I guess we can't rule anything out.'

Markham stood at the window, running a hand through his dark hair. Then he wheeled round and fixed the DS with a penetrating stare.

'Something's not right. From what you've told me, the earth had been recently disturbed in the underground section of the grottoes.'

'That's about the size of it. Four pits were newer than the rest – you could tell cos they were darker.' Noakes wrinkled his nose ruminatively. 'There was a different smell an' all. Peaty, like down the allotments when folk are getting a patch of ground ready to plant.'

'What did Preston have to say when you told him?'

Noakes shrugged. 'He thought the sub-contractors might've scooped out some irrigation canals. That or the archaeology boffins decided to dig a few cross sections.'

'For God's sake!' A wave of angry colour flushed Markham's cheeks. 'Isn't it the architect's job to know these things?'

'Seems to have been a bit stop-start, Guv. Reading between the lines, I'd say Preston's had his work cut out dealing with all the bickering. I mean, there's the authorities, the university, the cathedral ... plus Sir Philip putting his oar in. I think the poor sod bailed out now and again to work on other stuff and left them all to it.'

Seeing that Markham's fingers were drumming an ominous tattoo on the window sill, Noakes added propitiatingly, 'Should be possible to work out who was responsible.'

'I wish I shared your confidence, Noakes. What a shambles! Sounds more like Piccadilly bloody Circus than a place of devotion!'

Markham sat down heavily, his face unusually tense.

'Nat told Olivia something about a prowler doing the rounds at night. Did the boys say anything to you?'

Noakes scratched his head. 'Nat talked about St Mary's being haunted. Someone called the Night Watchman, I think he said. He's a caution that lad.' The DS smiled ruefully. 'Fancies himself a Ghostbuster.'

'I'm not so sure it's fantasy, Noakes.' As Markham placed his hand upon a manila file, Noakes was struck by his boss's suddenly careworn expression.

'That the report from Children's Services then, Guv?'

'Yeah.' Markham pinched his nose as if to ward off a migraine. 'It seems there were some safeguarding concerns raised in an ISI Inspection a while ago after children reported having nightmares about a hooded figure in the dormitories. The inspectors didn't make a big deal out of it – dispensed the usual bland advice about TV and internet access needing to be more strictly monitored, blah-blah.'

'Hmm.' Noakes sounded doubtful. 'You think they didn't take it seriously enough?'

'Hindsight's a wonderful thing, Sergeant. The inspection took place a year or so before those two students absconded

… stories about a night-time prowler take on a more sinister hue in retrospect.'

'Child Protection didn't get involved then?'

'No.' Markham sighed. 'Maybe with St Mary's being a choir school there was an assumption that students would be more "temperamental" than your average Tom, Dick and Harry … so it didn't set any alarm bells ringing and there wasn't any official follow-up as such.'

'Any connection with the matron's disappearing act? Irene something or other—'

'Irene Hummles. Could well be, Noakes. Apparently, she would have been the youngsters' first port of call for advice and support. The pastoral side of things was mainly down to her.'

Markham appeared to have come to a decision.

'I think we need to speak to the new matron. That's assuming they appointed someone.'

'Cynthia said Alex Sharpe's wife Kate stepped into the breach. She's still doing the job apparently.'

'Ah, a *de facto* appointment. Guess it makes sense with him being Director of Music,' Markham acknowledged.

Noakes thought back over his visit to St Mary's. 'The boys didn't seem very keen on Sharpe,' he commented, 'but they had to admit he's a brilliant musician. In fairness to the man, he's probably had it tough what with the last principal breathing down his neck the whole time.' The DS chuckled. 'Sharpe doesn't stand any monkey business from the boys, that's for sure.'

'Just as well. I had the impression Nat and Julian were in danger of being spoiled by Cynthia and the canon.'

Noakes was meditative. 'Woodcourt's a stand up guy … for a sky pilot.' He scratched his head. 'Could have sworn I've seen him some place before … can't think where.' He gave up chasing the fugitive memory and added, 'Nat's a nice little fella. Couldn't get a handle on Julian. Dreamy-looking, bit of a bookworm too. But handy with his fists apparently. Cynthia told me he's proper protective of Nat –

watches over him and fights his battles as though they were brothers.'

Markham thought back to his first sight of Julian in the visitors' parlour. Olivia had said the boy put her in mind of a portrait seen in a gallery, 'Unknown Young Nobleman'; that he looked as though he belonged in a mysterious, cypress-shaded Renaissance city where doubleted gallants lived hard and died young. Certainly, there was an aloofness, as though his thoughts were turned inward upon some dark conundrum that he did not choose to share.

The DI recalled his thoughts to the present. 'Yes, that's a very close bond between the two lads,' he said gravely. 'Rudderless little souls, but it looks like each has found an anchor in the other.'

It was clear to Noakes that something about Nat and Julian had struck an answering chord with his boss. He wondered idly if Markham had any thoughts of fatherhood. Thirty-one or two, wasn't he? What could be holding him back? Noakes vaguely recalled hearing canteen gossip about 'a tough childhood' but, by some unspoken compact, he and the guvnor had never exchanged life stories. Probably all the better for their working relationship.

He became aware that Markham was addressing him.

'*If I could intrude upon your valuable time, Detective.*' There was a decided edge to the DI's tone. 'I said we need to get back to St Mary's. I want to see Kate Sharpe and then take a closer look at the main building.'

'Isn't that just flats for Woodcourt and Sharpe plus some offices?' Noakes noticed that Markham's eyes were glittering with a peculiar intensity. What the hell was he driving at?

'There are attics too, Noakes, apparently disused. Do you remember our chat with Canon Woodcourt about that painting ... "The Forty Martyrs"?'

Noakes was nonplussed. 'Sure. The one with the saints who'd been executed for being Catholics. Pretty rum, I thought, showing 'em all together like they were at a party.'

'Never mind all that!' Markham was peremptory. 'Do you recall asking Woodcourt about one saint in particular?'

Noakes's brow cleared. 'You mean the fellow who built the secret rooms and hidey holes?'

'*The very one!*' Markham thumped the desk for emphasis. 'Don't you see, Noakes,' he continued intently, 'there could be concealed hiding places. Woodcourt mentioned rumours of a priest hole at St Mary's when he said that parts of the site go back to Elizabethan times.'

Noakes looked sceptical. 'Are you expecting to find another body, Guv?'

'Yes,' was the grim response. 'I have a feeling that Irene Hummles may never have left St Mary's. Olivia asked about the matron's quarters when the boys gave her the grand tour. Julian said the matron used to live on the top floor of the main building until she "went away".'

'But wasn't there a full investigation when the woman disappeared? Surely they'd have turned the place over.'

Markham pulled another manila file towards him, his lips a thin line.

'Looking at the case papers, I have a feeling the search was rather superficial.' There was a pregnant pause. 'DCI Sidney – DI Sidney he was then – seems to have been keen to save the cathedral authorities and Sir Philip Soames undue embarrassment, particularly in view of previous extensive coverage about missing students.'

Noakes might have guessed it! Typical Slimy Sid. No way was he going to put posh folks' noses out of joint as he slithered up the greasy pole! Aloud he said, 'We're not doing an official search then, Guv?'

Markham grimaced. 'This is under the radar, Noakes. Call it copper's hunch... Discovery of the bodies at the grottoes got me thinking about unsolved mysteries connected with St Mary's. Irene Hummles apparently vanished into thin air four years ago. But she took nothing with her—'

'So, not setting up a new life,' pondered Noakes, 'or faking her own death.'

Markham shook his head. 'Unlikely.'

'Could it have been suicide?'

'Highly probable given the depression and drinking. But they never found a body and – *get this, Noakes* – she'd made an appointment to see a counsellor at the Health Centre's Addiction Clinic on the very same day she disappeared.'

'Sounds like she'd turned a corner,' conceded Noakes, 'so why top herself?'

'*Exactly*! The timing's all wrong. So you see, Noakes, I think she's still there.' Markham shivered even though it was stuffy and close in his little office. 'As if,' he said slowly, 'a seam in the backdrop of one of those paintings had opened, drawn her in and closed, without leaving so much as a mended tear in the canvas.'

'Creepy,' agreed the DS with feeling.

'Let's go, there's no time to be lost!'

Alex Sharpe's better half was an unprepossessing woman. The Princess Diana hairstyle – superabundance of frosted highlights – couldn't compensate for protuberant eyes, doughy complexion and sad, downturned mouth. Her voice was equally dull, a low contralto without inflexion. As Markham shook hands, he caught a distinct whiff of alcohol, sherry at a guess. For all that she dressed the part of the school matron – calf-length, plum-coloured corduroy skirt and prim white blouse with pie-crust collar – there was the sense of troubled waters.

Markham's eyes exchanged telegrams with Noakes's. *They're not very lucky with their pastoral team.*

The Sharpes' flat too was depressing. Furnished as impersonally as a Premier Inn hotel room, the living room had no charm or character, no cosy little touches to indicate that the space was truly lived in. Just chintzy frills and flounces, lurid spongy carpet and anodyne chocolate-box pictures on the eau de nil walls.

Mrs Sharpe droned on colourlessly about Irene Hummles, giving no clue whatsoever as to the character of the woman.

For all the surface monotony of the recital, however, there were signs of repressed tension in the way Kate Sharpe's fingers kept restlessly pleating and unpleating a fold of her voluminous skirt.

At the mention of Nat and Julian, a look of genuine affection glanced across her features so that, for a fleeting instant, she looked almost pretty. Her hands too were momentarily stilled, but immediately afterwards the nervous fidgeting resumed with redoubled vigour. Something was troubling her, but what?

Eventually, Markham gave Noakes the look that meant, *Come on, we're getting nowhere fast. Let's wrap this up.*

'You've been very helpful, Mrs Sharpe.' Noakes did his best to force some conviction into the statement.

Markham took pity on his subordinate. With equally false bonhomie, he said, 'I believe Nat and Julian gave Noakes here the full VIP treatment.'

A blank look greeted this sally.

God, she was heavy weather!

'I mean, they took him into pretty much every nook and cranny. A comprehensive tour eh, Noakes?'

It was the DS's cue.

'Actually, sir, we didn't get around to this part of the site. Julian mentioned some spooky attics or some such but there wasn't time.' He smiled winningly at the lumpen woman opposite. 'Any chance of you showing us what's up there, Mrs Sharpe?'

Kate Sharpe turned so white that Markham thought she was going to faint. Instinctively, he put out a hand to steady her. Guiding her to the sofa, he asked, 'Are you feeling quite all right, Mrs Sharpe?'

'I'm getting over the flu, Inspector.' She laughed shakily. 'Probably a case of too much Night Nurse.'

One thing was clear. No way was she going to accompany the two men. No way was she going to climb the stairs to the attics.

In that instant, Markham knew with absolute certainty that he was on the right track.

The two officers emerged onto the landing outside the Sharpes' flat. On the other side of the main staircase was a door with a neat name-plate indicating Canon Woodcourt's residence. To the left of the Sharpes' apartment, a narrow flight of stairs led to the upper regions. The next floor up seemed innocuous enough – offices for the accountant and PA to the principal, and a little kitchenette from which came the clatter of teacups and a cheery hum of voices. Easy, then, for Markham and Noakes to slip unobtrusively past, continuing up the stairs to the floor above.

The door to the attic floor was unlocked. What lay beyond was disappointingly ordinary. Nothing to see save broad transoms in a musty, cobwebby space. A grimy skylight afforded the only natural light. Great louring clouds passed across the dormer like a dark hand before a face, blotting out even that feeble illumination.

A half-hearted attempt had been made to convert Irene Hummles' former flat to office space, but clearly the dormer was unused, loose wires trailing along ill-fitting skirting boards. Dreary porridge-grey carpeting covered the uneven floorboards.

Markham and Noakes stood silently for a few minutes while their eyes became accustomed to the gloom. Then they moved slowly forwards.

Despite its air of abandonment, the long space looked surprisingly clean. No beetles, rats or cockroaches.

Almost too clean.

Markham scanned the wainscoting. Nothing out of the ordinary. No unevenness or warping to signal a hidden space.

He began to feel foolish. What must Noakes be thinking? It was just like a modern loft. Nothing Elizabethan about it. Boxes, lumber, a pile of mouldy old clothes.

Lumber.

Markham caught his breath. Something was nagging at

him. The lumber was not scattered haphazardly about as one might expect. There seemed something almost contrived about that neat pyramid against the back wall at the gable end.

Cat-like, he moved swiftly across to the pile of jumble and cleared it away from the wall.

There it was. The tell-tale knot. Sinking to his knees, Markham gently pressed it and a panel slid open, exposing one end of a rough sack, like a winding sheet.

He could barely bring himself to touch what he had uncovered. Though there was no reek of putrefaction and he knew who was concealed beneath the hessian folds, it was still a moment of profound sadness.

Somehow Markham's legs were moving, taking him across the floor of the attic, far away from the pitiful package. His heart was racing. He felt odd, as though he was somehow there but not there. The blood rushing in his ears, it was as though he was pitching headlong down an abyss. Without a word, Noakes moved up on his other side.

All unknowing, the DS echoed Olivia's death knell for the two bodies excavated in the grottoes. 'It's OK, Guv. She *wanted* to be found. She was *ready* to be found.'

Outside, the night clouds trailed low, like medieval funeral pennants. A feeling of complete peace washed over Markham. As Noakes moved away to make the necessary phone calls, he bowed his head in silent respect and breathed a prayer for the repose of Irene Hummles's soul.

May she receive merciful judgement in the same measure as those who murdered her receive eternal damnation.

7

Let It Come Down

'This is a *disaster*, Markham, a *disaster*!'

Nothing like stating the blindingly obvious, thought Markham sourly, as he and Noakes sat 'in conference' with DCI Sidney.

While Sidney ranted, Markham's eyes wandered round the Hall of Fame, as the DIC's inner sanctum was irreverently known.

Bloody hell, talk about tooting your own horn! The walls were plastered with blow-ups of Sidney rubbing shoulders with the great and good, his Humpty Dumpty bonce bobbing up and down between celebrities like that of a demented photobomber.

Not that the man was remotely photogenic, reflected Markham as he watched Sidney's bald head glisten sweatily under the strip lighting, the overcrowded mouth stretching in something between a grimace and a snarl. His superior's fledgling beard – an uneasy compromise between five o'clock shadow and full face rug – entirely failed to produce the macho impression that was no doubt intended. Prominent on Sidney's desk sat a silver-framed studio portrait of a strong-jawed Valkyrie spouse and two sturdy, unsmiling boys; somehow, this undermined the message of all-conquering hero implicit in the photographic montage.

'*Well, what have you got to say about it?*'

Sidney's normally seesaw tones had risen to apoplectic pitch.

'I agree, it's a most unfortunate development, sir,' Markham replied leadenly. 'Not least for Irene Hummles.'

Sidney's sallow complexion flushed. 'Naturally, I'm appalled the poor woman ended up like that.'

Naturally.

'But my current priority is to fend off the press who are literally baying for blood over this fiasco. I mean, how the hell did the search teams manage to miss the body?'

The DCI looked at Markham accusingly as if holding him personally responsible for the catastrophe.

'Of course, you can talk about human error and promise an imminent review of search techniques,' continued Sidney.

Oh, so it's me in the hot seat for the press conference, thought Markham, his face impassive.

'They had sniffer dogs, for God's sake. And there must have been some stench of decomposition...' The DCI's face twisted with distaste.

'Officers thought they were on a missing person enquiry and looking for someone who was alive – suicidal and gone off to some lonely spot to end it all,' said Markham. 'In fact,' he continued, recalling a witness statement in the file on Irene Hummles's disappearance, 'didn't Preston's number two tell them he'd seen Irene leaving the school grounds on the day she vanished? That would automatically have set the team on the wrong track, so they didn't bother with cadaver dogs and the ordinary ones missed the scent. Then it could be the body wasn't stowed in the attic to start with but kept elsewhere in the school and quietly brought back up to the flat after the initial checks by police.'

'You know what the *Gazette*'s like,' chipped in Noakes helpfully. 'They'll get tired of calling us *The Keystone Cops* and move on to someone else.'

Sidney's basilisk glare would have turned a lesser man to stone, but Noakes gamely persisted. 'All we can do is the usual, sir. Apologize to the family, talk about valuable lessons being learned...' He trailed off as the other's face turned from red to purple.

'Oh, that's a *great* consolation!' the DCI exploded, glaucous eyes bulging. '*Guaranteed* to get the cathedral and school off my back. To say nothing of Sir Philip Soames, who has already called to convey,' Sidney air quoted savagely, 'his profound disappointment at the shadow which has been cast over St Mary's good name by recent discoveries which he believes to be unconnected with the school.'

Markham spoke quietly. 'I sympathize with Sir Philip's feelings, sir, given his family ties to the place, but he must accept there's a strong likelihood of there being a connection between those bodies in the grottoes and Irene's murder.'

'I don't think he accepts any such thing,' came the terse response. 'You and Noakes had better get over there post haste and do some damage limitation.'

As the two men got to their feet, Sidney snapped, 'Not so fast, Inspector. What's this I hear about your *lady friend*?' The appellation dripped with innuendo, but Markham kept his voice level.

'Sir?' Always best to play the dumb wooden top when Sidney went for the jugular.

'*Don't fence with me, Inspector.*' It was a hiss. 'I've heard that Miss Mullen has accepted a job at the school.'

Markham had always striven to keep his relationship with Olivia well under wraps, shrinking with proud sensitivity from any exposure of their romance to police canteen culture. He was clearly no match for Sidney's intelligence network, however. Best to admit what the DCI's informant had already told him.

'Olivia had been head hunted by St Mary's well before the latest developments.' Permissible to bend the truth in the circumstances.

'Well, you know your own business, I suppose.' The DCI's voice would have curdled milk.

Too bloody right, so back off!

'But I trust, Inspector, that the high standards of personal and professional conduct that I expect of my officers will not be compromised by any conflict of interest.'

For an instant, Markham wished passionately that he could give vent to a cathartic burst of contempt and punch the man's lights out. A glance at Noakes, mutely sympathetic, helped him bring his feelings under control.

'Of course, sir.' He did his finest impersonation of a plank of wood. It appeared to satisfy the other.

'Right, just so long as that's understood. Press conference later, and I'd advise you to be word perfect. One other thing. Have we got ID for the bodies in the grottoes?'

'Yes, sir. Though I'm not sure it takes us much further. It's in my report.' Markham passed over a folder. 'Two casual workers. Looks like they were on the payroll of one of the subcontractors via the Community Jobs Initiative for the long-term unemployed. I'll see if Edward Preston – he's the architect – can flesh it out for us.' Not the most fortunate choice of words, he realized, as Sidney's scowl deepened.

'You do that, Inspector.'

With a regal wave of the hand, the DCI indicated that the interview was over.

As they headed to the cathedral, Noakes stole a sideways glance at the DI who drove stony-faced, his knuckles white on the steering wheel.

He reckoned it was DCI Sidney's sneering reference to Olivia which had got under Markham's skin. For the umpteenth time, he wondered about the relationship between the red-haired schoolmarm and his guvnor whose chilly impenetrability repelled any exchange of confidential chit-chat. 'S. E. X.' was his wife's verdict, delivered with pursed lips. But Noakes sensed something much deeper. As though Olivia was somehow Markham's centre of gravity.

He blinked in surprise. Fancy his coming over all poetical. Such was the bewildering effect that Olivia had upon him, as though an exotic bird of paradise had strayed into a pigeon fancier's coop.

Completing the short journey in silence, they drew up in the cathedral car park.

Canon Woodcourt hurried out of the narthex to greet them before ushering the two men into a quiet office tucked away to the side. Observing Noakes's look of apprehension as he took in the prayer room sign, Woodcourt chuckled.

'It's all right, Detective. You don't have to worry about speaking in tongues or anything like that. This is just our all-purpose space for anything from Mums 'n' Tots to bereavement counselling.' Switching the *Vacant* panel to *Meeting in Progress*, he announced, 'Nobody will disturb us in here.'

Markham stifled a groan as he saw that a reception committee awaited them. Dr O'Keefe, Sir Philip Soames, and a third man who he guessed was Alex Sharpe were sitting at an oak refectory table.

They had barely taken their places before Sharpe went on the offensive.

'In the first place, I want to say that I strongly object to your badgering my wife when she was unwell and I wasn't available to support her.'

Some knight in shining armour you'd have been, thought Markham, flinching at the strident, hectoring tones which, from the way he shifted in his chair, also grated uncomfortably on Sir Philips's ears. The man's a bully, he said to himself, taking in the jutting jaw, double chins and suspicious currant eyes. No wonder that poor pug-faced woman looked as though she'd had the life sucked out of her.

'We paid the briefest of visits, Mr Sharpe, and there was no question of harassment. I apologize if any distress was caused to Mrs Sharpe, but we were anxious to speak to Irene Hummles's former colleagues.'

Markham's voice was courteous but his expression deadly.

'Naturally we appreciate you were just carrying out your inquiries, Inspector,' said Woodcourt pacifically, quelling Sharpe with a look. 'But this has been the most terrible shock to our community here. Distressing enough to learn that the grottoes had been defiled, but to discover that Irene's body was literally mouldering above our heads all this time …

she was a devout woman, but didn't even receive a Christian burial.'

Taking off his spectacles, the canon began to polish them vigorously with a snowy-white handkerchief.

Quietly and unobtrusively, O'Keefe left the group, reappearing moments later from what Markham assumed was a galley kitchen. Woodcourt gave him a grateful look and sipped from a glass of water.

'I suppose there's no doubt as to the identity of the remains, Inspector?'

This was Sir Philip.

'We'll receive formal confirmation later today, sir, but I would say no doubt at all.'

'I assume the tragedy has its roots in Ms Hummles's private life,' resumed Soames. He turned to Woodcourt, 'I'm sorry, Canon, but one must presume that all was not what it seemed.'

Markham declined to be intimidated. 'With respect, Sir Philip, it isn't as cut and dried as that. Given the discovery at the grottoes and the fact that Irene was known to be upset about two missing students, we must consider the possibility that the answer to these mysteries lies here at St Mary's.'

As though in response to some internal prompting, Markham made no mention of Nat, Julian and the Night Watchman.

Sir Philip leaned across the table and Markham felt the full blast of his personality.

'You know what this means. The proud heritage of St Mary's, devotedly nurtured by generations of my family, will be besmirched by prurient sensationalism and scandal-mongering.'

His voice was low but insistent, its fierce sibilance shredding the silence like a scythe. The remarkable eyes blazed in their deep, bruised sockets.

You had to hand it to the DI, thought Noakes in admiration, as Markham regarded Sir Philip calmly. The man had the strength of a steel wall.

'Be assured, Sir Philip, we will proceed as sensitively as possible and with all due respect for St Mary's reputation, but it would be negligent to focus exclusively on Irene's personal history—'

'That's rich, talking about negligence when your lot ignored what was right under their noses!' sneered Sharpe.

Markham continued inexorably as if there had been no interruption. '—and it stands to reason that we must focus on the place where she was last seen alive.'

'We are a family at St Mary's, Inspector.' The Canon sounded choked. 'Irene was well-loved. It's *inconceivable* that anyone here could have wished her ill.'

O'Keefe laid a concerned hand on Woodcourt's shoulder and patted it reassuringly. Clearly, the short period of their acquaintance was enough for there to have sprung up a strong mutual respect.

The principal raised his eyes anxiously to Markham. 'This has been terribly unsettling for the school, Inspector. My telephone has been ringing off the hook. Parents, journalists,' he sighed exasperatedly, 'and nosy parkers by the dozen. There was a gaggle of journalists and snoopers hanging around earlier, shouting intrusive questions and frightening some of the boys. Took me an age to get shot of them.'

'We can help you with that, sir,' said Noakes, pulling out his police notebook. 'I'll get our press office to field enquiries and generally run interference.'

A look of relief washed over O'Keefe's face, the strain of his baptism of fire suddenly very apparent.

'Of course, staff are deeply concerned as well,' he added. 'I mean, *three* bodies discovered on site in quick succession. I'm half expecting a flurry of resignations.'

'Let's get the weekend over,' advised Markham, 'and then I'll do a briefing first thing on Monday morning followed by interviews. We'll try to cause as little disruption to your timetable – and to the cathedral services – as possible.'

O'Keefe nodded. He shot Sharpe a warning look. 'I promise you'll be afforded every assistance, Inspector.'

At that moment, the door burst open and Edward Preston breezed into the room with the exuberance of a red setter.

Markham had to admit that Noakes's rather jaundiced pen portrait for once had not exaggerated. The architect's glowing good looks irradiated the prayer room, his bright handsome head casting Alex Sharpe into the shade. The Director of Music appeared to feel diminished by the contrast.

'Good of you to spare a moment of your precious time,' he muttered sarcastically.

'Not at all,' replied Preston, quite unruffled and in perfect command of the situation. Looking straight at Markham, he declared, 'I'm not sure I can shed any light, Inspector, but please let me know if there's anything I can do to help.'

Markham passed him a sheet of paper. 'We've got IDs for the bodies in the grottoes, sir. Jacob Smith and Colin Saunders, two casual labourers working for one of the subcontractors under a local enterprise scheme. Photos and details are there.'

Preston scrutinized the sheet carefully but his face was blank. 'Sorry, Inspector, I don't recognize either of them. But,' an air of constraint clouded the perfect features and a note of embarrassment crept into his delivery, 'as you probably know, there have been interruptions to the restoration work, so I haven't been on site throughout. But that's not to say one of my team mightn't remember them. Leave this with me and I'll ask around.'

Good, thought Markham, *at least I can count on O'Keefe and Preston. The canon's too shell-shocked to be much use right now and Sharpe has clearly decided we're fascist oppressors. Well, two out of four's something, I suppose.*

Woodcourt seemed to have drawn strength from Preston's youthful vigour. Rousing himself with an effort, he smiled bravely at his colleagues.

'Right, I must get ready for Evensong. There will be special prayers for Irene, of course, with a full requiem in due course for the repose of her soul, as she would have wanted.' His lip trembled. 'We'll pray for God's mercy towards her … and towards us all.'

O'Keefe accompanied the canon to the door, gently murmuring words of comfort.

Sir Philip intoned solemnly, 'May her soul be reborn in the astral light.'

That's not C. of E.!

The look Noakes sent Markham was more expressive than if the DS had uttered the words aloud. Luckily, Sir Philip promptly took his leave, not however before informing Markham that he looked forward to receiving a full briefing 'at your earliest convenience'.

Sharpe followed suit, ostentatiously consulting his watch, leaving Preston to escort the two policemen off the premises. He looked disturbed, and threw them both an apologetic glance.

'You're not seeing us at our united best, just now, gents.' The pleasant, genial tones were troubled.

'We understand, Mr Preston.' Markham was bracing. 'It's been a shock.'

The young man pumped their hands gratefully and strode off in the direction of the grottoes.

'Officers!'

Oh God, not some busybody parishioner-cum-rubbernecker. That's all we need!

On second thoughts, this was no gossiping bedlam, Markham told himself as he took in the fine-boned face, sleek grey bob and observant brown eyes.

With her neat tweed jacket and skirt, colourful silk scarf knotted at the throat in an understated bow, sensible handbag and sturdy brown loafers, she looked what she was. An English, middle-class gentlewoman, without artifice or pretension, who reminded him of a much-loved aunt lost some years before.

Noakes too seemed to approve, smoothing his hair and straightening his tie, as though ready for inspection.

'My apologies for ambushing you, gentlemen.' It was a well-bred voice. 'My name is Georgina Hamilton.'

Noakes did a double-take.

The one who'd reported desecration of graves in the cathedral cemetery. Miss Marple herself!

Fortunately, neither the DI nor Mrs Hamilton observed his confusion. Doing his best to look alert and intelligent while Markham performed the introductions, he cleared his throat. 'How can we help you, madam?'

Markham noticed that Mrs Hamilton was looking around furtively as though nervous.

'Why don't we pop back into the cathedral prayer room for a moment,' he suggested. 'It isn't locked and there's time for a chat before anyone arrives for Evensong.'

No sooner said than done.

'I was the one who called at the police station about interference with graves in the cemetery,' she announced without preamble after they had sat down. 'I know, I know,' she said dryly, rightly interpreting the awkward silence. 'No doubt I was dismissed as the archetypal neurotic female of a certain age.' Her eyes twinkled disarmingly. 'Possibly even alcoholic to boot.'

A flush crept slowly up Noakes's neck.

'We take everything of that kind very seriously, Mrs Hamilton,' he stuttered. 'I went and checked it out myself. Spoke to the groundsman too. Everything was as it should be... He wasn't aware of any unusual activity, but he'd been off sick for a few days and the company hadn't been able to arrange a substitute. So, he couldn't be one hundred per cent positive as to comings and goings.'

'No need to justify yourself, Mr Noakes. I'm sure you did everything by the book. I'd worked myself up into quite a state that night when I went to the station. When I look back, I can't even be sure that I didn't imagine the whole thing... But somehow I don't think so.' She gave a convulsive shudder. 'I can still hear the taller man's voice. There was something *evil* about it. I'd know it again anywhere.'

Markham felt a needle-sharp pain between his shoulder blades, all his senses suddenly on high alert.

'What was it exactly that you saw, Mrs Hamilton?' he asked levelly.

She smiled ruefully at him. 'It *looked* like an interment at the back of the Soames Vault. Afterwards, I wondered if it could have been *re*interment following an exhumation.' Her face fell. 'I remember my late husband Geoffrey saying that reburials generally take place in the small hours to ensure maximum privacy. But this was early evening and it didn't *feel* official.' She shook her head emphatically. 'No, it didn't feel like those gravediggers had anything to do with the cathedral. I think they'd counted on no-one being around at that time ... there was something sneaky and underhand about them...'

Interference with human remains in the cathedral graveyard. Discovery of three skeletons in the precincts of St Mary's Choir School. Markham did not believe in coincidences. Grimly, he made an internal resolution to re-visit the matter of the Soames Monument. If that meant putting various officials' noses out of joint – or the coroner's for that matter – then so be it.

'But I'm not here to talk about that,' Mrs Hamilton continued briskly. 'No. Joan the cook at St Mary's is an old friend of mine. She used to 'do' for me and Geoffrey until we moved into assisted accommodation not long before Geoffrey died.'

Georgina paused as though suddenly at a loss for words.

It was Noakes who gently encouraged her. 'Go on, Mrs Hamilton.'

'Well.' The earnest, intelligent face clouded over. 'This sounds very foolish, but Joan is an eminently level-headed sensible woman with no nonsense about her... Sometimes she sleeps over at the school if there's been a function or late dinner. There's a little room for her at the end of one of the boys' dormitories.'

Again, she paused, unknotting the scarf at her throat as if it suddenly felt too tight.

'Joan swears that something made her wake up one night. She listened for a while before convincing herself it was just the usual sounds and trying to settle back down to sleep. But for some reason she couldn't drop off.'

Georgina twisted her garnet ring round and round, looking pleadingly at the two men for reassurance.

'It's all right, Mrs Hamilton,' said Markham softly. 'Please continue.'

'She said she felt there was something out there. Something wicked that made her neck prickle. She slipped out of bed and looked round her door down the dormitory. There was a light flickering, she thought. It cast a shadow on the wall. Like a hooded figure. For one crazy moment, she thought perhaps it was the ghost of a monk come back from the dead. Then the shape seemed to bend over one of the beds before straightening up, almost as though it was aware of being watched. The light went out and everything was dark again. She doesn't know how long she stood there, rooted to the spot with fear. But eventually she went back to bed, though she didn't sleep a wink all that night.'

Georgina stumbled to a halt, looking flustered.

'As I say, it must sound a bit daft...'

'Not at all.' Markham was authoritative. 'You naturally wondered, in retrospect, if what Joan saw might relate to the discovery of bodies at St Mary's.'

'Yes, that's pretty much it, Inspector.'

'Has Joan spoken to anyone else about this, Mrs Hamilton?'

'No, she decided to hold her peace. Felt the poor new principal had enough on his plate without having to listen to what she calls her megrims.'

'*Excellent.*' The DI sounded upbeat. 'I'd like her to keep it that way. This is just between the four of us, understood?'

'Do you think it could be relevant, Inspector?' Georgina sounded uncharacteristically tremulous.

'Yes, I do. I can't tell you why at this stage, but you can take my word for it that this is very useful information.'

Her brow cleared. '*Thank you,*' she said with real feeling.

'Can we give you a lift anywhere, Mrs Hamilton?' Noakes enquired solicitously.

'No, I could do with a walk, Detective. Thank you,' she said again, 'it's a weight off my mind to have told you.'

The two men escorted her to the door of the cathedral. Markham watched her retreating figure until it disappeared. Then he turned to his DS.

'Right, Noakes, back to the station. We need to prep for that bloody press conference.'

Unseen by either of them, a figure flitted through the narthex from its place of shadowy concealment and disappeared into the dimly lit cathedral beyond.

8

Undivulged Pretence

At the end of Evensong, Nat felt he had acquitted himself well. There had been one wobble during the *Miserere*, but Mr Sharpe hadn't minded and even told him 'Good effort' at the end. Julian had sloped off, muttering that he had 'things to do' before Prep. Nat felt obscurely hurt by this desertion, but knew better than to ask what was wrong after having been rudely repulsed when he caught his friend crying behind the changing rooms before rugger. Julian was fierce and sullen by turns these days and sometimes seemed almost to despise him, though he was quick to lash out at anyone who bothered Nat. It was all very puzzling and Nat did not know what to make of it.

Sighing, he disrobed in the vestry then went out into the cathedral. This was his favourite time, when everywhere was peaceful, the vast space lit only by the sanctuary oil lamps and votive candles which flickered on stands in the side chapels. Magnificent floral arrangements glowed softly in the darkness against the stark white marble. Nothing disturbed the sacred hush, subtly perfumed with the mingled scents of blooms and incense. Slipping into a pew, he closed his eyes.

It had been exciting going underground at the grottoes. Exciting but scary too. He had been afraid they might find something bad down there. He could tell Julian was creeped out because he turned a funny colour and looked like he was going to puke. Suddenly he felt a fierce desire to help his friend. *Please let Julian be all right, please let him be like he was before, amen.* It wasn't much of a prayer, but he meant it with all his heart.

Maybe the police would solve the mystery of the Night Watchman. The hooded man's breath made a sort of whistling sound. Like he had false teeth or something. That's how he knew the prowler wasn't make believe. No-one made a weird noise like that unless he really existed.

He hoped Miss Mullen would stay at St Mary's. When she smiled at him, he felt warm from top to toe as if a light had switched on inside him and she understood him without the need for any words. Julian said she looked like the picture of Morgana le Fay, the fairy witch in Nat's picture book *Legends of King Arthur* that Mr Woodcourt had given him for coming top in Latin. But Nat could tell Julian liked her too.

Somehow Nat must have drifted off, drawn into the heartbeat of the cathedral like a small creature nestling up to its mother.

A creaking of the pews recalled him to the present. If he didn't get a move on, he would miss Prep. With a sigh, he rose to his feet and made his way out through the narthex (fortunately still unlocked) and round to the cloister garth.

It was twilight now, and he blinked in the gloom, still under the spell of the cathedral which slumbered behind him like some great beast. Gradually, the night air broke his trance and he shivered as the cold of the stone flags struck through to his bones.

Suddenly, he caught the odour of wood-smoke. Dimly, in a far corner of the garth, he made out a figure. Moving closer, he saw a strange and unexpected sight.

In the darkest corner of the cloister garth, Canon Woodcourt stood next to a still smouldering pile of embers which appeared to be the remnants of a small fire on which he had been burning papers. A few fragments, their edges curling brown, were all that remained. Woodcourt's face was troubled as he gazed unseeing at the dying blaze. Clearly, he had chosen the moment when he believed himself least likely to be disturbed, since Prep was sacrosanct and no students were supposed to be abroad at that time.

With the delicate sensitivity to another's pain which reflected his own love-starved childhood, Nat stole away, reluctant to obtrude upon a private interlude. But, quiet as he was, the canon heard him.

'Nat, my dear boy! Come and join me,' he called softly.

Nat was embarrassed. 'I didn't want to interrupt you, sir, or be a nuisance.'

'*You could never be a nuisance!*' Woodcourt declared firmly and was rewarded by a shy smile.

'I'm going to confide in you, Nat, because I know you to be loyal and true. Indeed, wise beyond your years.'

'I'll never let you down, sir,' came the earnest reply.

'If I am sure of anything, I am sure of that.'

The canon hesitated as if uncertain where to begin. Finally, as though each word was a red-hot brand, he said, 'I have uncovered some evidence of a most serious nature—'

'Is it about the Night Watchman, sir?' interrupted Nat eagerly.

For an infinitesimal instant Woodcourt's face appeared so altered – parchment-white, with the skin stretched taut over the temples – that Nat failed to recognize his friend. What, he wondered fearfully, could have caused such a transformation?

'I'm sorry, sir,' he mumbled. The man who had always been so good to him had obviously come upon something which wounded him to the core. 'I didn't mean to upset you.'

Woodcourt sighed. It sounded to Nat as though wrenched from the depths of his being by some almost unbearable pain.

'You are not the cause of my distress, Nat. But there is someone who has abused my trust and blackened the honour of our school. Those papers you saw me burn showed me what has been going on.' He stared down at the remains of the fire as though in the grip of some profound emotion. 'Now,' he said slowly, 'I must decide what to do.'

Nat's heart beat very fast. *It must be the Night Watchman,* he thought. *Mr Woodcourt knows who it is.* His thoughts were tripping over themselves. *Or maybe he's found out what happened to Miss Hummles and those people in the grottoes.*

Whatever the nature of the canon's discovery, Nat could see it had come upon him like a thunderbolt, so that he appeared to have aged a hundred years in the space of just a few seconds. Patiently, he waited for the clergyman to recover, confident that the man who had looked out for him from the moment of his arrival at St Mary's would know what to do.

Eventually, Woodcourt roused himself. 'But you're freezing out here! Let's go back inside. No, not that way,' as Nat headed for the little wicket which connected the cloister garth to the school quads, 'why don't we take a turn around the cathedral while we've got it to ourselves.' Correctly reading Nat's anxious expression, he added, 'Don't worry, you won't get into trouble. I'll clear it with whoever's taking Prep tonight.'

Back in the cathedral, it felt warm and safe.

They turned into The Forty Martyrs Chapel adjacent to the vestry.

Visitors to the chapel, expecting to see images of venerable saints in classical poses, were generally taken aback by the startling impact of its avant-garde design.

Nat, however, loved the sunburst fresco with abstract geometric shapes in white and grey which hung above a simple granite altar. He wondered what the artist meant by it and why he hadn't painted holy men and women with haloes around their heads. Perhaps he thought that was too boring. Perhaps he wanted people to imagine the martyrs' souls in glory, leaving the world of finite time on their journey out of darkness to the bright light at the end of the tunnel.

Under the fresco was a rectangular Perspex box with brightly coloured wood-block chalice, sword, pillar and whip vivid against swirling concentric patterns in blue, red and green. The canon had told Nat that these items represented Arma Christi, the instruments of Christ's Passion and the symbols of His victory over the Devil. They seemed to burn and pulse with a mysterious triumphant fire of their own, so that he could not look away.

'Come on,' murmured Woodcourt, smiling at Nat's rapt expression. 'Let's go up to the balcony, there's a good view of the baldachin from there.'

Together they mounted the spiral stone steps to the upper level with its tiered pine benches bounded by a low steel rail. Nat's favourite vantage point at the front afforded a bird's eye view of the aluminium crown of thorns, composed of multiple interlocking rods, suspended above the main altar. Like the implements in the chapel below, it seemed to defy time and space, beckoning him to come closer, making him feel almost light-headed...

The boy's head swam and his world seemed to tilt.

'*Woah, Nat!*'

Strong hands grasped him roughly round the waist and yanked him back.

'*Canon!*' It was Alex Sharpe, his voice rough with concern. 'Nat was very nearly over the rail! It's dangerous for him with his vertigo. Remember, we nearly lost him last Christmas from the organ loft!'

'I had forgotten, Alex. It was most remiss of me.' Woodcourt sounded dazed, as though he shared something of Nat's dislocation from time and space.

Nat noticed that Mr Sharpe was looking closely at them. He pulled himself together. The last thing the poor canon needed right now was a lot of fuss and bother just because he'd had one of his turns. If he'd toppled out of the balcony, it would have served him jolly well right.

'I'm all right sir, honestly,' he reassured the Director of Music. 'I lost track of time after Evensong. Mr Woodcourt knows I like it up here and was going to bring me back.' No need to mention what he had seen in the cloister garth.

'C'mon then.' Sharpe spoke gruffly but his expression was kind. 'You can walk back with me. Prep's over but you'll be in time for tea. Assuming the others haven't wolfed the lot.' He turned to Woodcourt. 'I'll see you later this evening at the committee meeting then?' The canon nodded absent-mindedly, as if his thoughts were far away.

Nat felt a pang as he looked at his friend. He had always thought of him as indestructible – a giant-slayer – but, slumped there in the shadowy cathedral, Woodcourt suddenly looked infinitely sad and spent, as though all his strength had leached away. Gently, Nat touched his sleeve. 'Thanks for looking after me, Mr Woodcourt. I'll be all right now. After Prep I'm going to read your book about King Arthur. I've got up to where the knights expel Sir Mordred.'

He was pleased to see a gleam of animation pass across the other's face. 'Ah yes, Nat. Sir Mordred, destroyer of Camelot. A traitor indeed.' Woodcourt chuckled. 'Right, off you go now.'

Alex Sharpe led Nat carefully down the stone spiral and they disappeared around the corner of the vestry.

Woodcourt sat on in the cathedral, motionless as one of the figures in the stations of the cross below, his head bowed. The evening wore on and still he remained, preserving his lonely vigil.

A short time afterwards, a trim upright figure passed through the cloister garth. Georgina Hamilton was feeling unusually buoyant. Tea had, of course, been excellent as ever. Such a wonderfully light hand as Joan had with scones. And so generous to give her the recipe. That should guarantee victory at the next Women's Guild Bake Off!

Even better than the tea had been Joan's tearful relief when Georgina told her about the meeting with Inspector Markham and Constable Noakes.

'I'd almost convinced myself I must have imagined the whole thing, Georgina,' she confided, 'but I just couldn't get it out of my mind. I wanted to tell someone, but it sounded so far-fetched, like something only a madwoman would dream up. Do the police *really* think there could be something in it?'

Georgina had replied in the affirmative before impressing upon her friend the need for absolute discretion. Giddy with gratitude, Joan clutched her hand.

'I can sleep easy now I know the police are taking care of things. I was just,' the plump face creased with worry, 'afraid in case it had something to do with what they found in the grottoes or, God forbid, poor Miss Hummles ... though I can't for the life of me see how.'

Suddenly, as she found herself doing increasingly often, Georgina thought of her dead husband. 'Be you ever so high, the law is above you', Geoffrey was fond of quoting as he went about his civic duties. Was it possible, she wondered, that what she had told the police might bring down a murderer who thought to have evaded the inexorable reach of justice?

Deep in her own thoughts, Georgina skidded on something lying in her path, almost turning her ankle.

Hold on a moment, it looked like she had trodden in some ashes mixed with fragments of paper scattered amongst the smoking remnants of a fire.

Gingerly, she bent down and picked up a few shreds which appeared to have survived the conflagration. It meant the end of her brand new gloves, but that couldn't be helped. Far more important to retrieve what looked like pages from a diary.

The moonlight was Georgina's ally as she hastily skimmed their contents.

It was the work of minutes.

'My god!' she whispered, her arms falling heavily to her sides. 'I *know* that handwriting! But surely he could not be involved in anything so evil!'

What was that?

She glanced around apprehensively, certain that she had heard the soft whistle of indrawn breath, had seen a shade detach itself from the depths of the cloister before melting into the opaque blackness beyond.

The moonlight and shadows mocked her, fluctuating in the night wind that had suddenly blown up from nowhere. At that moment, Georgina felt uneasily convinced a baleful influence haunted the very air of the cloister and venomous eyes watched her closely. Was it some resurrection of the flesh or a risen ghost?

Time to take herself firmly in hand. What would Geoffrey think of her giving way like this?

With shaking fingers, she stuffed the scraps of paper into her handbag and stood irresolutely as though waiting for inspiration.

What should she do? Confront the writer? Go straight to the police? No, surely not that. She owed him the chance to explain.

The thought of Inspector Markham briefly steadied her. She recalled the compassionate, searching gaze, the calm air of authority. Remembered too the quiet earnestness of his manner when he requested that she should say nothing to anyone about Joan's story. For the first time since being widowed, she had felt valued – not dull and dreary, like a remaindered volume with no story worth hearing.

She would write the inspector a note as soon as she got home and deliver it to the station first thing in the morning. Nothing explicit, not yet, but enough to point him in the right direction. If it was the right direction. Heaven help her, could she even be sure this was not some hideous misunderstanding – that she was not looking through the wrong end of the telescope and distorting what she saw?

Abandoning the heap of ash on unsteady legs, Georgina never noticed the figure standing, frieze-like, against the wall of the cloister. Never noticed the silent watcher in the dark.

Later that same evening, with the students at last packed off to bed, lights blazed in the common room at St Mary's. The low-ceilinged, sprawling room, adjacent to the chaplain's cottage, was comfortably furnished with a chesterfield and several wing chairs. Joan had wheeled in the tea trolley which, unusually, featured her celebrated melt-in-the-mouth scones in addition to the usual bourbons and custard creams.

'You'll be needing to keep your strength up, sir,' she told the principal with a kindly pat on the arm. Desmond O'Keefe, poleaxed after a day spent reassuring staff and students, made no demur as he sank gratefully into a chair and held out his hands to the aromatic log fire.

He was pleased to see that the cook was looking much more cheerful than she had done of late.

'I was worried you were coming down with something yourself, Joan, and we might have to do without you for a while,' he observed, watching as she busied herself with cups and saucers.

Joan swelled like a bantam in her outrage. 'And leave it to those flibbertigibbets of schoolgirls to see to things! I think I know my duty better than that, Dr O'Keefe!' She cast a critical eye round the common room. 'Now, I think you're all cosy in here, sir, so I'll be off.'

'Thank you, Joan. It was all hands to the pumps today. I don't know what we'd have done without you!' said the principal with quiet sincerity. Mollified, she bestowed a motherly smile on him before bustling away.

O'Keefe stretched out his legs in front of him. God, he felt demolished. Utterly bone-tired! What a nightmare start to his new job! 'And the hits just keep on comin'!' he muttered as Alex Sharpe slouched into the common room.

Watching as Sharpe helped himself to tea before disappearing behind a copy of the *Gazette*, O'Keefe chided himself for being uncharitable. The man, admittedly, was unprepossessing, but he must be under considerable strain. That wife of his looked as though she was on the verge of a nervous breakdown, for a start. Then there was what he had heard referred to as the previous principal's 'reign of terror'. O'Keefe surmised that the Director of Music had no doubt borne the brunt of that.

The principal's thoughts turned to the canon. If ever a man was unsuited to the unpleasantness of cathedral intrigue and municipal in-fighting, it was him! He had looked alarmingly frail today. A holy old man like that would have no more chance against the likes of Sir Philip Soames and Sharpe than a rusty nail against a pair of pliers.

On the plus side of the equation, thank heaven for Cynthia Gibson, dependably supplying the acting matron's deficiencies. Though she too had looked quite wretched today and was uncharacteristically fierce with the boys over some misdemeanour or other. Understandable, given the ghastly business with Irene Hummles. Rumour had it that Cynthia and the startlingly good-looking Edward Preston were 'an item'. They seemed an unlikely couple, which perhaps explained her strained appearance and air of constant watchfulness.

Cynthia's friend was likely to prove an asset. He'd warmed to Olivia Mullen at first sight and was untroubled by her rumoured connection to Inspector Markham. Thinking back to his first impressions of the faunlike English teacher and the gravely courteous policeman, he found he was not surprised by their liaison...

The next moment, O'Keefe was startled by the arrival of Sir Philip Soames in the common room. Leaning heavily on Edward Preston, he gestured at an armchair with his elegant silver-topped cane. 'I'll sit there, Preston. Hopefully this won't take long.'

'I'm sorry, did we schedule a meeting?' The principal sounded confused. That was all he needed, he told himself savagely, some interminable committee convened to appease Sir Philip's seigniorial sensibilities!

'Nothing for you to worry about, O'Keefe.' The patron was very suave. 'Preston is going to describe developments at the grottoes since,' he gestured eloquently with his cane, 'I cannot visit the site in person. If the mountain will not come to Mahomet...'

'Quite.'

O'Keefe wondered irritably why Preston could not have called on Sir Philip, but then it occurred to him that the latter no doubt wanted to flex the muscles of his power to be sure that they – unlike his rapidly atrophying physique – were still in working order.

'I daresay Mr Sharpe may even condescend to share his plans for this year's Christmas programme.'

Abashed, Sharpe emerged from behind the *Gazette* and shambled over to join the other two.

'Good evening, gentlemen, Sir Philip. Ah, tea!' Canon Woodcourt came in rubbing his hands.

He looks absolutely *flattened*, thought O'Keefe. What a change since this morning!

Conscious of the principal's concern, Woodcourt pulled a tragi-comic face. 'I know, I know. I'm a superannuated old crock fit for nothing but the knacker's yard!'

'I apologize, sir. I didn't mean to suggest...' The principal was embarrassed to have been caught out.

The canon laughed. 'Your face is an open book, O'Keefe. In my world of church diplomatists, that's actually quite refreshing!'

He settled himself in a chair next to the chesterfield and looked attentively at Sir Philip.

Just like a medieval court, thought O'Keefe in amusement, wondering how soon he could slip away.

'No need for you to stay, O'Keefe.' Sir Philip had an uncanny ability to read his thoughts. 'Unless you want to, that is.'

O'Keefe needed no second prompting. Rising to his feet with alacrity, he made his farewells.

Some forty minutes later, with the main business of the evening completed, St Mary's common room was winding down. Preston and Sharpe had left together, but Sir Philip and Canon Woodcourt lingered a few moments longer. The weary night cleaner, passing her hoover desultorily across the deep pile carpet, heard nothing more enlivening than the following exchange.

'Good to know you've pre-empted that difficulty for us, Canon.' Sir Philip's deep tones expressed satisfaction. 'Sharpe obviously requires monitoring,' he continued, 'but it's all a question of developing some backbone. Between us I am sure we can supply the necessary resolve. Preston certainly seems sound enough.'

The canon's response was drowned by the hoover.

'Right, I believe we can call it a day. Forgive me, Canon, necessity compels me to make use of you, so I'll ask for your arm to my car. My factotum will be growing anxious by now.'

Slowly, they moved towards the door. 'Would you like me to keep the *Friends of St Mary's* advised of developments, Sir Philip?'

'Oh, I think so, don't you?'

The swing doors, swooshing shut behind them, let in a draught of ice cold air. Shivering, the cleaner's pace quickened. Five minutes later, silence reigned once more.

9

Quiet Consummation

As she walked up the front path of Cathedral Mansions the following morning, Joan looked approvingly at the beautifully landscaped communal gardens lying under a sun-spangled frost. Even on a winter day, their meticulously clipped herbaceous borders, pergolas and flower beds neatly stocked with bedding plants offered a pleasing prospect. Joan knew that Georgina missed The Old Rectory's wildflower meadow, but at least her move to the assisted living complex – just off St Mary's Lane and a stone's throw from the cathedral – had not robbed her of year-round vibrancy and interest. Her green-fingered friend also delighted in the apartment's tiny balcony, where she tenderly nurtured dwarf orange trees and coaxed an amazing variety of plants into a profusion of beauty.

It had been good to see a return of the old decisive Georgina the previous evening. After Geoffrey's death, she had seemed somehow adrift and strangely wistful, as though all the old familiar landmarks had disappeared and she was groping in the dark. Which was only right and proper for a widow, Joan supposed, but she missed the familiar confident bossiness. That business with the police had been a bit of a godsend. There has been a definite glint in Georgina's eye when they were discussing the police investigation, and Joan could tell she had taken a shine to Inspector Markham.

Joan waited outside the ground floor foyer. She had a swipe card and her own set of keys, at Georgina's insistence, though the apartment was so small that it only required a fortnightly clean. Pressing the intercom, she waited to be buzzed up.

No response. Joan tried again. Nothing.

She felt the first stirrings of unease. Georgina was such a creature of habit that you could set your watch by her. Saturdays, she was at home until twelve o'clock then off to the cathedral to join the ladies' church workers group. After that, it was the Bridge Circle and home for tea by three.

Joan hesitated, uncertain. She and Georgina had the greatest respect for each other's privacy – one reason why their friendship had endured for so many years – but she had never known such a deviation from routine. What if Georgina had been taken ill and was lying helpless upstairs? She decided to risk her friend's displeasure and let herself through to the ground floor using her swipe card.

The little lift whisked her up to the second-floor apartments in a jiffy. Nothing looked awry or out of place, two tropical potted plants standing sturdily as usual like sentinels on either side of the landing window. The strains of Classic FM came softly from the flat opposite.

And yet, for all the well-carpeted warmth, Joan felt a sliver of ice cold apprehension stiffen her spine.

Something was wrong. A subtle change in the chemistry of the place. A sense that someone else had recently stood where she was standing now. Someone who should not have been there.

Joan knocked hard at Georgina's door. Not a well-bred knock, more like a pounding. She called her friend's name again and again.

The Classic FM halted and Derek Hart, the retiree from across the way, emerged onto the landing, his kindly face anxious.

'Morning, Joan. Can I help?'

'I'm worried about Georgina.' Her voice, even to her own ears, sounded oddly remote and quavery. 'There's no answer and it's not like her. She's normally at home this time of day. I'm going to let myself in.'

The apartment was very quiet. Joan turned left, making straight for Georgina's living room with her favourite armchair. Almost as though she knew what she would find.

Georgina was sitting there. She looked very peaceful, eyes shut tight, hands folded neatly in her lap and lips curved gently upwards in a strange secret smile. She wore the same ensemble as the previous evening when she had visited Joan at St Mary's. The antique rosewood writing desk on one side of the armchair was open, though no writing paraphernalia was visible and the little drawers and dockets appeared undisturbed. The glass-topped side table on the other side held a half full whisky tumbler. What made Joan catch her breath was the empty bottle of Diazepam next to it.

Oh no, Georgina, no!

She became aware of Derek gently guiding her to a chair before quietly going back out into the hallway and telephoning the police.

Joan did not know how long she sat there dejectedly contemplating her friend's body. Through the half-open curtains, she saw the little orange trees standing jauntily to attention on the balcony, haloed by the nimbus of the morning sun. Suddenly, she was flooded by the conviction that Georgina would never have taken her own life. However lonely the furrow she ploughed, however much she missed Geoffrey, such a staunch believer would never have taken the easy way out. 'Plenty of time for rest later when the recording angel says "Time no longer"!' she was wont to declare at any shirking of duty. Tears brimmed in Joan's eyes at the realization that she would never hear those forthright tones again.

'Come on, Joan, drink this.' Derek Hart was at her elbow with a well-sugared cup of tea. Looking at the still figure in the armchair, his face was sad. 'She was a real lady and a good neighbour.' He hesitated delicately before adding, 'I would never have thought she was the kind to kill herself. Just goes to show we never really know what's going on in someone else's life.'

Joan drank the tea and kept her counsel. She would speak to Inspector Markham. Georgina trusted him and he would know what to do for the best. In the meantime, sitting in the flat opposite the tranquil corpse, she made a silent pledge to her dead friend to help the police trap whoever had staged this cruel charade.

A short time later, Markham stood in the doorway of Georgina's living room watching silently as white boiler-suited SOCOs flitted like ghosts in the background.

Thoughtfully, he contemplated the tableau.

Yes, tableau. There was something too perfect and contrived about it, right down to Georgina Hamilton's legs, crossed modestly at the ankle as though the proprieties had to be observed even in death.

Joan had been dry-eyed and composed when Markham got there, adamant that her friend would never have taken her life. Listening to her in Georgina Hamilton's living room, with an uncanny sense that the dead woman's soul was hovering a little way above their heads, Markham acknowledged her logic. The two women had enjoyed a happy evening, swapping recipes and gossip. Joan felt that Georgina had begun to haul herself out of the bereavement pit at last.

'She liked feeling useful, Inspector. Talking to you made her feel she was back in the thick of things, that she could do some good. It was the cheeriest she'd been in ages. She was a very religious woman too. I remember watching a documentary with her – about that Dignitas place where people go to kill themselves when they're terminally ill. Georgina didn't hold with it at all. She said suicide was a great sin. Kept quoting from the Bible. "The Lord giveth and the Lord taketh away" – those were her very words. She would never have ended it all, Inspector, no matter how bad things got. She was a fighter, you know.'

Markham *did* know and felt a sharp sense of personal loss. Having summoned a uniformed officer to take Joan home, he continued to study the scene.

Questions raced through his mind in dizzying procession. Who could it have been?

Someone who had followed Georgina home from St Mary's that night? Someone known to her? An unexpected visitor whom she had nonetheless admitted to the apartment?

What was the motive? Markham remembered Georgina's keen, terrier-like gaze. Had she come upon another piece of information about St Mary's? Something of a scandalous or incriminating nature? Had she been weighing what to do when the power to decide was taken out of her hands forever?

Noakes appeared, his boots creaking, treading gingerly as though conscious of the incongruity between his bear-like frame and this doll's house with its dainty furnishings.

'All neat and tidy, Guv. Well, she wasn't the sort to do anything messy. Always very considerate according to the neighbour.' He coughed uncomfortably. 'Although I think it gave him a bit of a turn seeing her propped up there like a dummy.' He stopped short at the expression on Markham's face. '*What*?'

'That's just it, Noakes,' the inspector said intently, 'don't you see, she was propped up – positioned for us to find.' He moved closer to the armchair and looked down meditatively at the shuttered face. 'I think whoever did this felt bad about it, regretted it. Maybe even felt protective towards Georgina. It's almost *genteel*. Nothing sordid, nothing ugly.'

'What makes you think someone offed her, Guv?' Noakes sounded genuinely bewildered but then launched into his usual verbal shorthand, ticking off bullet points one by one. 'Widowed not that long ago. Finding it difficult to cope. Counselling for bereavement, leaflets in the kitchen drawer. Sleeping pills in the bathroom cabinet. Decided she'd had enough. Finito.'

Markham pointed at the bottle of Diazepam. 'If you look closely, Noakes, you'll see that has a label from the chemist in Wellgrove.'

'What of it?' Noakes sounded mutinous.

'*Think, man!* Why would Georgina go all that way to pick up medication? It's a fair hike.'

Noakes was not going to concede without a fight. 'Maybe she happened to be out that way – a day's shopping or some such. Or maybe she didn't want folk seeing her at the chemist here. She was the private type, so she might not have wanted people knowing her business.'

'*No.*' Markham's voice held an obstinate note that Noakes knew all too well. 'No, I'm not buying it. I think the murderer was cautious and collected those tablets out of town. No chance of being recognized that way.'

The inspector walked over to the French windows and looked out at the balcony garden that had been the dead woman's pride and joy. There was something so gallant and hopeful about the winter pansies and violas bobbing in their large white tubs and the enticing citrus trees with their succulent fruit. He wondered who would look after them now.

'I think Georgina was over the worst.' Markham spoke with conviction. 'That's what Joan says and I agree. It didn't make sense for her to have come home from a happy evening of tea and chat and then kill herself. I mean, how could she have been so upbeat if she was planning something like that?'

'Maybe the calm kicked in cos she knew that next day there wouldn't be any more pain.' But Noakes sounded less confident now and Markham knew he had won the day.

'I want a post-mortem on this one,' rapped the DI. 'Too many unanswered questions. It's not just the bottle. How come the tumbler's still half full? She'd have needed a full glass to knock back that many tablets. And another thing … why's the writing desk open? Was she writing something yesterday evening when she was interrupted? Could mean nothing, but she was an organized woman and I don't like loose ends.' He shook his head. 'I think we were meant to take this at face value. Lonely widow coming apart at the seams so took her own life. Case closed. But what about when she came to see us, Noakes? That wasn't some pathetic attention-seeker. She was totally on the ball and keen as mustard to help her friend.' The inspector spoke with a sudden fierceness which make his subordinate jump. 'Trying to make us think Georgina took the coward's way out was downright evil. I don't think it happened that way at all.' He gestured at the armchair. 'I'm willing to bet she was forced back in her seat and smothered with one of those cushions – wouldn't have been difficult if she'd had a drink, been slipped something, or lulled into a false sense of security. There's no sign of a struggle, so she must have been taken by surprise.'

'Not much flesh on her neither,' said Noakes, 'so likely she wouldn't have been able to put up a fight.'

'Exactly.' Markham jammed his hands into his pockets. He took one last look at Georgina Hamilton's serene face, wordlessly vowing that he would call her killer to account. Passing into the tiny hallway, he suddenly noticed an old-fashioned framed sampler on the wall. Beautifully stitched in embroidered silks and threads, mythical birds and beasts roamed its borders while the central panel bore a single verse: *On that day, the secrets of all hearts shall be laid bare.* Oh yes, he told himself, I am going to drag all the hidden malignity into the light. Then he and Noakes quietly left the SOCOs to their work.

Back at Bromgrove station, Markham viciously jerked down the blinds on the glass partition wall which formed one side of his office. CID was largely deserted, but he craved freedom from prying eyes.

Sighing deeply, he slumped behind his desk. Events were moving faster than he could control them, as though he was being drawn inexorably into the centre of a whirling vortex. *Calm.*

He reached listlessly for a stack of papers. Staff interviews at St Mary's had so far yielded nothing new about the matron. But Markham felt convinced Irene Hummles had been killed for what she *knew*, and that somewhere in the bundle of statements lay the key to her murder.

There was a knock at the door.

'Come!' He was half grateful for the interruption.

It was Desmond O'Keefe. Markham could see what Olivia meant about the man. Slight, spare, almost Spanish-looking, he had a Jesuitical aura all right. But for all that, Markham instinctively liked his lack of ecclesiastical priggishness – the total absence of those airs and graces which might have been expected to form part of his job description.

'What can I do for you, Dr O'Keefe? As you know, there's been another tragic incident, possibly unrelated to events at St Mary's, though we're not currently able to say.'

'I heard, Inspector, and I'm truly sorry. I didn't know Mrs Hamilton, but I believe she was a good friend of Joan, our cook.'

That was it. No fishing for information or details.

Markham felt some of his tension ebb away.

O'Keefe cleared his throat. 'In the circumstances, I'm reluctant to bother you with this. Something and nothing, really.'

Markham somehow mustered an encouraging smile. 'Why don't you let me be the judge of that?'

'There's a society connected to St Mary's. Called *Blavatskya* or some such. Named after the woman who founded the theosophy movement, apparently. I don't pretend to understand the half of it, but the idea is to explore connections between different mystical traditions.'

'Very worthy, I'm sure. However, I must say you look sceptical.'

'It's Sir Philip's baby, Inspector.' Markham suppressed a groan. 'Between you and me, I think he's a bit of a crank. But the canon rates him, and he's been incredibly generous to St Mary's over the years. So, it seems mean-spirited to begrudge him his pet project...

'But—'

'I received an anonymous letter the other day accusing the society of "unwholesome practices".'

O'Keefe took a folded sheet from his pocket and passed it

across the desk. Markham scanned it quickly and looked up in puzzlement.

'*Nairatmya*? What the hell's that all about?'

O'Keefe grinned. 'Some Buddhist doctrine of personal self-conquest, so Sir Philip tells me. Transcendence through purity and mortification of the flesh.'

'Hmm. Problem is, your poison pen doesn't seem to think there's anything very pure about it.' Markham looked straight at O'Keefe. 'Doesn't come right out and say so, but I'd say whoever wrote this is driving at child abuse. Let's see...' Markham consulted the letter. '...*inappropriate behaviour ... warped effect on adolescent sexuality ... brainwashing ... perverted conditioning ...* and so on. Hold on a minute, that's interesting. *Disordered and potentially violent impulses ... possible tragic outcomes.* I wonder...'

'You think there could be a link with the truanting and other, er, safeguarding concerns? Maybe even a connection with the murders at St Mary's?'

'Don't you, Dr O'Keefe? Isn't that why you brought this to me?' Markham was blunt.

'Yes.' The principal met his gaze frankly. 'I can't afford to ignore it. Speaking personally, I think it's just one of Sir Philip's hobby horses – that's what Edward Preston says and I'm inclined to agree with him. *Blavatskya* meets in school every fortnight – one of the large music rooms. The canon or Sir Philip reads a paper, the boys have a short debate and that's about it. Oh, and there's a little newsletter or magazine too; the *Friends of St Mary's* helps with that. Pupils make the occasional trip to look at Sir Philip's curios, but Cynthia Gibson always takes the boys down and brings them back. All quite inoffensive. You could call it part of students' PSHE – that's Personal, Social and Health Education to the uninitiated. Certainly doesn't amount to a cult or anything sinister from what I can see.'

'And yet, you're not one hundred per cent certain.'

'I don't want to be heavy-handed, Inspector, and start off on the wrong foot with Sir Philip. And I certainly don't want to be closed-minded and parochial – opposed to the boys developing an interest in other cultures. But ... well, I thought I should mention it ... the children's welfare is paramount, and I didn't want to hold anything back.'

'I'm grateful to you, Dr O'Keefe. Leave this with me.' Markham rose, signalling that the meeting was over. 'I promise you absolute discretion.'

The principal slipped from the room, leaving the inspector to his thoughts.

While Markham brooded in his office, DS Noakes was chatting with an old friend down in the bowels of the building.

'Don't often see you down in Records, Noakesy.' Sergeant Ivor Harrison, having a quiet day in his musty domain, was delighted by the diversion, even going so far as to rustle up a pot of tea and illicit cream cake in the back office.

'Ah well, I'm too grand for the likes of you now.' Noakes grinned through a mouthful of cake. Unruffled, the other responded with a two-fingered salute and swilled his tea.

Finally, patting his paunch with the satisfaction of a connoisseur, Noakes declared, 'Wonderful cake that. Much better than anything upstairs.'

'It's the missus' turn to bake for the Women's Guild, so I get the leftovers.'

'Lucky you,' replied the DS with feeling. 'Remind me to come down here more often!'

Harrison got down to business. 'So, what's your guvnor after then?'

'Intel on three lads who disappeared from Bromgrove around twenty years back.' Noakes consulted his notebook. 'Yeah, 1997 that would be.'

'Mispers?'

'Two mispers and a suspected homicide. Let's see, here are the names. Jonathan Warr, David Belcher and Adam Waring. Two of 'em – Belcher and Waring – came from the Hoxton Estate. Warr lived in Bromgrove Park, so I'm guessing he was a few rungs higher up the ladder.'

Harrison's eyes glazed over with a reminiscent, faraway look.

'I remember them,' he said wonderingly. 'Even after all this time. Saw quite a bit of them when I was on the beat. Fourteen and thought they knew it all, the great daft lummoxes. Never thought there was any great harm in them, to be honest, though they always seemed to be at the centre of any mischief that was going down. Belcher and Waring were tearaways, pretty much left to drag themselves up. Warr's parents were a cut above – teachers, I think. He was a quiet lad, not really the type to kick over the traces. Would have outgrown the other two in time.'

Noakes was startled to see the grizzled veteran's eyes fill with tears. Wiping a sleeve across his eyes, Harrison said almost in a whisper, 'Poor silly lad. Time wasn't on his side. They found his body in a shallow grave round the back of Bromgrove Spinney a few years after the three of them did a flit. Identified him using dental records.'

Noakes looked down at his stewed tea in an agony of sympathy.

Eventually, Harrison recovered his composure.

'I was at Jonny Warr's funeral in the town cemetery. It was a miserable day. Stair rods. But the whole place turned out. I'll never forget his mother's face. She taught part-time at St Mary's and played the organ at the cathedral, so the students had the music sorted.' The sergeant's face twisted. 'They did Jonny proud. Sir Philip was there an' all. He wasn't an invalid in them days. Spouted prayers in some foreign lingo that nobody understood, but I remember he looked proper upset. Someone told me a nephew of his drowned in an accident around the same age when they were on holiday, so it must have brought it all back.'

Noakes frowned. 'The other lads weren't there for the funeral,' he said flatly.

'No.' Harrison sounded weary and defeated.

'Could they have killed Jonny, d'you think?'

'I've often asked myself that. But look, David and Adam

had no nastiness in them. Even that lot down the Hoxton won't hear a word against them.'

'An accident, then, and they ran away.' Noakes was doggedly persistent.

'They'd have faced the music those two, not gone on the run.' Harrison's face was very serious as he looked the other in the eye. 'I think someone did for them. Same as happened to Jonny. They're out there rotting in some ditch or cesspit, you mark my words, Noakes,' his voice shook, 'waiting to come home.'

The two men sat silently as dismal images scrolled remorselessly across their minds.

'Is your boss re-opening the investigation then?' Harrison tried to glean some comfort from Noakes's visit. A thought occurred to him and he shot a shrewd glance at his friend. 'Is there some connection with St Mary's? You know, they had a couple of lads supposedly hightail it from there a while back...'

'Yeah, we're considering them too,' admitted Noakes. 'I've pulled their case files from St Mary's. Justin Furlong and Ned Pettingill. Not so much a case of heading for the bright lights with them though. More like teenage angst. They were both thirteen when they ran away. Justin was wound up over his voice breaking and Ned had problems coping with his parents' divorce... No obvious similarity with David, Adam and Jonny beyond the fact that all of them melted into thin air. I've got the usual from CAMHS on Justin and Ned, but I'll take anything you've got down here on the other lads.'

Harrison responded with alacrity, disappearing into the stacks and returning a few minutes later with a stack of manila files which he plonked down in front of Noakes.

'Your guvnor might want to have a chat with Mike Bamber. Retired now, but he worked the case. Between you and me, I think it did for 'im. He was never the same man after. Always hanging round Jonny Warr's grave, smoking and talking to himself. Any road, his details are in there. Let me know how you do, won't you, my son?'

Noakes recognized the plea.

'Wilco.' Clumsily, he slapped the other on the back. 'I know you were right cut up about those boys, Sarge. Don't know if anything'll come of it, but looks like we may have a pattern of young fellas going missing in Bromgrove, and my guvnor doesn't like coincidences. Leastways not when we've got an outbreak of unexplained homicides in the mix as well.'

The two men shook hands. Noakes lumbered upstairs to the upper regions, leaving Sergeant Harrison alone with his memories.

'Right,' said Markham when Noakes arrived in his office with the files. 'Let's clear our heads. Get out of the office for a bit. Maybe it's a long shot, but we can check out the Bromgrove Park address for Jonathan Warr's parents. I don't feel up to the Hoxton today. Not without Kevlar vests and backup, at any rate!'

Nothing loath, Noakes led the way to the car pool and selected his favourite Ford Mondeo. The journey passed in companionable silence, both men feeling they had somehow secured a reprieve.

The light was failing when they drew up outside the Warrs' address in Bromgrove Park, a quiet close on the outskirts of town lined with detached modern homes set in extensive manicured gardens.

The door was answered by a slim middle-aged woman with a faded platinum bob and tired eyes. On learning who they were, a thin sigh escaped her, but she smiled wanly and ushered the two officers through to an airy and spacious conservatory overlooking the back garden.

Catching Markham's eye as he took in the incense burner, meditation chimes and delicate brass prayer bells dangling from a lacquered ivory frame, Mrs Warr told him, 'My husband and Jonny were mad for all that New Age stuff.'

'Is your husband around?' Ideally, it would be good to see the parents together.

'We separated a year or so after they found Jonny,' came the quiet response. 'It was perfectly amicable. Something shifted after he died and we couldn't seem to find our way back.'

The interview flowed easily, but there was frustratingly little to add to what they already knew. Jonny's mother could only tell them that her son had become withdrawn and secretive in the months before he vanished.

'You have to give them their freedom,' she said brokenly, her eyes begging them to agree. 'He was that age, you see. I don't blame the other boys. There was no real harm in them.' It was almost an exact echo of Sergeant Harrison's words. 'Jonny was a clever boy, came with me to St Mary's sometimes for band practice, but he was happy at Hope Academy and none of his teachers reported any problems.'

'How do you think he ended up in the Spinney, Mrs Warr?' Markham's voice was very kind.

'I know what you're thinking!' She flashed. 'That he was into drugs or underage sex or … something horrible.'

'I promise you, Mrs Warr, we're coming to this with a completely open mind, making no assumptions. Your son was a *victim*. That's our starting point.' Markham was firm.

'I'm sorry, it's just that it's been so long.' She faltered. 'Can I ask … are you reopening the case because of the bodies at St Mary's?'

Markham looked at Noakes.

'We're treating it as a cold case review, luv,' the DS said earnestly. 'We never like to close the book on any investigation, see. Especially if it involves a child.'

Shortly after that, it was time to go. As they walked through the hall, Noakes gestured to a framed studio portrait on the wall. A slender, blond, mild-eyed boy with a frank, open gaze.

'Very striking, your Jonny.'

'Yes, he was. But he took his looks for granted, wasn't vain at all.'

The poignant contrast between the pitiful decomposed corpse of the crime scene photographs and the glowing youth of the portrait – looking out fearlessly at the world – was not lost on either man.

As they drove away, Mrs Warr stood watching, a desperate entreaty in her eyes.

Tell me what happened to my son!

10

Ancient History

'So, you want to know about the Warr case. Ah, Markham, that was the one that got away. But before we get on to that, tell me, how's life treating you?'

Mike Bamber regarded his former protégé with an expression of rueful resignation belied by his shaking hands, chain-smoking and frequent slugs of Famous Grouse.

The two men were sitting in the retired DI's snug, his wife Cath having tactfully left them to it.

As Markham updated his old mentor, part of Bamber's mind was reliving the dreary day of Jonny Warr's funeral, all those years ago. He could recall the exact date, now: Friday 12 December, 1999.

Despite his stout frame, wispy grey hair and high colour, Bamber still radiated authority, so that for a moment Markham felt himself transported back to the days when he was a nervous young detective learning his trade.

'Relax.' Bamber chuckled at Markham's discomfiture. 'I'm retired now, remember! Just a decrepit old has-been—'

'Hardly that!'

'—while you're the Commissioner's blue-eyed boy. And for God's sake call me Mike. After all this time, I reckon you've earned the right!'

Markham gave the shy smile which was so much at odds with his normally austere demeanour.

'I'm grateful to you for making the time, Mike.'

'What else have I got to do? Keeps me out from under the missus' feet any road.' Bamber's rheumy blue eyes were shrewdly speculative. 'Now then, the Warr investigation. As I say, mothballed way back. Why the sudden interest?'

Markham spread his hands helplessly. 'You'll have heard of the discoveries at St Mary's.'

'A right hornet's nest you've stirred up there, lad. I won't ask if you've got anywhere. Your face at that press conference was a picture.'

Markham grimaced. 'Damage limitation, Mike. And the investigation's dead in the water. But the murder of Irene Hummles—'

'Definitely murder then?'

'No doubt about it. The hyoid bone was fractured.' Markham frowned then continued. 'We screwed up badly over that. Took Irene's disappearance at face value. Swallowed the PR – sad middle-aged woman who'd bailed out when life became too much.'

'So, what do you reckon was *really* going on?' Bamber was suddenly alert with interest.

'Apparently, she'd gone into meltdown over a couple of lads who absconded on her watch. I began thinking we'd got this the wrong way around.' Markham's voice was urgent. 'D'you see, Mike? It started with *two missing boys*. Two boys who disappeared and were never seen again.'

Bamber sucked down another lungful of smoke. It seemed to aid the thinking process. 'You went back through the files looking for missing teenage boys and came up with those three. Jonny Warr, David Belcher and Adam Waring...'

'I'm sorry, Mike. I know Warr and the others got under your skin.' It was an open secret that Bamber had received treatment for PTSD since leaving the force. Markham wondered if he and Cath had taken a conscious decision not to have children – not to bring new life into a world where danger lurked.

'It was a long time ago. But you're right, I've never forgotten those boys. They'd be coming up to forty now with families of their own, like as not.' Bamber took a long draught of whisky.

'All that was taken away from them,' he said heavily. 'And out there someone thinks they've got away with it.'

'You think the same killer – or killers – murdered all three?' asked Markham.

'Yes, I do.' Bamber was quietly certain. 'You couldn't get a fag end between them, they were that close. Depend upon it, the same evil shit did for them all.'

Markham remained silent for a moment, anxious to signal his sympathy, before wandering over to the window as though to admire Bamber's immaculate herbaceous borders.

'It's all right, lad,' said the older man wryly, 'you can sit down now. Round here we don't wear our hearts on our sleeves!'

Markham returned to his chair. 'What we could be looking at here is a pattern. A killer starting up again.'

'Perhaps they never stopped,' said Bamber in a low voice.

Markham stared at him.

'I mean to say, what if there've been other disappearances over the last twenty years – say from outside the area – but no-one's joined the dots?'

Markham felt as though he was drowning in quicksand. *His worst nightmare.*

Bamber continued in a remorseless catarrhal rumble. 'Or maybe one killer did for the first three and an associate, or copycat, abducted the two from St Mary's.'

'What can you tell me about Jonny, David and Adam?' Markham's voice was hoarse. 'C'mon, Mike, *anything at all.*'

'Sparky, liked to lark about. Jonny was quieter than the other two – did a stint as an altar server at the cathedral before he went off the rails. David and Adam were into martial arts – some sort of kick-boxing, or perhaps it was taekwondo ... I can't remember now.' He laughed. 'Fancied themselves Jackie Chan.'

Markham thought back to the conversation with Mrs Warr.

'Jonny's mum said something about a band at St Mary's...'

'Yeah, that's right. Played the sitar did Jonny.' Bamber

grinned at Markham's bemused expression. 'Always had to stand out from the crowd. No *Floral Dance* brass whatsit for him!'

'Were the other two musical?'

'Nah. But they went through some sort of hippy phase.' Bamber shrugged. 'Pretty harmless stuff, the odd spliff at most. At least they weren't doing hard drugs or mugging old ladies.'

'No real harm in them then,' said Markham slowly.

'That's about the size of it. Though...' he hesitated.

'Go on,' the younger man urged.

'All three of them were naïve, *gullible*.' Bamber's face darkened. 'A predator picks out the weak from the rest of the herd, right? Well, those kids were vulnerable. Belcher and Waring were from broken homes, while Jonny had been bullied at school and was a bit of a loner. They could have been drawn into something without seeing the danger until it was too late. Oh,' he broke off, exasperated with himself, 'I'm not making much sense.'

'No, Mike,' Markham reassured him. 'Those boys are more real to me now. Not just grainy photos in a folder.'

Later, back in his car, Markham kept revolving that one word in his mind.

Gullible.

Olivia looked around her new classroom with pleasure.

Not bad. Not bad at all.

It had been a good idea to come into St Mary's and take the measure of her new kingdom, she decided. With it being a Saturday, the boys were all out doing sports, so everywhere was quiet.

The room was in a corner of the first quadrangle: fifteen desks were arranged in a horseshoe, so smaller than average class sizes. A world away from Hope Academy.

Yes, all perfectly satisfactory. Computer, interactive whiteboard, flipchart easel, and gunmetal filing cabinets. There was also a book case, tucked away behind the door, for her own personal collection. Happily, she began arranging her treasured classics and anthologies.

Suddenly, Olivia heard voices. Raised voices. She froze behind the open door, feeling like a voyeur but reluctant to obtrude herself into what sounded like an intimate conversation.

She recognized Cynthia's voice. Who was the other? Ah yes, the delectable architect. From the flutter in her friend's manner when she had introduced Edward Preston, Olivia guessed she was smitten. She could understand why. Early forties, handsome as a dream, humorous and good with children. Diplomatic too, given the invidious tightrope he had to walk at St Mary's, caught between the local authority on the one hand and Sir Philips's myrmidons on the other.

On this occasion, however, he sounded uncharacteristically harsh, if not angry.

'For God's sake, Cyn, what the hell did you want to do that for? I thought you understood ... got to be careful...'

The soft reply was inaudible, but it appeared to mollify Preston.

'I'm sorry, sweetheart, but I thought we trusted each other. You could have ruined everything ... don't need outsiders...'

Cynthia's voice was breathy, needy, insinuating. Olivia only caught muffled snatches of speech.

'...thought you'd like it ... didn't know she was with *him*...'

There was a fade out, as though the speaker had momentarily moved just out of earshot, then Olivia heard Preston again, his voice fading in and out.

'We need to keep it between ourselves. Remember what the Master said...'

'I've been so worried, Ed ... that horrible business with Irene...' Cynthia was shrill now.

Olivia craned forward as far as she dared. It would be incredibly embarrassing if they caught her eavesdropping like this.

Preston's voice was soothing. It sounded as though he was embracing Cynthia, speaking into her hair.

'Nothing to do with us... Some maniac, sweetheart... Most likely, she hooked up with someone she shouldn't have. Let's face it, the poor woman wasn't the full shilling, was she? I mean she was incredibly emotionally vulnerable ... unstable ... the Master really put himself on the line persuading the governors to give her a second chance...'

Their voices died away, and Olivia heard footsteps receding down the corridor.

She remained stock still for a few minutes before slowly emerging from behind the door.

What to make of that conversation, she wondered. What had Cynthia done to upset her boyfriend? Was she, *Olivia*, the outsider?

And who was the Master? Was it the same person who'd persuaded the governors to give Irene Hummles a second chance?

She sat down at the nearest desk, her earlier bright optimism giving way to a creeping unease. There had been something clandestine and unwholesome about Preston and Cynthia. As though whatever they were negotiating was far darker than a lovers' tiff.

'Miss Mullen! Miss Mullen!'

Nat and Julian peered round the door, fresh from their exploits at rugby.

'My team won!' crowed Nat, hopping from one foot to another in his excitement. 'Against the under fourteens! And I scored the winning try cos Julian fumbled a catch!'

Julian grinned wryly at Olivia. 'He's never going to let me live this down, Miss Mullen.'

Despite the weight on her mind, Olivia could not help but be amused by Nat's braggadocio, his narrow chest puffed up with pride at having triumphed over the big boys. Julian's eyes were fond as he watched his friend strut. Olivia suspected he might deliberately have muffed it to give Nat his moment in the sun.

'P'raps you can come and watch us tomorrow,' Nat said to Olivia with studied casualness.

'I'd like that, Nat, though I don't know much about rugby.'

Nat was giving the new member of staff no wriggle-room. 'Don't worry, I'll teach you,' he said before adding kindly, 'you look like a quick learner.'

'What have you been up to since I last saw you?' Olivia adroitly turned the subject before she could be commandeered for other touch-line assignments.

'We had an adventure last night,' said Nat with an air of importance.

In the silence that followed, the world seemed entirely still. Julian, who had turned very pale, stiffened like a soldier preparing for battle.

Nat glanced uncertainly from his friend to Olivia and back again.

Olivia got up and closed her classroom door. 'You can trust me not to blab to the other teachers, cross my heart and hope to die,' she said.

Perching on a desk, Nat launched into a garbled story about how they had got up in the middle of the night to look for the Night Watchman. Olivia's heart sank like a stone when she heard this, but she forced herself to laugh. 'And did you track him down to his lair?'

Nat said with some *hauteur*, 'Well not him 'xactly. But we saw something weird down at the little cemetery by the—'

'We shouldn't have been there, Miss Mullen,' Julian cut in, correctly intuiting Olivia's concern, 'but we were curious.'

Nat was annoyed with Julian for stealing his thunder. *'Don't interrupt, Julian!* Anyway, it was Mr Woodcourt. He was doing a funeral, he said.'

Olivia leaned forward. 'Oh, you spoke to him?'

'Well, not right *then* cos he was busy. But we asked about it today.'

Olivia waited. *Don't rush him*, she told herself.

Nat beamed. 'He had to take care of some ancient remains for Mr Preston.'

Observing Olivia's look of mystification, Julian explained. 'The dig turned up some human fossils from the Middle Ages,

Miss Mullen. Mr Woodcourt was giving them Christian burial – you know, saying prayers and stuff—'

'—an' sprinkling holy water.' Nat was not to be outdone.

'He should really have given the fossils to the archaeology people,' Julian continued, 'but Mr Preston agreed to let him have a prayer service – like a blessing...'

It appeared to cross Nat's mind that the canon's actions might be negatively construed because he piped up defensively, 'It wasn't stealing, Miss Mullen. The bones didn't belong to anyone and Mr Woodcourt didn't think it was respectful to put them in a glass case in a museum so people could come and gawp at them. He said that way their souls wouldn't rest in peace.'

Olivia nodded solemnly.

'They'd wander the earth for ever and ever, jus' like vampires,' Nat added with evident relish.

Julian's voice was emotionless. 'Mr Woodcourt wouldn't be able to do that for all the bones down there, but he said the service was sort of symbolic...'

'Like an exorcism!' exclaimed Nat.

Julian rounded on the younger boy. 'He did *not* say exorcism, Nat!'

'But that's what he meant!' Nat was determined to have the last word.

'*Wow*, lads!' Olivia decided it was time to intervene. '*An adventure indeed!*'

'You won't say anything to the other teachers will you, Miss Mullen?' Nat looked worried.

'Mr Woodcourt wanted to keep this a secret. He and Mr Preston might get into trouble if anyone finds out.'

'None of the teachers will hear about it from me,' she replied and was relieved to see the narrow shoulders relax. 'Now, you must be famished after all that exercise, and I'm feeling a bit peckish myself.'

It was an effective distraction. 'Cook's sure to get out the biscuits if *you're* with us, Miss Mullen,' whooped Nat joyously. 'C'mon!'

*　*　*

A while later, having left Nat and Julian conducting a vigorous post mortem of the rugby over orange juice and snacks, Olivia walked slowly back to her classroom for a last check.

She was just shutting the door when from behind her came the sound of a discreet cough.

Whirling around, she found herself face to face with the principal.

'I'm sorry if I startled you, Miss Mullen. Can I walk you to the front door?'

'Thank you, Dr O'Keefe.' Olivia paused, somewhat unnerved by his cat-like stealth and unsure how to broach the subject which now held a burning interest for her.

'You're looking what Nat would call discombobulated, Miss Mullen,' the principal observed. 'It was the same for me at first. Mercifully, the canon was there to see me through.'

Here was an opening.

'Mr Woodcourt must be a tremendous asset to St Mary's,' she said carefully. 'How long has he been here? Did he work in parishes first?'

Easy, don't want to sound nosey.

But the principal – clearly something of a fan – saw nothing amiss.

'He's a marvellous man,' he said warmly. 'Seventy-one, but roars round like a teenager with the boys ... apparently quite a demon on the cricket pitch.'

'Aren't Anglican clergy normally retired by his age?' Olivia blushed. 'Sorry, I don't mean to pry...'

'No need to apologize,' answered O'Keefe smoothly. 'No, Dick's good for a few more years. Career-wise, he's criss-crossed the country. Studied at Ridley Hall. Then started out as a curate in Gracechurch. Later on, let me see, I think he was vicar of St James's, Cedar Hill and rector at Holy Trinity in Bude ... or was it the other way around? Anyway, I know he did sterling service for the Diocesan Youth Service in various places – plus he co-ordinated the Crusader Gap Year Scheme – before being poached by the cathedral here and eventually ending up as Residentiary Canon. Does lots of outreach with schools and Bromgrove Education Team, as well as being part of the furniture for the last twenty years. Genuinely humble. He wouldn't allow a full profile on the St Mary's website, so, ironically, he has the shortest entry of any of the staff. Low Church, of course, so the Dean's Anglo-Catholicism must sometimes raise his hackles, but he's the soul of forbearance.'

Olivia murmured some conventional words of admiration. The shadowy doubts that had been floating just below the surface of her mind were dispelled by O'Keefe's enthusiastic recital. Woodcourt might have deviated from orthodox practice, but his service for the medieval dead, seen in a certain light, was arguably a poignant tribute to the indestructibility of the human spirit. She felt ashamed of her suspicions, which she now realized had been fanned by the partly overheard exchange between Cynthia and Preston.

'You're looking tired, Miss Mullen.' The principal sounded concerned. 'Be off home with you now,' he added as they reached the front entrance, 'and forget all about St Mary's.'

Olivia felt a change in air pressure – as though someone somewhere had opened a door or window and was listening intently. But then the impression vanished and she was bidding Dr O'Keefe goodbye.

Forget about St Mary's.

The words hung in the stillness as the front door shut behind her.

11

On The Scent

'I felt a bit of a fool, to be honest, Gil.' Olivia grimaced as she concluded the account of her morning's activities. 'I was all ready to pin everything on Canon Woodcourt when, from what Dr O'Keefe says, the man's next door but one to a saint!'

A wave of compunction hit her as she contemplated Markham's heavy eyes and white, tired face. 'Oh Gil, I'm sorry,' she said. 'You wanted a night off and here I am blethering on about my half-baked theories!'

Markham smiled across the table in their secluded corner of the tiny pizzeria. However busy it was, Giuseppe somehow always managed to conjure up a private nook for favoured customers. The swarthy, fierce-looking little major-domo had a soft spot for Markham ever since the latter rescued his underage daughter Maria from the clutches of James Foley, kingpin of the Hoxton estate and a thoroughly bad lot. The Italian had also capitulated to Olivia's charms hook, line and sinker. *Bellissima*! was his invariable sigh of satisfaction whenever he saw her with Markham.

At Olivia's reference to Woodcourt, Markham was suddenly alert. It wouldn't do to let her become fixated on the canon.

'I'm not ruling anything out, sweetheart,' he said. 'I agree, the canon sounds an unlikely suspect at this stage. But there is something seriously out of joint at St Mary's... Oh, and by the by, that silver-tongued principal of yours was round at the station earlier to tell me about some school society which raised eyebrows.'

'Oh, you mean *Blavatskya*.' Olivia laughed. 'All perfectly

harmless. Papers on secret societies and occult symbolism, with the odd wonder-worker thrown in for good measure. The last one was all about some character called the Count de St Germain, if you please – Robin Hood crossed with the Scarlet Pimpernel! The kids love seeing Sir Philip's knick-knacks and trinkets—'

'The kids? What kids?'

Olivia was startled by the sharpness of Markham's tone.

'Well, boys from the choir school. Nat and Julian told me all about it. The kids go to look at Sir Philip's treasures, and he spins exotic tales for them – masters of ancient wisdom fighting for the poor and oppressed. *Boys' Own* stuff. Cynthia says they really lap it up. There's no harm in it surely.'

Markham pulled a comical face. It was an attempt to reassure Olivia, but secretly he felt a growing disquiet. With assumed nonchalance, he forced a clumsy laugh.

'I hadn't figured Sir Philip for Jules Verne! Well, it's certainly a little unconventional, so I can understand why O'Keefe covered his back by letting me know.'

At that moment, they were interrupted by Giuseppe bearing two plates of *cassata* 'on the house'. His face lit up as Olivia clapped her hands together like a child and exclaimed in delight over the layers of cake, ice cream and fruit.

'That's a work of art, Giuseppe. Almost too beautiful to eat … though I'm going to force myself!'

In that instant, Markham decided not to tell Olivia about the three Bromgrove teenagers whose disappearance twenty years earlier he felt increasingly sure was somehow linked to St Mary's. Far safer for her if he kept those details to himself for the time being.

Looking at his girlfriend tucking happily into her pudding, her delicate features irradiated by the pool of candlelight, Markham's mind roved uneasily over what Olivia had told him about Woodcourt's peripatetic career. Mike Bamber's question echoed relentlessly in his head like a hammer on an anvil. *What if there've been other disappearances over the last twenty years – say from outside the area – but no-one's joined the dots?* The notion that an elderly and well-respected clergyman like the canon could be implicated in a ready-made paedophile ring – running undetected for years – was hard to swallow, particularly when he recalled Woodcourt's gentle affability and unaffected kindness. And yet ...where better for a serial abuser to conceal himself than within the stronghold of the Church of England, smack bang in the heart of the establishment? Due to the epidemic of historical sex abuse cases, men of the cloth could no longer count on slipping under the radar. But twenty years ago, it would have been a very different story.

The syrupy juices of his cassata suddenly filled Markham with an overpowering nausea. In his mind's eye, he was watching Woodcourt dig down into the spongy clay of the little cemetery. Sickened, he abruptly pushed his plate away.

'Gil?' Olivia's voice was full of tender concern. 'Are you OK?'

Markham somehow summoned up a smile, though he felt beads of sweat breaking out on his forehead. He needed to keep his mounting suspicions of Woodcourt to himself at all costs. Any alteration in Olivia's demeanour towards the canon could put her at risk.

And there was no *proof.* It was all 'rumour, painted full of tongues'. What if his suspicions of Woodcourt were nothing but an appalling, unspoken slander?

'It's been a long day, my love,' he conceded, reaching across the table for her hand, 'and the pressure to crack this one is well and truly on. I feel—'

'—like Saint Sebastian shot with arrows!'

Olivia's anxious eyes belied her merry tone.

Markham held her gaze. 'You just concentrate on getting ready for next week. It's been a while since you were up to your neck in lesson plans and curriculum targets, remember. Leave the detecting to CID!'

'You don't think Cynthia and Edward Preston have got themselves into some sort of trouble do you, Gil?' Markham noticed that Olivia was nervously plucking at Giuseppe's spotless napery, a sure sign that the conversation she had overheard was preying on her mind.

'It was probably just personal stuff. Can't be easy trying to have a relationship in a goldfish bowl like St Mary's,' he said firmly, 'particularly with the likes of Sir Philip and that beady-eyed principal taking it all in. Preston probably has a tough time of it as piggy-in-the-middle between the two of them.'

'I thought you liked Dr O'Keefe.' Olivia was surprised.

'I'm reserving judgement. That fellow's almost too good to be true.' Markham flashed Olivia one of his rare, impish grins. 'Or maybe I'm just jealous that you've succumbed to his well-oiled charm.'

Olivia giggled. 'It *is* a bit practised, I suppose.' Markham was pleased to note that the restless fingers were stilled and the cloud had lifted from her face.

'One thing's for sure,' she said brightly. 'Cyn and her beau were obviously completely in the dark about poor Irene Hummles. From the sound of it, the canon tried to save Irene's job ... had to have been him cos I can't imagine Alex Sharpe playing the Good Samaritan...'

'God, no.' Markham yawned. 'Right, better get the bill before I end up face down in the *cassata* and Giuseppe tells me never to darken his door again!' He hesitated, somewhat embarrassed. 'I left Noakes holed up in the office doing some research and...'

'...you want to check with him before coming home.' Olivia punched Markham playfully on the arm. 'And they say romance is dead!'

Arm in arm, the couple weaved their way somewhat unsteadily to the door and were eventually allowed to depart in a flurry of affectionate *arrivedercis*.

Outside, they stood for a moment looking up at the gauzy, navy blue sky pricked with myriad gem-like constellations. Markham found himself hoping passionately that the poor victims in his current case had now left evil far behind and found peace.

A pulse in the eternal mind, no less.

Olivia slipped her hand into his and squeezed it. There was no need for words.

Back at the police station, DS Noakes was also contemplating the night sky from the window of the CID office, though his thoughts were running on potential opportunities for overtime rather than anything more poetic.

Wearily massaging the back of his neck, he turned back to his desk, cleared away the detritus of his lonely fish and chip supper and reflected with some satisfaction on a good evening's work.

He thought he might be on to something with the canon all right. Cross-referencing *Crockford's Clerical Directory* against missing persons and unsolved homicide indexes had thrown up such a glaring set of coincidences. that it seemed incredible no-one had ever made the connection.

But to Noakes it was clear as day. *Wherever Woodcourt had served, one or more young boys subsequently went missing.* A couple had eventually turned up in waterlogged trenches, but in such an advanced state of decomposition that the forensics were worse than useless. It was all there for the guvnor on the spreadsheet. Dates, locations, the lot.

Noakes picked up one of the sheets of notes that he had made and glanced over it. In all cases, Woodcourt had figured as a volunteer of information.

Stephen Harper, aged twelve, had sung in the choir of St James's, Cedar Hill. 'He was a dear, devout boy,' said the Reverend Mr Woodcourt, thirty-two, vicar of St James's. 'Only a madman could have contemplated harming such a child.'

Then there was Henry Lewis, aged thirteen. 'He was a shining light here at Holy Trinity,' said the rector, the Reverend Mr Woodcourt.

It was the same story with other lads who had somehow slipped through the church's net.

Woodcourt was invariably on hand to offer a soundbite.

What was it they said about Jimmy Savile? *Hiding in plain sight.* Well, the same could be true of Woodcourt too. The ultra-respectable clergyman living a double life.

The DS thought back to Nat's shining-eyed hero worship of St Mary's Chaplain. He had been curate, then vicar, and rector. Why had he suddenly decided to do chaplaincy work? All right, he was made a canon, but he wasn't running a proper parish. Was he lying low, out of the limelight? Replaying his conversations with Nat and Julian, Noakes felt the undigested chip supper churn inside him. Come to think of it, Julian hadn't appeared to share his friend's enthusiasm for Woodcourt. Possibly the older boy had picked up on signals that went right over Nat's head...

It occurred to Noakes that Woodcourt had pulled the wool over his own eyes as well. Not your typical sky pilot, and he'd been taken in by the lack of airs and graces. Markham too, he reckoned.

They'd have to do any investigating of Woodcourt on the QT. Apart from the fact that it wasn't their job to re-open old crimes, they could hardly charge around turning out every cupboard in the canon's life over the past twenty years. Slimy Sid would never stand for it. And the church would no doubt batten down the hatches at the merest whiff of scandal, whisking Woodcourt well out of reach. What they needed was someone discreet, someone on the inside...

And he knew the very man! Steve Sinnott. When Sinnott had announced he was leaving the police to train for the Anglican priesthood some fifteen years previously, Noakes had been as bemused as the rest of CID. But they'd stayed in touch over the years, exchanging Christmas cards and the odd e-mail. Muriel had derived a certain cachet from the connection, peppering her conversation at the Women's Guild with references to 'George's friend the vicar'. Well, time for His Reverence to do Noakes a favour. He looked at the office clock: 10.30pm. Not too late to make a phone call. After all, it wasn't as if the guy would be out whooping it up. He'd probably be glad of the diversion.

* * *

When Markham arrived at the office half an hour later, he found his DS looking like the proverbial cat that got the cream. But as he listened to Noakes describe his 'man in the know', it turned out the preening was more than justified.

'Steve's a diocesan youth leader for North Cornwall, Guv. Ex-job too, so you can count on him being discreet.'

'Well done, Noakes.' At last they were getting somewhere! 'How soon can he get the intel?'

'I've set up an appointment for Tuesday. That'll give him time to work his contacts.'

Markham ran a hand over his face. He felt sandbagged with exhaustion, but beneath the fatigue was an undercurrent of elation. This had to be the break they were looking for, *had to be.*

'D'you think the canon's still, you know, *at it?*'

Markham winced. Noakes was never one to beat about the bush.

'If you're asking is he an active paedophile, then I think the likely answer to that is yes, Noakes. But it's complicated, and I can't work out how all the pieces fit together. What I think we can hypothesize is that Irene Hummles, Georgina Hamilton – and likely those two poor lugs in the grottoes – were killed to stop them revealing what they knew.'

'What about the kids at St Mary's? Are they safe?' Noakes spoke gruffly, but Markham knew that Nat and Julian had somehow wound themselves round his weather-beaten old heart.

'With St Mary's being a crime scene, I've arranged twice-nightly patrols. Despite the press sensationalism, parents aren't clamouring to remove youngsters from the school—'

'Cos it's a handy dumping ground!' Noakes was indignant.

'Oh, for God's sake, Noakes!' Markham exploded in tones of purest exasperation. 'Get that chip off your shoulder. We're not talking Dotheboys Hall! In case you've forgotten, this is a *choir school*. Christmas is the biggest gig of the year. The only thing that matters is who's going to snag the treble solo for 'Once In Royal David's City'!'

Noakes was momentarily distracted from class warfare.

'They did Bromgrove proud last year,' he said reminiscently. 'Sang like angels. Better than Aled Jones, Muriel thought.'

'There you are then,' Markham said hastily before the DS proceeded to share further musical insights from Mrs Noakes. 'It'll be business as usual for the cathedral.'

'What about the Night Watchman bod?' Noakes had the bit between his teeth.

'Given the level of police scrutiny, I'm willing to bet he'll take a back seat for the time being. Too risky. But I'll brief Dr O'Keefe as a precaution.'

Markham swayed on his feet, causing the DS to eye him narrowly.

'Look, Guv, you're all done in. You need to head off home and get some kip. Won't, er, your girlfriend be wondering where you've got to?'

Exhausted as he was, the DI was amused to note Noakes's self-consciousness when alluding to Olivia. No doubt he imagined she had some sort of sexual marathon lined up!

'You're right, time to call it a night.' He bit his lip and turned to go. Noakes would only think he was 'losing it' if he articulated his acute sense of foreboding. He suspected five children had been abducted and murdered. *Five that they knew of.* It looked increasingly likely that there were others. His former mentor's words kept ringing in his ears like a death knell. *The same monster did for them all.* Somehow they had to break the pernicious cycle.

Saturday at St Mary's was a half day, usually taken up with choir rehearsals and sporting fixtures. After prayers in the chapel at 5pm followed by tea between 5.30 and 6pm, students generally had the evening free so that they could unwind before the rigours of cathedral services the following day. Then it was lights out – 8pm for the juniors, then the seniors an hour later.

Nat always liked Evensong. Tired out from his exertions on the rugby field, he found something very soothing in the gentle chanting of the cantors and soft diapason of the little organ. Wedged between his classmates, the half hour usually passed in a cosy dream, his scurrying thoughts gradually succumbing to the drowsy antiphonal hum, incense and flickering candlelight. With his eyes shut, he could pretend he had a family and home. Aunt Emily *meant* to be kind, but Nat knew she found him a nuisance. Here at St Mary's, there were other boys in the same boat, and Mr Woodcourt always said it was more important to lend each other a helping hand than to shine in class.

Best of all, there was Julian. An instant liking had sprung up between them from the very first day of Nat's arrival at the school. Almost imperceptibly, the older boy had become his friend, his patron and the comforter of all his woes. Sometimes proud and stand-offish with others, Julian watched over him with a grim protection which never faltered. Any lads inclined to pick a fight with Nat soon found themselves confronted by an opponent whose listless manner concealed a fierce loyalty, with the result that they quickly learned to keep a respectful distance from his fists.

But something was wrong with Julian. Terribly wrong. Worst of all, Nat did not know how to put it right.

Opening his eyes, Nat surreptitiously glanced along the line of boys to where Julian stood, haughty and withdrawn as ever. His face gave nothing away, but Nat *knew* it was an act. He remembered how he had come upon Julian weeping behind second quad just two weeks earlier, his shoulders heaving with choking sobs which had alarmed Nat far more than any angry outburst. He had been tempted to steal quietly away, keenly aware how little his friend would appreciate being caught crying like a girl; but Julian's frantic grief compelled him to act.

'What's the matter, Julian? Has something happened at home? You can tell me.'

He had timidly placed a hand on Julian's shoulder, but

the older boy had flung him off with something approaching terror. 'No! Get off me! Don't touch me! Leave me alone!' he had cried. 'You don't know... You can't – I couldn't tell you what I've done. You'd hate me.'

He had turned away from Nat, cringing with some kind of shame, and Nat had quietly walked away, his heart pounding with fear.

Since then, Nat had watched Julian closely and seen that he was out of sorts. All his timid enquiries had been gruffly, almost rudely, repulsed, however, and he took it sadly to heart that his chief prop and steadfast supporter would not share his troubles. Julian had seemed cheerier with the arrival of Miss Mullen – going so far as to call her 'cool' – but this revival of spirits had alternated with fits of gloom and silent moodiness, so that Nat could not get anything out of him. Even Mr Woodcourt couldn't jolly Julian out of his depression, despite holding out the lure of try-outs for the cricket First Eleven. If the prospect of sporting glory could not rouse him, Nat reflected, his friend must be in a very bad way.

Nat made a sudden desperate resolution to collar Julian after tea and get to the bottom of it. They'd pull through whatever it was together. *They had to.*

After tea, Nat looked anxiously around the boys' comfortable, though rather battered, recreation room situated at the back of first quad. While the other students clustered in front of the television, happily engrossed in *Dr Who*, Julian sat in the shadows, so preoccupied with his own thoughts that he seemed scarcely aware of what was going on around him. Nat's heart sank at the realization that his friend was shunning him, when this was usually their favourite moment of the week. Nevertheless, he bravely sat down next to Julian on the sagging overstuffed sofa and summoned up all his courage.

'What's the matter, mate?' he asked in a rush. 'Are you sick or something? Why won't you tell me?'

Slowly, as though coming out of a trance, the older boy looked at Nat with a strange expression in his dark eyes. Half-fierce, half-imploring, he muttered huskily, 'S'all right, I'm OK. Don't worry about me.'

Nat looked so hurt and distressed, as though bankrupt in the eyes of their small community, that Julian tempered his abrupt dismissal with a clumsy laugh, though the tears stood in his eyes and his lips trembled.

'Honestly, mate, it's nothing for you to worry about... Just, well, personal things.'

Nat felt obscurely reassured by this answer. St Mary's code of honour meant that you didn't pry into another fellow's domestic circumstances. He had never said much to Julian about his dead parents or Aunt Emily, so he could understand the other's reserve about family. He knew Julian didn't like his stepfather and guessed he was unhappy at home. That had to be the reason why he was so dejected and unlike himself. Nat could not expect any further revelations and would just have to wait until the cloud had passed.

And yet... Looking down, Nat noticed that his friend's hands were bruised and criss-crossed with scratches.

Julian saw him looking.

'Punched my locker when I was feeling a bit wound up,' he said with an embarrassed laugh and averted gaze. 'Then I fell over in that patch of nettles round the side of Chaplain's House... I'll get some ointment later.'

It sounded unconvincing. Nat thought that Julian might have made those scratches himself.

There was nothing of the sneak about Nat, but at that moment he decided he would have to tell someone about Julian. Someone who would know what to do. Someone who would say the right thing and not blab to everyone.

Mr Woodcourt.

Yes, that was his best bet. *He'd* know how to get Julian to open up. Nat always felt better after he'd brought a problem to the canon. 'There is nothing either good or bad, but thinking makes it so,' he liked to tell Nat.

Awkwardly, Nat clapped his friend on the arm, happy now that he had made his decision. 'Joan's sure to have some cake left over from tea,' he said. 'I'll go and nick some for us to take upstairs later.' Smiling reassuringly, he headed for the kitchen, leaving Julian to his thoughts.

12

On Our Watch!

The cathedral service for the Second Sunday of Advent went without a hitch. Greatly relieved not to have muffed the solo vocals for 'O Come, O Come Emmanuel', once the opening hymn was over, Nat felt he could relax.

Mr Sharpe was usually very strict about the choristers maintaining what he called 'custody of the eyes', but today for some reason the Director of Music sank into the choirmaster's stall without even glancing in their direction. Nat took advantage of this unusual lapse to steal a few glances at the congregation. There was Mr Noakes a few rows from the front, looking rather uncomfortable, as though his tie was strangling him. The big, bossy-looking lady next to him, must be his wife. Her hat was so big, it looked like she had a rhododendron bush on her head. The people sitting behind didn't look very pleased. Julian gave a warning cough from the other side of the aisle, which made Nat realize he had been staring. Smothering a grin, he tried to look prayerful and devout.

Nat was happy to see that Julian was looking brighter than on the previous evening, though something about the set of his head and the way he squared his shoulders – as if settling some load upon them – suggested he was making a conscious effort.

He wondered what Julian had done. Something so dreadful that he couldn't tell Nat about it.

Nat's mind began to race. He thought back to the recent craze for voodoo that had swept St Mary's. Maybe Julian had put a curse on his stepdad – made a doll and stuck pins in it like Timms Minor – and something bad had happened. Then there was that craze for the occult and Ouija boards. What if Julian had been contacting dead people or, even worse, worshipping the Devil? Mr Woodcourt had said you got excommunicated in the Middle Ages for unleashing dark forces and stuff like that.

Nat didn't like to think of his friend doing anything dodgy, recalling that Julian had been unimpressed by his fascination with *Harry Potter* style wizardry. Myths and legends, or tales of chivalry, were more to the older boy's taste than what he scornfully dismissed as 'hocus pocus'.

No, on balance he didn't think Julian's trouble was anything to do with the black arts... Perhaps he'd been a grass and snitched on another fellow... Perhaps he'd stolen something, or lied, or cheated... But Nat couldn't imagine Julian doing any of these things, or anything mean and sneaking for that matter cos he was as honest as daylight.

He thought back to how Julian had cringed away the other night at his touch. Almost as though he was afraid Nat would catch something from him! What if he had done something bad with another boy? Nat wasn't sure precisely what this might entail, but he knew from certain sly winks and nudges, as well as from scraps of conversation overheard in the locker-room and various embarrassing allusions to 'abomination', that such things were possible. Perhaps it was like leprosy and you got something horrible from doing it. Just like the Black Death. Nat broke out in a cold sweat at the very thought.

Create in me a clean heart, O God, and renew a right spirit within me.

The psalm rang out clear and true. This was the lay vicars' moment, and they did the sonorous text full justice. Distracted from images of buboes and pustules, Nat revelled in the glorious sound. Looking across at Julian's face – his countenance as sternly remote as that of the recording angel on the altar reredos – it was impossible to imagine him being yucky.

So, if it wasn't *that*, what was it?

He'd been fast friends with Julian since, well, forever. Couldn't be any closer, not if they were blood-brothers, just like the Spartan warriors Miss Gibson had told them about. They hadn't taken an oath or cut each other's veins, but they knew it just the same.

At that moment, Nat remembered the scratches on Julian's hands, the ones he said he'd got by falling in nettles – the ones Nat thought he'd done himself. From a distance, they didn't look so sore and angry any more. But what could have made Julian hurt himself like that? Perhaps he wanted to give another fellow a black eye, or pummel him senseless for some slight or insult, but couldn't because it was against the rules, so he worked off the anger by taking a pen-knife to his hands. Julian was someone who could stay pent up for a long while before exploding in rage; maybe when in this mood, he figured it was safer to punish himself rather than pitch into a classmate.

Nat became aware of a pair of kindly eyes fixed on him in some concern. Oh Lordy, everyone else was standing for the collect while he remained seated. No wonder Canon Woodcourt was staring at him. The Director of Music's expression was altogether less indulgent. Julian drew a finger across his throat to indicate that Nat would 'catch it' after the service. This gesture of complicity, and the accompanying smile, suddenly made Nat feel much better. It was a glimpse of the old sunny Julian, the one he knew was still there behind all the storm clouds. After the service, he would speak to Mr Woodcourt about his friend and ask for help to find out what was wrong. The canon wouldn't just bang on about God or quote the Bible like their Religious Studies teacher. No, he could be counted on to *do* something.

Ducking his head apologetically in the direction of Mr Sharpe, Nat prepared to listen to the Gospel.

* * *

After the service, all too aware that the Director of Music would be on the warpath, Nat exited the robing room in double quick time and whisked round to the vestry. Technically it was out of bounds, but he hoped by some fluke to catch the canon's eye.

Luck was on his side. Almost as if he had been expecting Nat, the canon had removed his heavy vestments and was looking across the room to the door. Jerking a thumb upwards, Mr Woodcourt mimed the words *Forty Martyrs*, which Nat interpreted as a signal for him to go to that chapel once the coast was clear.

Melting into a gaggle of altar servers, he disappeared into the outer sacristy and waited anxiously until the post-service hubbub had subsided. The echoing of many voices, the clattering of many feet and the clinking of precious vessels being removed by the sacristans, all swelled forward in a mass like the heave of waves withdrawing across the shingle. Finally, Nat felt it was safe to emerge and climbed the stone steps to the balcony of The Forty Martyrs Chapel where the canon was waiting for him.

It was where they had sat before.

'Nat, my dear boy.' Mr Woodcourt's voice was very gentle. 'I thought we'd lost you during the service. You seemed to be in another world!'

Nat's face began to work at the mild raillery.

'Oh sir,' he cried, clasping his hands in consternation, 'I'm frightened about Julian and don't know what to do!'

The canon was very still. Eventually he spoke in the familiar steady and compassionate tone.

'What makes you think there is something wrong with Julian, my boy?'

'He's just not the same anymore.' Nat's voice gained in conviction. 'I think something very bad has happened cos he has these moods and things.'

The canon's expression of kindly concern never altered.

'I nearly got it out of him the other day, sir,' Nat continued headlong, the words tumbling out of him. 'He said he'd done something – something that would make me hate him if I knew... I've seen him crying as if his heart would break... An' he's got cuts on his hands – he said it was nettles but I think he did them himself, sir.'

Nat put his head in his hands. When he looked up, he was half-blind with tears and he could no longer see the canon's face. Swiftly, he drew his sleeve across his eyes and the scene swam back into focus.

The other clapped him on the shoulder, saying firmly, 'You did well to tell me about this, Nat. It must have been a great weight on your mind but now you can set it down. I will consult with Dr O'Keefe and, between us, I am sure we can get to the bottom of whatever is troubling your friend. Sometimes family trials—' he paused delicately, 'can cause great distress.'

From this Nat understood that the canon would find a way to win Julian's confidence and loosen his tongue about whatever was upsetting him – probably something to do with home. Being a grown-up, he would know the right words.

Nat took a deep breath. *'Thank you, sir.'* An afterthought struck him. 'You won't tell Julian I came to see you, will you, sir? Otherwise he'll think I ratted on him.'

'You're quite safe on that score, Nat,' came the jovial response. 'Now run along before Miss Gibson sends out a search party!'

With that, the boy pitter-pattered away as the canon contemplated his retreating figure with a look of tender regret.

DS George Noakes wrenched off his scratchy new paisley tie and rammed it savagely into the glove compartment of his Ford Cortina. Running a finger round the inside of his collar, he breathed a prayer of gratitude that Muriel had suddenly decided her presence was indispensable to the success of the cathedral's Third World Lunch, leaving him to his own devices.

Little Nat had looked a bit peaky and preoccupied during the service, he thought. Kept glancing across at his chum as though there was summat up with him.

Noakes thought back to Julian's discovery of the little *Star Wars* toy in the grottoes and their subsequent conversation over tea. There had been something oddly intense and wistful about the lad, and he had looked downright wretched when they were exploring that creepy catacomb. *Freaked out*, Nat had said. At the time, Noakes had put Julian's reactions down to claustrophobia. But what if there was more to it than that? What if he was holding something back?

The DS felt a prickle of anxiety. Was it possible that Woodcourt had made a move on Julian? Or did the boy perhaps know something that he was keeping a secret out of fear or misplaced loyalty? The teenager hadn't seemed nearly as keen as Nat on the canon, but maybe he thought it was uncool to slobber over a teacher. He was such a self-contained lad, it was difficult to tell what might be going through his head.

Then there was Julian's unexpected request that he should have first dibs on the plastic figurine. The DS had taken it as a reflection of the boy's lonely and love-starved home life. But now he wondered...

His hands on the steering wheel, Noakes looked thoughtfully across the cathedral car park towards the school buildings. He felt a sudden overpowering urge to check the whereabouts of Nat and Julian and satisfy himself that they were safely tucking into their Sunday roast.

Then he caught sight of his crumpled face in the car mirror and the moment passed. Self-consciously, he rearranged his features and checked to see that no-one had observed him daydreaming. It was Sunday for heaven's sake! What did he imagine was going to happen to the two boys on a weekend? Everything in CID was strictly need-to-know, and as far as the outside world was concerned they were following several lines of inquiry – not a whisper of paedophilia or sex abuse. There was no reason to suppose Nat or Julian was in any danger, and it would only put backs up if he hung around the school like a bad smell. Might even put the wind up Woodcourt if the police seemed to be taking too close an interest. 'Sides, the patrol boys were keeping an eye out as well. All safe as houses.

With one long parting look, abashed by his curious reluctance to quit St Mary's, Noakes drove slowly out of the cathedral car park.

Now, what to do with the unlooked-for bonanza of some free time away from the ball and chain?

Whoa… Acacia Avenue … now, why did that name ring a bell?

Oh yeah, he remembered seeing the address at the bottom of one of those booklet thingies – there'd been a little stack of them on a table in the entrance hall at St Mary's. The *Friends of St Mary's*, that was it. He'd picked one up and taken it back to CID. Seemed harmless enough. A few short articles and blurred illustrations of the school magazine variety. There were pieces on signs of the zodiac and the lost race of Atlanta, and another about an exhibition of Kabbalistic manuscripts at the British Museum. All double Dutch to Noakes. Even more mystifying was a weird little item entitled *Maha Chohan* – not an Indian takeaway, he recalled ruefully, but something to do with spiritual enlightenment. Sounded a bit far-out, but alternative religion was likely on the school syllabus, and anyway Markham had said Sir Philip was majorly into this theosophy hoo ha; he was the school patron, after all, so no surprise that he tried to get the kids interested.

O'Keefe had got his knickers in a twist because some busybody do-gooder suggested the school society – some poncey-sounding name – was a cover for perviness. For the life of him, Noakes couldn't see how. The whole thing sounded boringly virtuous and above board. A big yawn in fact.

That was the trouble, he reflected. All this hysteria about 'historical' sex abuse meant people were seeing bogeymen all over the shop. Why, even Edward Heath had been suspected of running a satanic sex cult. *Edward Heath*, Noakes chuckled to himself, *I mean, I ask you!*

The DS sobered up abruptly at the thought that the current investigation meant he and Markham were having to think the unthinkable. About a highly respected – even *revered* – senior clergyman and pillar of the community no less. The stakes were frighteningly high. If they got it wrong, Slimy Sid would have them directing traffic for the rest of their careers... But somehow, he felt certain they were on the right track. Those spreadsheets spoke for themselves, and Steve would help them nail the bastard.

Now, what the hell was the address for the *Friends of St Mary's?* Come on, *think!*

Number 32, that was it!

Couldn't hurt to have a quick dekko. Prob'ly no-one even there on a Sunday.

But Noakes was wrong. As he watched, a tall gangly young man with a long narrow face and dark, dead-looking wispy hair came around the corner and disappeared down the steps to the basement of number 32.

The DS waited five minutes then did likewise. A small metal plaque next to the doorbell informed visitors that this was the *Friends of St Mary's Head* (and no doubt sole) *Office.*

'Good afternoon, can I help you?' The young man was surprised but polite as he answered the front door.

Noakes flashed his warrant card and asked if he could come in. The other's smile of polite mystification deepened, but he courteously led the way into a poky front room, screened from the road by rather dingy net curtains, which obviously functioned as an office. A pervading aroma of Pot Noodle gave a clue as to preparations for Sunday lunch. No wonder he was such a scrawny specimen.

'I'm Jack King, one of the volunteers, Officer. Sorry about the mess. We're in the middle of a fund-raising mail shot,' the young man said, gesturing apologetically at piles of envelopes covering every inch of sludge-coloured carpet. Shifting a pile of stationery from one of the two uncomfortable-looking armchairs, he waved Noakes to a seat.

Nothing doing here, the DS said to himself. *Still, no harm asking a few questions.*

'What's the set up then, son?' he enquired, plonking himself down and sending up a cloud of dust in the process.

'Well, there are a couple of us Bromgrove Uni students from the Comparative Religion faculty doing a sort of internship here – expenses only, nothing flash. Essentially, we run the admin side of *Friends* in shifts. Good for the CV and community relations ... kind of school-uni outreach scheme. Bromgrove LEA lobs us the odd grant, but basically Sir Philip Soames funds the office.'

The young man was earnest and helpful, thought Noakes approvingly. Not at all your typical hippie layabout. A good advert for higher education.

'All very worthy,' he said reassuringly. 'How long has it been going?'

King scratched his head. 'God, forever. More than thirty years, I think. There's a decent subscription list, but we don't take it for granted – try to do some PR and hustle local businesses for sponsorship.' Rentokil had taken out a full page spread in the last issue, Noakes recalled wryly.

'D'you have a list of subscribers I can take away?' the DS asked. 'Don't worry, you haven't done anything wrong,' he added as he saw a nervous look come over the other's face, 'purely background stuff. Trying to build up a picture of St Mary's and so forth.'

The young man's expression cleared. 'No worries, just give me a sec and I'll photocopy it for you. I'll root out the minutes for the last quarterly meeting too and get you some back numbers. You might find it interesting.' Unlikely.

Ten minutes later Noakes was out on Acacia Avenue, leaving Jack King to his Pot Noodle. Not a particularly productive interview, but then you never knew. He'd slip over to CID (might as well get full value from being off the leash) and review what they'd got. No doubt Markham would be along later.

A passer-by on the other side of the road who had apparently paused to tie a trailing shoelace straightened up, watched the car till it was out of sight and then moved purposefully in the direction from which Noakes had just come.

Markham and Olivia had also attended the cathedral's Sunday service, sitting inconspicuously in a pew right at the back.

The hour is at hand. Let us cast off the works of darkness and put on the armour of light... then on that last day, when Christ shall come again in his glorious majesty to judge both the quick and the dead, we may rise to life immortal...

Advent and Eschatology. The end of days.

As the gloomily apocalyptic clarion call echoed around the cathedral, Markham glanced at a marble statue to the left of their bench. It depicted a fiery archangel, in full armour and with outstretched wings, thrusting his sword into a huge coiled serpent which writhed beneath his feet.

Put on the armour of light.

Looking at the celestial combatants locked in their epic struggle from time immemorial, Markham felt a shiver of apprehension. What if the forces of darkness were too much for him this time? If Noakes was right, then evil had prevailed for decades and its perpetrators had flourished like the bay.

At that moment, a shaft of sunlight picked out Canon Woodcourt on the altar. As though conscious of the DI's scrutiny, he looked up. It seemed to Markham that the clergyman looked straight at him before once more bowing his head.

Clamorous doubts assailed him once again. Wasn't it possible that he and Noakes had somehow got this whole thing horribly wrong and that Woodcourt was exactly what he seemed – a decent and devout man of God? Could they exclude the possibility that Woodcourt's connection to the missing teenagers was simply an unfortunate coincidence? Had he and Noakes allowed themselves to be swayed by popular prejudice against priestly 'kiddy fiddlers'?

Markham recalled Olivia's invariable mantra against pessimism. *Angels are bright still, though the brightest fell.* Well, he would not rush to judgement without proof. Please, God, it would be forthcoming...

The service seemed never-ending. Normally he would have gained pleasure from the richness and beauty of the liturgy, but today the lighting of the advent wreath – four slim crimson candles round a central gold taper – merely served to remind him of lives brutally snuffed out.

Looking up at the stark vault of the cathedral, Markham thought back to his moment with Olivia under the stars the previous night and felt a searing sense of dislocation. What did his poor victims signify in the cosmic scheme of things?

At that moment, Olivia leaned trustingly into him, stray wisps from her ungovernable chignon tickling his chin. Imperceptibly, he felt the tension leave his body, as though magically banished by her touch. Suddenly God did not seem quite so remote. In the silence which followed the prayers of intercession, he sent up his own desperate petition: *I believe, Lord, help thou my unbelief!*

At the end of the service, Markham felt a mysterious reluctance to leave the cathedral. Watching the retreating backs of the choristers as they disappeared down the processional ramp to the sacristies, he had the oddest compulsion to call the boys back.

Olivia sensed his anxiety.

'D'you want to pop round to the school and check things, Gil? I don't mind, honestly.' She laughed. 'I know how it is, sweetheart. That motto *Not on my Watch* runs all the way through you like a stick of rock!'

Markham smiled shame-facedly. 'Am I that obvious?'

Linking Olivia's arm in his, he made a snap decision. Best to steer clear of the school today.

The boys were in safe hands, and Woodcourt had no reason to suppose the police were on to him. Time to enjoy a Sunday stroll and the company of his girlfriend like a normal human being…

'How about the Municipal Cemetery?' he asked.

It was a quirk of Markham's that, with so many victims of crime consigned to unmarked graves at best and sludge, silt and slurry at worst, he derived curious satisfaction from visiting graveyards where the dead lay tidily at rest in serried ranks under their grassy mounds and sombre headstones. Olivia fancied that this was where he communed with all those discarded uncoffined innocents he secretly held in his heart.

At the cemetery, the couple slowly wandered hand in hand between the graves underneath a sky bleached of colour save for a huge blood-red sun trembling on the horizon.

Olivia preserved a sympathetic silence. She knew that when Markham was ready he would talk. Meanwhile, she contemplated the poignant doggerel on tombstones and wove little histories around generations that lay deep underground.

As he walked, Markham's thoughts were running on Georgina Hamilton. The autopsy had revealed cancer of the womb, but her GP was unaware. Markham suspected she might have been seeing someone privately, in which case it would take time to unravel the thread. His conviction that Georgina would not have committed suicide remained unshaken – no coward soul hers – but DCI Sidney would no doubt be delighted at the prospect of such a verdict. He kicked a stray pebble on the path, relieving his feelings by imagining that it was a sensitive part of the DCI's anatomy. *Never fear, Georgina, I'll get justice for you and the others. Judgement Day is coming, I promise!*

'Ouch!' yelped Olivia.

Markham became aware he was squeezing his girlfriend's hand so fiercely as to cause pain.

He kissed the little palm and tucked it into his coat pocket. Mollified, Olivia smiled up at him.

'I'm sorry, Liv,' he began.

'No need. I'd rather you took it out on my mitts than a suspect!'

'It was DCI Sidney, actually.'

'Ah!' said Olivia in a tone of deep comprehension.

Time to return to the real world.

'Right, dearest, I'm going to drop you back at home and swing by the station. I can take my bad mood out on Noakesy if he's around.'

Reluctantly, they made their way towards the lights of the High Street.

In the offices of Bromgrove CID, an unaccustomed peace reigned, the steady hum of strip lighting the only sign of life.

The rest of CID would have been amused if they could have seen DS Noakes sitting in his fusty cubicle surrounded by back issues of *Friends of St Mary's*. With a view to killing some time, he had embarked rather unenthusiastically upon the reading material thrust at him earlier as he left the unprepossessing little office at number 32 Acacia Avenue. Despite himself, however, he had become increasingly absorbed, his posture rapidly shifting from slumped apathy to alert interest.

Sex and secrets. That was the thread running through it all, he realized with growing unease. It kept cropping up. '*You must cherish the Master's "hidden knowledge".*' Noakes read the text aloud, following the words with a stubby forefinger. '*A bid to recover the innocence of childhood via the renunciation of grosser sexuality ... finding pure warmth in the lap of young friends.*'

Bloody hell, no wonder O'Keefe had got the jitters.

Then there was something called *mystical regression*. '*The way of spiritual childhood ... rejoice in the touch and warmth of young companions to conquer the forces of evil and enmity in the world, just as Christ called for eunuchs for the sake of the kingdom of heaven.*'

As he read these unsettling words, another Biblical text bobbed unbidden to the surface of Noakes's mind. *Better for the man who harms one of these little ones to be thrown into the sea with a millstone around his neck.*

A shower of loud taps at the window next to his cubicle made the DS almost jump out of his skin. Just the branches of a spindly elm directly outside the office, but the sound unnerved him nonetheless, as though the insistent rapping was a spectral call to attract his attention.

Noakes's eyes dropped once more to the text in front of him.

A sentence immediately leaped out at him.

Death is no skeleton with a scythe but rather an angel bearing a golden key.

Skeletons.

Noakes felt his chest tighten, his breath come short. Again, in the stillness of the room, he had the feeling that someone was calling to him, begging him urgently to decipher the code.

Memories bubbled up like boils being lanced.

Jonny Warr had played the sitar. He was mad for anything 'alternative'. The missing boys had been through a hippy phase...

Noakes felt as though some hideous poison was creeping through his system. Was O'Keefe right, then? Was this apparently innocuous little society the nucleus for an evil network of abusers?

That list of subscribers. Perfect cover for paedophiles hiding in plain sight.

With suddenly shaking hands, Noakes thumbed through the magazines.

Yes, each issue featured *Students of the Month*. Bright-eyed handsome lads gazing out at the world from the pages of the little booklets, their sunshiny innocence undimmed by the cheap paper and amateurish photography.

And then a note from a nightmare. The picture of Julian Forsythe staring up at him.

A noise behind him.

'Are you all right, Noakes? You look as though you've seen a ghost.'

Markham's whole body tensed as he saw the picture of Julian.

Oh God, no, please, no!

There was no need for anything further. Noakes snatched up his mobile, moving with unaccustomed speed and decision. When he spoke, there was an undercurrent of hoarse urgency in his voice that Markham had never heard before.

'Dr O'Keefe. DS George Noakes here. I need you to check the whereabouts of Julian Forsythe and get back to me on this number as soon as you've located him. Now!'

The two officers gazed at each other in mute horror waiting to hear what they already knew.

Julian was gone.

'On our watch,' groaned Markham.

It sounded like an epitaph.

13

Lengthening Shadows

In the wan small hours of the following morning, Markham dragged himself through the front door of his apartment. Although badly in need of comfort and reassurance, he decided not to disturb Olivia and headed to the spare room to snatch a few hours' broken sleep.

Curled into a ball, peristaltic shudders coursed through him as he reviewed the night's events.

Most harrowing of all was the memory of Nat Barton's shocked and bewildered face. His eyes red with crying, the boy was bustled away by protectively hovering staff once it became clear he could shed no light on the disappearance of Julian Forsythe. Nat was out of bounds to the police for the time being. Or at least until the school doctor had checked him over.

Just before he was whisked off to the infirmary, however, Nat had sobbed out a question which reverberated agonizingly in Markham's mind.

'What made Julian go and leave me in the night?'

This piteous reproach unlocked memories which Markham had thought were long buried. Memories of someone who had left him in the night never to return. The fair-weather father who had walked out on his family when Markham was nine years old, leaving behind a scorched earth legacy of silence and repression. They had never talked about it afterwards. Not once. Part of him closed off that night. Died.

I should be glad of another death.

Markham wondered how Nat would come to terms with

•

the horror of Julian's almost certain abduction and murder. Perhaps he too would simply embark on a project of denial – unhitch his friend from time and space, think of him as rolled round diurnally with rocks and stones and trees. Well wadded with pragmatism, he could only survive by erasing the past.

Somehow, recalling Nat's fine-boned spiritual face and the intensity of his bond with Julian, Markham felt it more likely that he would be eternally tormented by the dreadful irreversibility of his friend's disappearance. The trusting peace of his confiding little soul would be forever poisoned, leaving a sense of loss that deepened every hour.

Markham's gut twisted with self-disgust at the realization that he had failed Julian Forsythe. Logic told him that there had been no reason to suspect that Julian or Nat was in any immediate danger, but emotion was a different story. He'd had an extrasensory awareness of danger or evil after the service in the cathedral. He'd felt it lurking there somewhere in that cool vaulted space. Wanting very much to get away from it, he had ignored the nagging sixth sense that something was off centre and admonished himself for being caught up in the hysteria of unfounded suspicion.

Unfounded suspicion. Woodcourt.

The canon, alerted by O'Keefe, had arrived quickly on the scene tonight. Amidst the chaos and confusion, he showed such fatherly concern for Nat and the frightened lads who clustered round him – counselling against the 'grave sin of despair' – that Markham doubted all over again. Could the man so earnestly exhorting staff and students to remember that God was with them really be a counterfeit priest?

Police units had scoured every inch of the school complex, not excluding the chapel, basement shrine and grottoes. The search yielded no trace of Julian Forsythe. His bed in the little dormitory was neatly made up. Impossible to know if he had ever been in it that night. No-one could be certain of having seen him after tea. As though he had melted into the swarm of boys before slipping away unnoticed. As for the cathedral, it had been locked up earlier that night. A sweep of the premises had disclosed nothing.

Again and again, Markham replayed that memory of the cassock-clad choristers vanishing down the cathedral processional ramp after the Sunday service. This time he called out to Julian to come back. But the slight dark figure never turned. He felt as though the sound of those receding footsteps would haunt him all his life.

The abduction had to be an inside job. *Had to be.* How else could Julian have been spirited away from under the noses of staff and students? And yet, preliminary interviews indicated nothing out of the ordinary had occurred until just after 7pm when Noakes raised the alarm and a flurry of staff converged on the senior dormitory – the Sharpes and Woodcourt from the direction of their respective flats, O'Keefe from the Chaplain's House and Cynthia, trailed by a sheepish Edward Preston, from her cottage on the north side of the cathedral. An emergency assembly was hastily organized, the junior boys blinking like little owls and the seniors affecting a desperate insouciance which deceived no-one. As word spread through the ranks that Julian Forsythe was missing, a ripple of disquiet passed through the room like an icy gust. Outside a gibbous moon hung in the black arcing sky as search parties fanned out across the grounds.

At least they'd been spared Sir Philip Soames. A flare up of myasthenia gravis had left him too ill to leave the house. Markham felt a growing conviction that the *Friends of St Mary's* was somehow a perfect breeding ground for the evil in this case. He did not relish informing St Mary's patron that his cherished theosophical society had served as camouflage for a twisted commerce in children's bodies.

Markham's thoughts turned back to the lost boy. He had no doubt that he was already dead. Just like the owner of the little plastic figurine he had found down in the grottoes.

There had been something strangely touching about Julian, he reflected with wrenching sadness. *Noli me tangere.* It was that cloak of reserve – a sense of something withheld – which made him reluctant to violate the boy's privacy. Lying there in the darkness, he admitted to himself that there had been another more selfish reason for his inhibition. The dread of touching a painful nerve and stirring up dormant memories of his own unhappy childhood.

But he should have gone in harder. Should have pressed Julian about the Night Watchman. Should have…

Markham ground his teeth in an agony of frustration. This self-flagellation would only divert his energies from the task in front of him. The utmost he could do for Julian was to crack the conspiracy. The meeting with Steve Sinnott would need to be brought forward as a matter of urgency…

Markham's exhausted mind began to drift, his thoughts flashing frantically hither and thither.

Noakes. The DS had interrogated staff and students like a man possessed, his usual shambling gait and lazy affability nowhere to be seen, every barked instruction eloquent testimony to a gnawing self-reproach.

Olivia. Her tender heart would break over Julian. How would he ever find the words to tell her?

With that last despairing thought, oblivion finally claimed him.

Three hours later, Markham and Noakes sat grim-faced in the DI's office at CID.

Outside, a light dusting of snow turned Bromgrove Green's familiar shop fronts to silvery filigree, the gaudy festive fripperies taunting the two men with their reminder of Christmas cheer. Toystop, in particular, with its *Star Wars* themed window display, was a heart-rending reminder of the missing boy's enthusiasm for all things Jedi.

Breaking the news of Julian's disappearance to Olivia had been an ordeal.

'*Oh no, that poor boy*,' she whispered, her voice tight with distress. 'He was so proud and excited when he showed me the school's relics. And so protective of Nat. He didn't have anyone else...' Like Markham, she berated herself for negligence. 'I didn't do enough. I knew Julian was holding back, but he was so private that I didn't like to pry. His thoughts were all he had.' Tears ran down her face. *'Tread softly because you tread on my dreams.'*

A lump came into Markham's throat as he recalled his girlfriend's passionate plea.

'Julian never had much of a shot at life, Gil. Promise me you'll nail the lowlife who did this.' He had done his best to comfort her without, however, mentioning Woodcourt. The spinners of the spider's web must be allowed to go on hatching their schemes until the time came to lure them out from their dark hiding places.

Noakes too was taking Julian's disappearance badly. Pouchy under the eyes, and sending up a shower of scurf every time he scratched his frowsy head, the DS looked even more shop-soiled than usual.

'Friends of St Mary's! Nowt but a cover for nonces!' he exclaimed bitterly, flailing at the pile of magazines which fluttered like confetti about him. 'Should have seen it right away.' He gnawed impotently on his fist. 'An' that poor little bastard. Just didn't get the breaks ... life over before it'd even begun.' Honking into a dingy hanky, he scowled at Markham as though daring the guvnor to contradict him.

The DI's intercom sputtered into life, making them start.

'There's a Reverend Sinnott 'ere at reception asking for DS Noakes.' The desk sergeant sounded suspicious. 'Says it's about St Mary's.'

Noakes was galvanized into action.

'Sinnott's kosher, Sarge,' he barked into the intercom. 'I'll be right down.' Turning to Markham with a faintly apologetic air, he added, 'Figured we couldn't wait till Tuesday, boss, so asked Steve to come in soonest. He's a family man himself, you see...'

'You did right, Noakesy.' Markham's voice was warm. 'We need something to break this case. I'll take whatever your mate has to offer.'

*   *   *

The Reverend Sinnott, Markham reflected, looked more like a prop forward than a priest with his burly frame, crinkly ram's wool hair and plug ugly features. But his hazel eyes were astute and compassionate. It was the steady gaze of a man only too familiar with the darkest recesses of the human heart.

There was no time for polite preliminaries.

'What can you tell us about Canon Dick Woodcourt?' Markham asked bluntly. 'We're investigating a possible paedophile ring going back many years and Woodcourt keeps turning up.'

Sinnott exhaled deeply before replying with an air of quiet deliberation which commanded respect.

'Woodcourt's a very able administrator, Inspector, and highly regarded for his pastoral gifts. I'd heard rumours over the years about pre-pubescent boys... There always seemed to be a coterie of young lads in attendance, so tongues tended to wag. In fairness to him, though, I'd say stories like that are pretty much par for the course if you're wearing a dog collar and working with young people.'

'Not for you!' Noakes was outraged.

Sinnott's smile was rueful. 'I have a wife and kids. That was a protection of sorts. Being ex-Job helped too. But a guy like Woodcourt ... well, there's something a bit finicky and precious, about him. That's what fanned the flames.'

Markham frowned. 'It was an issue for the church authorities, then?'

'Well, Woodcourt got moved about a fair bit.'

'But that's normal, isn't it?' Noakes was playing Devil's Advocate.

Sinnott shrugged. 'From what I heard, he had made one or two places too hot to hold him. There was gossip about Black Masses too, which didn't help.'

'*Black Masses*? What do you mean?' Markham leaned forward intently.

Sinnott emitted a rumbling laugh. 'Oh, it was just a load of hokum due to him dabbling in fringe stuff outside the mainstream. Theosophy, as I recall. A talk to some historical society or other about occultist philosophies ended with him being denounced to the bishop as a practitioner of the dark arts and devil-worshipper to boot!'

'Hmmm.' Markham was thoughtful. 'Isn't theosophy meant to be non-diabolic and peaceful?'

'Oh sure.' Sinnott nodded vigorously. 'Woodcourt was banging on about its origins in alchemy and astrology. He gave another talk later about its links to the great world religions, but by then all sorts of nonsense was doing the rounds.'

'You didn't find anything sinister about it?' Taut as a bowstring, Markham watched as Sinnott considered the question.

'To be honest, at the time no, I didn't. After all, it's a common enough aspersion in religious circles, Inspector. The Early Christians were accused of cannibalism and all kinds of occult practices. Then, a few centuries down the line, the anti-semitic brigade accused Jews of kidnapping and murdering Christian children to siphon off their blood.'

'The blood libel.'

Sinnott looked at Markham with heightened respect. 'Quite so.'

Noakes stared from one to the other in bafflement.

'Let's skip the *University Challenge* bollocks, Steve,' he pleaded. 'You said you didn't find anything sinister about the Black Masses shitstorm at the time.'

'That's right.'

'But what about *later*? Did anything happen to make you change your mind?'

Markham held his breath. He could tell from the sudden stillness which came over Sinnott that the DS was on to something.

'Something close to home?' he prompted gently. 'Something to do with your kids?'

The other stiffened. 'It's personal—' he muttered gruffly.

'Nothing's personal in a murder inquiry, mate,' interjected Noakes.

'*Murder!*' Sinnott's ruddy cheeks blanched.

'Ongoing inquiries,' Noakes confirmed portentously.

'Look, Mr Sinnott,' said Markham, trying to suppress a rising tide of impatience, 'if Woodcourt's our man, then he's a predator. We're dealing with someone who camouflaged himself as a priest to target his victims and cut the weakest from the pack. The perfect disguise.'

As his friend's head sank lower, Noakes attempted some bluff reassurance. 'The canon certainly fooled *us* good and proper.'

Sinnott looked up at the two officers with a hunted expression. 'Could be something and nothing,' he murmured, 'but I noticed a change in my younger boy. It was a while back when I was starting out in Boscastle. Woodcourt was doing lots of outreach with the Youth Group, and my lads belonged to a Junior History Club or some such. It all seemed harmless enough. Kept them out of mischief.'

Markham and Noakes exchanged a long wordless look.

'Gabriel became moody and withdrawn,' Sinnott continued. 'Thirteen's a difficult age, of course, hormones running riot and all the rest of it. But there was something not right. Then when I picked him up one evening from a JHC meeting, I noticed Woodcourt watching him when he didn't realize I was looking. Something about the expression on his face gave me the creeps. Like a fox in a chicken coop. And then it was gone so quickly that I could almost believe I'd imagined it. But I felt an overwhelming urge to get Gabriel away from the man...'

Some colour washed back into Sinnott's cheeks.

'I was a coward, Inspector. I never voiced my suspicions. Just found something else for Gabriel to do on JHC nights. Gradually prised him away from Woodcourt and decided to let sleeping dogs lie. I didn't want to upset my wife by making a fuss – especially since Gabe hadn't mentioned anything untoward. Also, I didn't want to screw my career by offending Woodcourt. He had a fair amount of clout in those days.' He grimaced. 'And I could have got it wrong. Some parishes can be a right nest of vipers – you wouldn't *believe* the bigotry and petty-minded hypocrisy – so I felt I just *had* to give Woodcourt the benefit of the doubt, whatever my own personal misgivings about the man.'

Markham felt a headache coming. There was something hovering just at the outer reaches of his peripheral vision. Whatever the phantom was, he could not pin it down.

With an effort, the DI recalled himself to the present.

'Who was pulling strings to protect Woodcourt, then?' Noakes returned to the attack. 'C'mon Steve, we need *names*. Who else was involved in this freaky theosophical mumbo jumbo? College types, hippie priests, those whatchamacallits … gurus – the wacky baccy crowd – or what?'

'Heavens no, it was all quite scholarly really. Just a bit far-out for the more conservative congregations, which led to misunderstanding. I mean, Woodcourt had some perfectly respectable backers...' Sinnott's eyes narrowed in concentration. 'Let me see. There was Sir Philip Soames for one and Colonel McIn –'

'*Say that again!*'

Noakes sprang to his feet, his eyes locking onto Markham's.

Startled, Sinnott looked from one to the other.

'Sir Philip Soames,' he repeated falteringly. 'He's quite well known in Bromgrove, isn't he? Local philanthropist and all that... Look here, Inspector, are you all right?'

Markham had turned very pale, but brushed aside the enquiry in a hoarse voice. 'I'm fine, Mr Sinnott. Please go on.'

'I'm not sure I can add much more,' Sinnott replied reminiscently. 'Woodcourt and Soames both read Greats at Balliol. Then Woodcourt went on to Besant Theological College while Soames dabbled in antiquities – he's an amateur archaeologist and orientalist... Of course, the family fortune helped. But he's been a generous patron of the church – sponsored restoration work at the cathedral and St Mary's and helped any number of struggling clergymen …

stuck to Woodcourt through thick and thin, otherwise he'd have been out on his ear … swung him the canonry too, I shouldn't wonder. Got some sort of terminal illness now, but still turns out for diocesan youth pilgrimages. Amazing willpower. They don't make them like that anymore.'

Sinnott paused, alarmed by Markham's lowering taciturnity. He turned anxiously to Noakes who looked equally grim.

'Surely you can't imagine…' he stammered. 'You're not seriously suggesting that Sir Philip… *My god*.'

Markham's face was like a carved mask. Ignoring Sinnott, he addressed Noakes.

'So *that's* the connection.'

Noakes nodded slowly.

The DI gave an almost imperceptible jerk of the head towards the door. It was the signal for his subordinate to conclude the interview. Within a matter of minutes, the Reverend Sinnott was on his way.

'Can't tell you more at this stage, mate,' Noakes said as they shook hands on the station steps.

'I understand. Good luck, Noakesy.'

The interview had stirred up unwelcome memories for Sinnott who stared unseeing at the downy snowflakes dancing past in chilly drifts, softening Bromgrove's stark architecture with their crystalline monogram.

Suddenly, as if from nowhere, a gust of wind whipped up bearing the sound of gleeful childish shrieks.

Sinnott grasped Noakes's arm. 'Those poor kids…'

The other didn't trust himself to speak, but he wrung his friend's hand once more. As much as to say, we'll nail the bastards!

Back at the threshold of CID, Noakes pulled up short at the sound of stentorian bellowing.

Chuffing hell. DCI Sidney! That's all we bloody need!

He put one ear to the door. Best not to burst in while the DCI was giving it to the guvnor with both barrels.

'The very idea is simply *preposterous*, Markham!'

Slimy Sid's fury was off the Richter Scale.

'Do you have the *slightest* idea of the implications for the Local Authority Policing Partnerships? Investigating a distinguished clergyman based on malicious gossip and innuendo – it's clutching at bloody straws and I won't have it, Inspector. You'll make us a laughing stock.'

Markham's response was inaudible but it clearly didn't mollify the DCI.

'*Total supposition!*' Sidney was withering. 'You've got nothing except coincidence and...' There was the sound of outraged spluttering. '...that Father Brown misfit you've just smuggled into the station.'

A wave of heat travelled up the back of Noakes's neck. *Father Brown!* Still, he stayed where he was. Sidney was bound to run out of steam sooner or later.

But it sounded as though the DCI was merely getting his second wind.

'I've also received a serious complaint from Sir Philip Soames...'

The decibel level dropped somewhat, but snatches of indignant accusation floated into the corridor.

'...gratuitous harassment ... needless distress ... besmirching reputations ... years of service to the community ... appalling ingratitude to a benefactor...'

On and on it went, with allegations that Markham was looking for a scapegoat to cover his own deficiencies as Senior Investigating Officer.

From the way Sidney was wheeling out the rack, Noakes figured that the cathedral clique had got the wind up. But how far did the conspiracy go, he wondered. Who could they trust at St Mary's?

'You will drop this ridiculous vendetta, Markham. *That's an order.*' Sidney was inexorable. 'You can forget Mike Bamber and his half-baked theories.' A further twist of the thumbscrews. 'The man's a crank and leading you up a blind alley with his obsession about the Warr case. Obviously, there's a maniac out there with some sort of deranged religious fixation – possibly something to do with the shrine and its relics. Make local mental hospitals your focus. *And leave Sir Philip Soames alone.*'

Silence.

Clearly the guvnor was resorting to his usual strategy for dealing with the DCI. Polite compliance masking a determination to go his own way regardless.

Tetchy harrumphing heralded Sidney's imminent exit from CID. Thinking quickly, Noakes reversed down the corridor and slid into the stationery cupboard, his usual hiding place on such occasions.

A soft whoosh of the lift indicated the DCI's departure to the upper regions.

'You can come out now, Noakes.' Markham's voice was sardonic. 'Thanks for your support back there.'

'Figured you had it covered, boss.'

Noakes looked anxiously at Markham.

The inspector's voice was devoid of emotion but his eyes blazed with determination.

'Right, Noakes,' he said, 'this is what we're going to do.'

14

No Comfortable Star

Their unmarked police car sped through streets blanketed with snow. The winter night seemed particularly tense, as though holding its breath in anticipation of some frightful revelation.

'I've checked with St Mary's.' Noakes's voice was level, with an undercurrent of suppressed vehemence. 'Apparently Woodcourt's at a meeting in the cathedral.' He frowned down at his notebook. 'Dr O'Keefe said something about him having to see the suffragan or summat like that.'

Markham's hands tightened on the steering wheel.

'That's the assistant bishop, Noakes. Sounds as though the church authorities are gearing up for a spot of damage limitation.' He added in a bitter aside, almost as though speaking to himself, '*God, it's enough to make you puke.*'

Realizing Noakes was scrutinizing him with unusual intensity, Markham shook his head as though to slough off his sleepy befuddlement.

'Sir Philip's a sick man. As things stand, we've got nothing on him. But this connection with Woodcourt, which he took good care not to disclose to us, puts him in the frame for those cold cases in Bromgrove—'

'Jonny Warr, David Belcher and Adam Waring,' Noakes interrupted eagerly.

'Yes. And perhaps for other unsolveds as well.'

For all his hirsute dishevelment, Noakes was alert as any bloodhound. 'So, we're going to have a crack at him then, Guv?'

'I've logged us as attending St Mary's,' answered Markham, 'but in fact,' he smiled grimly, 'we'll be taking the scenic route via Thurston Lodge.'

'What about Sli – I mean, DCI Sidney?'

'What about him? He's a good man, but he'll cosy up to the establishment, because he sees himself as one of them. If there's a meeting at the cathedral, I shouldn't wonder if Sidney turns up there to give moral support, as it were. So, if he wants to know what I'm up to, let's say I'm concerned for Sir Philip's wellbeing. Alternatively, I have reason to believe that he could be in danger. Take your pick.'

It was clear from the quick rising light and fire on Markham's face that he had determined to defy his senior officer and to hell with the consequences. Noakes felt an answering glow. *Good on you, boss!*

As they drew up in front of Thurston Lodge, Markham thought back to his visit with Olivia on that other cold still day, when Nature had denuded the dilapidated house down to the bare bones so that it seemed to have kicked off its clothes, defying the casual visitor to find it wanting. He recalled the curious gargoyles which had seemed to sprout from the building's various corbels; little diamond-shaped faces, with the glazed blankness of death masks. Now, however, the place had quite a changed aspect, gilded as it was by a sort of faery fretwork. Stark angles and crumbling downspouts were softened and transformed by a gently gleaming coat of powdery snow, while the garden looked almost too delicate to be sullied by their rough feet.

For all the sugar-spun airiness and damply clinging flakes, which caressed his hot aching skin with their welcome chill, Markham found the place no less sinister than before. What secrets lay beyond the shroud-white physiognomy of this house? Whose voices were muffled in its depths?

'*Guv. You OK?*'

Noakes's voice recalled Markham to himself.

'Fine,' he replied curtly. 'You lead the way, Noakes. I

imagine the manservant will be screening visitors. We'll just have to play it by ear.'

Noakes's hand was raised to the brass bell pull when, to their surprise, the oak door was wrenched open.

Sir Philip's factotum stood before them frantic and wild-eyed, his features glistening with sweat. The mysterious inscrutability and impenetrable calm that had struck Markham on his first visit were gone.

Noakes and Markham stared at the apparition as though trapped in some infernal hall of mirrors. For a moment, no-one spoke.

Then the vision broke into a flow of hysterical supplication.

'Help me, please! He was fine when I left him, but now he's gone!'

'*Easy, mate, easy.*' Noakes laid a kindly hand on the flailing arm. 'What's up? Is it Sir Philip?'

Clutching Markham as though fearful of losing him from sight, the manservant drew the two policemen through to the back of the house, his limp even more noticeable than on the DI's first visit. Nothing had changed. They went along musty winding corridors papered in lurid sea-green, passing the same sombre paintings and tall cabinets towering like catafalques.

Finally, they reached a cubby-hole behind the kitchen which was evidently some personal sanctum. A faded picture of a dumpy little woman in a headscarf adorned one wall. The dresser beneath it held a cheap tea-light holder with a solitary burning candle. Markham recalled a similar stencilled image in the *Friends of St Mary's* magazines. Presumably this was Madame Blavatskya, the enigmatic foundress of the theosophy movement. Was this man Sir Philip's disciple? His partner in corruption? Or simply a devoted family retainer?

'*For God's sake, do something! Anything could have happened!*' their guide pleaded brokenly, a deformed shadow against the wall repeating and parodying his overwrought gesticulation.

'Gone where?' enquired Noakes patiently. 'What was he doing when you last saw him?'

'Reading in his library. He'd had a restless night. I wanted to stay with him, but he told me to go and rest, otherwise the doctor would end up with two patients, not just one.'

The asperity behind those words was authentic Sir Philip, concluded Markham.

'How long ago was this?' asked Noakes.

'Three, four hours... I only found out he was missing when I looked in the library just now. I was going to search the house when you arrived.'

'Check upstairs, Noakes,' instructed Markham. He turned a steady gaze on the manservant. 'You have a cellar here, yes?'

The other's face contracted with anxiety and hope. His breaths came as thick as sobs. Snatching up a torch from a rusty tool box, he cried, 'This way!'

As he followed, impressions crowded in upon Markham like phantasmagoria. Slippery walls. Ceilings stained by streaks of smoke and dust that stretched out like crooked fingers. Funguses resembling monstrous misshapen caricatures.

And then, finally, they were underground.

Markham did not need the domestic's shrill exclamation of horror to tell him that they had found Sir Philip Soames. There he sat, still clad in his dressing gown, propped up against the wall at right angles to the spiral stone stairs. Most ghastly of all, his glittering eyes were wide open, the sensual lips drawn up over his teeth in a grimace, and the brow contorted in an expression of agonized defiance. A livid weal round his neck betrayed the mark of a garrotte.

Feet thundered down the stairs. As Sir Philip's man started towards the body, with eyes dilated, Noakes reached out and grabbed him.

'No, fella,' he said kindly but firmly. 'You can't do anything for him now. Leave it to us.'

The response was a series of high-pitched inward screams alternating with the deep moans. The servant's face now ran with saliva and tears, as well as sweat. The spectacle filled Markham with a profound repugnance. Observing Noakes's gentleness, he wondered at his subordinate's compassion and felt ashamed of his own intolerance. In a matter of moments, the object of his disgust had been manoeuvred out of the cellar, his departing imprecation echoing round the desolate space: 'Find the devil who did this! Find him!'

Markham turned back to the corpse. It was a sight to chill any beholder. Death had stared Sir Philip in the face, and the arrogance of his dynasty, bred in the bone, had dropped away in an instant of pure terror. It was the look of a soul on the brink of everlasting torment.

But who had hurried him on his way and why?

Markham's eyes moved from the ghastly face, with its frenzied stare and clenched teeth, to Sir Philip's hands. His gaze rested on the delicate fingers for some time as he wondered what they might have done. Revolted, he struggled against an impulse to vomit. What had happened in this strange shell of a house? Had children been abused within its walls? Had the school society Blavatskya been a cover for torture and worse? Where did Sir Philip fit in?

Markham stood lost in thought for some time. Then he shivered. It felt as though the damp of the cellar was rising up from the earth like a disease. Taking one last look at the body, limp as a marionette but with traces of its former power, he mounted the stairs to rejoin Noakes.

Mercifully, there was no sign of the manservant.

'What a bloody mess.' Markham looked helplessly at his subordinate.

'Well, you were right about one thing, boss,' Noakes said phlegmatically. 'Sir Philip was in danger.'

'But *why*, Noakes, *why*?' The DI sounded at his wits' end.

'P'raps he'd found something out... Yeah, an' then he was killed so he couldn't spill.'

Noakes was warming to his theme.

'In which case, he could be innocent?' Markham thought back to the body in the cellar. Somehow, all his instincts screamed otherwise.

'One thing's for sure,' the DS said sententiously.

'What's that?'

'That poor bastard of a servant had nothing to do with it. He was practically gibbering out there. Thought he would collapse on us.' Noakes frowned at the memory then roused himself to ask, 'What next, boss?'

Markham ran his hands through his hair in a characteristic gesture of frustration. Noakes was struck by the look of naked despair on the DI's face. Something about this case was really getting to the boss. As if the investigation was somehow personal.

Markham jerked his head towards the front door. 'Let's get back to the cathedral.' He couldn't define the sudden uneasiness that had seized him. 'I want Woodcourt where I can see him.'

'He's going nowhere for a while yet, boss. Won't he still be tucked up in that meeting with the suffragan bloke?'

'Woodcourt's the answer to the riddle, Noakes. If he's covered his tracks all these years, then we're dealing with something uniquely evil here.'

The SOCOs had arrived. Time to go.

As they made their way outside towards the car, Markham heard a sound in his inner ear. Like a soft growl or chuckle. As though some animal slouched at his heels. He whirled around and looked back at the house, now a sepulchre.

Nothing stirred.

Noakes was looking at him curiously.

'Not enough sleep, Noakesy.'

The other grunted sympathetically. 'I'll drive, boss,' he said and Markham subsided with relief into the passenger seat.

God, it was nearly Christmas. A time of innocence. A time for children. And here they were following a coffin trail to the House of God.

He felt almost light-headed.

The star went forward and halted over the place where the child lay.

The age-old Christmas story. But no comfort to him. There seemed precious little chance that any sign or portent would lead them to Julian Forsythe. *Unless* they could break Woodcourt.

Again, that spasm of unease.

'Step on it, Noakes,' he said tersely. 'Blues and twos if you must.' Then, his voice sinking almost to a whisper, 'Can't afford to let him out of our sight. Not even for a moment. I think we've got ourselves a serial killer.'

The cathedral car park was deserted. Not a vehicle to be seen.

Markham's heart skipped a beat.

'Where the hell's the surveillance van?'

Noakes shot the DI a look. Such vehemence from his self-contained boss was rare. Again, he had the feeling that something about this case came closer to home than Markham cared to admit.

Still, there was supposed to be a static unit covering the cathedral. *So, where was it?*

The two men stood uncertainly by their car under the gunmetal sky.

Suddenly, Dr O'Keefe appeared around the corner of the cathedral. Markham's heart contracted once again as he took in the principal's anxious countenance and uncharacteristically headlong gait.

'Everything OK, sir?' Noakes's voice sounded unnaturally hearty.

'Not really, Officers.' The usually suave O'Keefe sent Markham a glance of mute entreaty. 'I seem to have, well, mislaid Canon Woodcourt.' He gave an embarrassed laugh, but the forced levity could not disguise the shapeless suspicions dimly stirring in his mind. In that moment, Markham could tell that O'Keefe was filled with compunction for having wronged the canon even in his thoughts. Seeing this, he would have staked his life on the principal's innocence of involvement in the conspiracy.

'When did you last see Mr Woodcourt, sir?' asked Noakes, stolidly unflustered.

'Let me see ... the meeting with Dr Harris – that's the suffragan – had to be adjourned when he was called away. Some sort of pastoral emergency at the university apparently. The canon and I walked back to school together.' O'Keefe scuffed his feet guiltily through the snow. 'Dick suggested to your lads they drive round to the back and Joan would rustle up some hot drinks and food.' Again, that nervous laugh. 'Figured they'd drawn the short straw, you see. Not exactly *The Sweeney.*'

'And then what?' prompted Noakes inexorably.

'I went off to check on Nat Barton. I'm almost certain Dick said something about needing to catch up with paperwork. It was a while before I thought to look for him.' O'Keefe looked wretched. 'I had some idea that the staff ought to stay together,' he concluded miserably.

The cathedral, thought Markham, the cathedral. Its bulk brooded before them like some great somnolent beast. As he looked towards it, the whole edifice seemed to vibrate with a mysterious warning.

Snow blindness, the DI told himself as his vision suddenly blurred and dark spots danced behind his eyelids.

His heart beat thick and fast, but through its throb he felt something else. A feverish tingling like an electric shock. As though a voice somewhere within the sanctuary cried out to him, 'I am here! Help me!'

Julian Forsythe! The murdered boy was beckoning him wildly, eerily, urgently to the site of his annihilation.

I am coming!

'The crypt.' The words fell almost involuntarily from Markham's lips. Under the same irresistible influence, he turned to O'Keefe. 'Who has access to it?' Markham's voice was faint, as though the air had been sucked from his lungs.

'They must have missed it in the sweep. Or been directed away from it. *Do not disturb the dead!*'

'The undercroft is open most days between 10am and 4pm. Anyone is welcome to worship in the side chapels, though the Bishops' Chapel is generally kept locked as it contains graves.' O'Keefe now sounded distinctly strained. 'Look, Inspector, you're surely not implying—'

Noakes cut across him. 'Who has keys to the Bishops' Chapel?'

'Well, members of the Cathedral Chapter – the Dean, Precentor and Canons.'

Canons.

The two police officers looked at each other before moving as one towards the cathedral. When O'Keefe made as if to follow, Noakes barred the way.

'Best you wait here, sir,' he instructed in tones which brooked no argument.

Later, Markham was unable to recall their route through the shadowy spaces down to the underbelly of the cathedral. But he would remember for the rest of his days the sight that greeted them at the threshold of the Bishops' Chapel. The cavernous chamber was brilliantly lit by candles in great sconces, the air thick with heat and the smoke of some foul parody of incense. Woodcourt, clad in Eucharistic vestments, seemed oblivious of their presence. Had he used drugs to induce some hellish auto-erotic trance, Markham wondered in stupefaction.

Julian Forsythe lay stretched out on a granite altar, seemingly asleep, surrounded by an array of vessels in brass, silver and copper. He had been dressed in some obscene outlandish garment which left his neck and shoulders bare.

Woodcourt's gaze met Markham's, but it was empty, no vestige left of the civilized clergyman who had welcomed him to St Mary's with such avuncular charm. The DI knew then that he had failed to see behind the mask of a killer who was right beside him.

There was no time to process the transformation. Even as Markham threw himself at the deranged cleric, part of him noted the ornate candlesticks that he had last seen on the high altar. Curse him! Perhaps he should kill him, send him to his infernal master... He looked once more at the unconscious boy, and then at the curved scimitar gleaming in Woodcourt's hand. Uttering an incoherent cry, he launched himself at the canon and felled him to the ground. The weapon clattered to the stone floor. Woodcourt's expression remained the same, the cold flat eyes devoid of all expression. Initially transfixed by the scene, Noakes must have followed close behind, because he was lifting the unconscious boy from the altar, crooking him tenderly in his arms.

Markham waited until Noakes, who had not spoken a word, had left the chapel, and then he proceeded to overturn the vessels from the filthy altar on top of its sacrificing priest.

The red mist descended.

As he loomed over the ordained killer, the blood roaring in his ears, the past caught fire from the present. Suddenly, Markham was back in that bedroom where the demon lurked and his childhood had ended. The beast beside the cradle. The stepfather whose memory he thought to have buried fathoms deep rose before him. He could almost hear that malevolent chuckle. Blindly, his heart full to overflowing, he seized a candlestick.

15

Exhalations Laden
With Slow Death

Two hours later, Markham and Noakes sat waiting in a small side-ward at Bromgrove General Hospital.

Markham hated these places with their endless corridors, harsh strip lighting and whitewashed walls which leached the colour from the faces of visitors and patients alike, so that everyone wore the same blanched pallor. He closed his eyes, transported to those last awful days at his mother's bedside in this same hospital when, with pitiful incoherence, her face grey with effort, she had broken down and begged forgiveness for her failure to protect him. As dissolution beckoned, a film of contrition clouded her eyes like a shadowy harbinger of the final veil. He could still see the outlines of her cancer-ravaged body under the bedclothes and the softening of her drawn features as the morphine took effect. However deep her sleep, she clutched his hand as though it was a talisman she feared to relinquish – proof that she was absolved of guilt for those years of childhood abuse to which she had turned a blind eye. Somehow, he had found the words to set her free, compassion overcoming years of banked down rage. After it was over, looking down at her serene features, Markham felt that she was once again the carefree parent of his earliest impressions whose pale lips bore traces of the smiling tenderness she had always shown him. Like a spring that had long been buried underground, his anguish had gushed over him in a scalding flow. Around him in the hospital, babies were being born into the world. He found himself praying fervently that his mother was beginning the world. The world that sets this one right.

While the DI was wrapped in his thoughts, Noakes studied his boss with an intentness he did not normally risk. Even with a quarter of an inch of stubble, his face putty-coloured and his suit crumpled, Markham had attracted a steady flow of admiring glances. His dishevelment and the violet shadows under his eyes mysteriously enhanced his air of distinction and gaunt, brooding abstraction. And then there's me, thought Noakes resignedly. Talk about Beauty and the Beast!

The guvnor had almost lost it back there. Hadn't looked like himself at all. As though he wasn't seeing the cathedral but was somewhere else entirely. His expression was murderous, full of black churning hatred, the veins on his forehead standing out like ropes and his face running with sweat. He looked capable of anything. Woodcourt would have copped it then and there but for the principal's arrival on the scene. Thank God O'Keefe had ignored the instruction to stay put. His calling out to Markham broke the spell.

Although oblivious of Noakes's covert observation, the DI's thoughts were running in the same groove. Back in the cathedral, the parameters of the rational world had dissolved so it seemed that his long-dead stepfather peered out at him from behind Woodcourt's eyes. The demon had slipped his leash, plunging Markham into hell.

If he had succumbed to the vile intoxication of violence which momentarily unhinged him, then it would have been game over. Glittering career and stellar prospects snuffed out in one fell swoop. Olivia's faith in him shattered. Markham supposed he should feel grateful to O'Keefe for his intervention – the sharp cry which had brought him to his senses before he could smash Woodcourt to a pulp and beat him until he screamed for mercy. A small shameful part of him, however, craved that bloody retribution which as a child he had been powerless to exact.

Of course, the principal *knew*. The long look he had exchanged with Markham held shrewd knowledge mingled with a pensive sympathy. Yet the DI felt obscurely reassured that O'Keefe would preserve *omertá*.

How had it come to this, he wondered despairingly. Over the years, he had somehow managed to seal off that childhood violation, locking his squalid secret in a box. That box went into a second box, which in turn was enclosed in another. Like those sinister Russian nesting dolls which, when taken apart, resemble a series of miniature coffins.

But the memories would not stay buried, swarming to the surface in an unstoppable vampiric eruption.

The pain. The shame. His stepfather's rancid breath and questing, rasping fingernails.

Seeing Woodcourt hanging over Julian Forsythe like some great bat had touched a hidden chord in Markham's mind, bringing back the searing recollection of his own degradation in an illuminating flash more terrible than any lightning stroke.

Oh God, Noakes was going to think he was off his trolley and liable to start climbing the walls any minute!

'Right, Sergeant.' Markham mentally congratulated himself that his voice was steady. 'What's happening with Woodcourt?'

He grimaced at the other's suddenly wary expression.

'It's all right, man, I just want an update on his mental status.'

'The uniforms who delivered him to HQ said it was really freaky,' replied the DC. 'He just kept talking total gobbledygook while snickering one minute an' crying the next.'

For all his rigid self-control, Markham shivered.

'The worst bit came when they went past Bromgrove Crescent,' continued Noakes.

Sir Philip's residence.

'Woodcourt gave a sort of shriek. Then he began gobbling and growling. Like an animal. Gave the lads quite a turn.

Felt as though they had Hannibal Lecter in the squad car. They had to hold him down.'

Markham fought down bile as he recalled the canon next to the crib in the entrance hall at St Mary's – his hand resting proprietorially on Nat Barton's shoulder – chatting cosily about the tradition that oxen in the farm sheds would be kneeling by moonlight in homage to the infant Christ at midnight on Christmas Eve, just as they knelt at His birth so many hundreds of years ago.

Woodcourt, the Devil's walking parody, narrating the sacred Christmas story.

What a grotesque perversion.

'Not fit for interview then,' was all he said.

'No way, boss. It'll be the men in white coats for him.'

So, he gets away with it.

Noakes had an uncanny ability to read his guvnor's mind. 'Look on the bright side, sir. At least we've nailed the bastard. Folk in high places will put it about that Woodcourt was a grade A nutter on some sort of mad crusade. Religious mania or some such. Remember the Yorkshire Ripper and all that 'Mission from God' malarkey. The *News of the Screws*'ll lap it up. No headlines about pervy priests and a vice ring, just some moonshine about hearing voices.' He gave a bleak chuckle. 'DCI Sidney can sleep easy. It'll all be squared away.'

'*Not if I have bloody well have anything to do with it!*' The DI's tone was so venomous, that Noakes flinched. 'Woodcourt was likely behind half a dozen murders,' spat Markham. 'Him and Soames. And God knows who else.'

He laughed. It was a horrible sound without any merriment. Noakes flinched again.

Suddenly, Markham slumped in his chair.

'I'm sorry, Noakesy.' His voice was gentle now. 'They *can't* spin this. For God's sake, *they can't!*' Almost pleadingly he added, 'What about the cold cases? Those kids from way back. Jonny Warr and the other poor little sods chucked away like trash.'

'Woodcourt's lost his wits and ain't going to recover any

time soon, Guv. Sir Philip's dead.' Noakes's voice held a warning. 'They'll lay everything at Woodcourt's door and close the book.'

Markham sat still and cold as marble, his head sunk between his shoulders.

Noakes cleared his throat. 'Alex Sharpe and his missus seem to have done a bunk.'

The DI's head came up. '*He* could be the weak link, Noakes,' he whispered. 'That downtrodden wife of his certainly knew something... Now I think about it, Sharpe seemed oddly watchful of Julian and Nat. Almost as though he was afraid to let them out of his sight.'

'Yeah.' Noakes nodded thoughtfully. 'When we were up at the school searching for Julian, I overhead one of the kids talking about him and Nat being jinxed. Turned out that Nat had nearly gone over a balcony in the cathedral when he was on his own there with Woodcourt. Apparently, Sharpe arrived in the nick of time and grabbed hold of him.'

The hope in Markham's bloodshot eyes was painful to witness and his breath was shorter now.

'We'll have to wait for the forensics on Sir Philip, boss.' The warning note was back again. 'Even if Sharpe turns up, there's no saying we'll get answers. He might decide to keep shtum...'

'You mean they'll have him lawyered up before we get a decent crack at him.'

The little colour in Markham's face had gone in a moment. His features were working and he looked close to tears.

Again, Noakes wondered what was eating him. He had never seen the DI this close to losing it over a case. As though what had happened to Julian, Nat and those lost boys had reawakened some secret agony. As though it had raised a curtain on something that Markham had hoped to keep hidden...

Was it possible his guvnor had been a victim of child abuse?

Noakes looked at Markham as if seeing him for the first

time, noting the hollowed temples and jaws, the deep lines round his eyes and mouth, the expression of despair.

Will he ever tell me?

When hell freezes over.

'Gentlemen?'

A crisply efficient voice cut across this silent colloquy.

An attractive blonde wearing a sharply pressed red tunic had materialized in front of them.

'I'm Christine Green, the Sister with responsibility for this ward.'

She looked at Markham with some concern, seeming to trace, with her experienced clinician's eye, the history of the case in the sunken rings round his eyes and the tight set of his lips.

'I'm sorry you've had a long wait,' she said in softened tones. 'Can I arrange some hot drinks and sandwiches for you?'

The DI uncoiled his tall, spare form from the uncomfortable plastic chair.

'Thank you for your consideration, Ms Green.' His voice was eager. 'If it's all the same with you, we'd like to see Julian.'

'Of course.' The woman smiled at them. 'I should warn you, he's still quite drowsy and disorientated but otherwise fine.'

'Has he been, like, interfered with?' Noakes blurted it out, his beefy pugilist's face brick-red with embarrassment.

'As far as we can tell, no.' Christine Green paused delicately. 'Which isn't to say that he might not have suffered some form of abuse.'

'You mean he was being groomed?' Markham demanded abruptly.

'I'd say it was a strong possibility.' She smoothed non-existent creases from her uniform. 'Coming round from the opiate, Julian was incoherent and rambling at first. But clearly something nasty went on. He kept shouting about the Devil lying in wait for him. There's old bruising and some scarring on his arms and legs, and he was frightened of physical contact – got hysterical when the SHO was examining him.'

Markham looked as if he was going to be sick.

'He calmed down when he realized he was safe,' the Sister said hastily. 'Cried his eyes out, though, and kept asking for his friend Nat.'

Seeing that Markham was beyond speech, Noakes took over. 'Julian's mum and stepdad are abroad. We're trying to locate them. Nat's back at school being looked after.'

'Well,' the Sister's voice was determinedly bright, 'let's hope Nat can be some comfort. It's good that the tears came. Means he's not so emotionally numb that we can't reach him.'

Markham found his voice. 'Julian's very reserved. Turns everything inward.'

Like you, thought Noakes.

The DI shot him a flinty look as though he'd spoken his thoughts aloud. Flustered, Noakes asked. 'How long can we have with him, luv?'

'Well, I'd be grateful if you didn't overtire him. Quite apart from the abduction, I'd say he's been in a state of unconscious nervous tension for a good while.'

Noakes frowned. 'You mean he's lost his mind?'

'Oh, Julian's a long way from that.' The note of authority was unmistakable. 'No, it's more a case of overstrain. Living all this time with something fearful beneath the surface of his mind tormenting him.'

'A secret,' observed Markham, his eyes clouded and remote.

The observation won him an approving look. 'Exactly, Inspector. I imagine he was bribed, or more likely threatened, not to tell anyone what was going on. And I think he was afraid not only for himself but for Nat – terrified that they might start on him too.'

She sighed. 'Some good angel must have been watching over Julian. For all the trauma, there's something innocent and unselfish about him. He would have done anything to protect Nat. I think he would have died for him.'

Again, Markham's throat was too full for speech. Filled with a quick vision of his own little brother, long since lost to drink and drugs, he was overwhelmed by a wave of grief quite startling in its intensity.

I didn't manage to save you, did I?

As the silence lengthened, Noakes stepped into the breach. 'Right then, miss, reckon we're ready to see the lad now.'

Julian was in a private room with a uniformed policeman standing outside.

In the pool of light cast by a bedside lamp, his handsome face, stamped by a forlorn wistfulness, broke into a hesitant smile at the sight of the two policemen. The DI noticed the small, wet ball of a handkerchief clutched tightly in the boy's hand, his red-lidded eyes fixed unwaveringly upon the visitors as if they alone held the key to unlock his prison.

Looking at the earnest, tear-stained face, Markham swallowed hard.

The squeaking of Noakes's boots sounded unnaturally loud as he manoeuvred himself into one of the two fabric-covered tub chairs placed at right angles to the bed. Markham took the other, indicating to the DS by an almost imperceptible nod that he should take the lead.

'Good to see you, mate.' As always at moments of high emotion, Noakes's voice was gruff. 'Thought we'd lost you for a bit back there. But you can't keep a good man down.' He gave a clumsy laugh ending almost in a sob. 'Feel like we should have brought you grapes or summat.'

Julian flashed a watery grin. 'Oh, I won't be staying long, Mr Noakes. I want to get back to Nat and the rest of 'em at St Mary's.'

No mention of mother or stepfather. It was clear where his allegiance lay.

'D'you feel able to tell us about it?' The DS was very matter-of-fact. 'Just between the three of us for now. Then mebbe later, you can help us put the bad guys out of circulation.'

Noakesy's good at this, thought Markham. Doesn't say much, but somehow makes kids feel safe.

The skinny body went rigid under the bed clothes then relaxed.

'It started about a year ago, Mr Noakes, with *Blavatskya.*' With heart-wrenching pride, he informed them, 'That's St

Mary's History Society. Me and some of the other fellows would have meetings and debates—'

Suddenly he faltered.

The silence stretched but Noakes made no attempt to fill it, just held Julian's eyes with his steady gaze.

Julian gulped and took up the thread again.

'Sometimes the meetings were at Sir Philip's house. Miss Gibson would take us down there and then disappear off to the back parlour with her marking.' He smiled reminiscently. 'She said we could only have a proper old ding-dong once she was out of the way.'

Markham stiffened. Cynthia. *Was she complicit in the abuse?*

He pulled himself back to Julian's narrative.

'...we usually went into the library.'

The boy faltered again before plunging into his story anew with the desperation of a drowning man.

'B-b-but...' He was stuttering now and clutching the damp handkerchief more tightly than ever.

'Sometimes there were v-v-visitors there too. Grown-ups.'

Another pause.

'I didn't really take much notice of them. Thought they were teachers.'

Drops of perspiration stood out on his forehead.

'One day I had to go into another room with two of them away from the rest. I d-d-didn't really like it, but the canon said it was an important life lesson.'

Markham's hands curled into fists.

'I don't remember their faces.' Sheer terror had wiped out the memory. 'Just that one of them smelt of Vicks and the other,' he gave a convulsive shudder, 'had fat little hands with fingers like chipolatas.'

Julian had begun to talk in a sing-song tone, like someone in a trance.

'Sir Philip gave me something to drink. It burned. They put something over my eyes so I couldn't see. They touched me and they made me do things to them. Dirty things. They were sweating and dribbling. I heard a voice say our bodies are temples of the Divine Being. I think it was the canon.'

Dear God in Heaven.

Julian's face seemed suddenly ancient and careworn, his despair filling the room.

Markham's heart was thudding in his chest, but he willed his features into an expression of benign tranquillity.

'Afterwards, Mr Woodcourt told me they were helping me and talked about the tree of good and evil. He said never to tell and I'd get into terrible trouble if I went blabbing. An' no-one would believe me anyway...'

Julian's voice had grown fainter and fainter during his terrible account until it had sunk to a whisper.

'Well, we believe you, mate. One hundred per cent.' Noakes spoke softly.

Julian looked trustfully up at him.

'Sir Philip said there were other special souls at St Mary's who needed a guardian spirit.'

The Night Watchman.

'Nearly done now, mate,' Noakes said gently. 'Did you have to be with those men again?'

A mute nod.

'But you never said a word?'

Another nod.

Noakes waited.

'Though I threw up once in the minibus when Mr Preston was taking us back to school.'

Preston. Cathedral architect. Keeper of the grottoes. Guardian of the catacombs.

'Helping Miss Gibson out, was he?' The question was very casual.

'Oh, he liked coming to the history meetings.'

The room was very still. Not by the flicker of an eyelid did the two men show their intense interest in Julian's answer.

'Once when I was in the library with ... them... I thought I heard Mr Preston. But then I realized it couldn't have been him cos the voice sounded rougher and deeper... Anyway, they called him Ned...'Sides, Mr Preston wouldn't have let them do those things to me...'

Ned. Short for Edward.

Something in their faces must have alerted Julian. With a shivering effort, he raised himself up in bed and looked from one to the other uncertainly, his eyes troubled and a shadow stealing over his face.

'N-n-not Mr Preston?'

With a pang, Noakes thought of his visit to St Mary's grottoes. He recalled how proud Nat and Julian had been of the architect's notice – translated into the seventh heaven of bliss at the prospect of hitching a ride on the works digger. Now Julian looked as if the world was crashing down about his ears.

Carefully avoiding Markham's eyes, Noakes moved to the bed and put an awkward arm around Julian's shoulders. The boy did not flinch, nor did he move away. He simply gazed up at the shambling figure with a confiding expression.

'There's nowt so queer as folk, lad,' Noakes pronounced. Then he added firmly, 'Whatever happens, just remember you did nothing wrong.'

'My mum said I had a black streak and would turn out badly,' came the mournful reply.

'Then she needs setting straight!' Noakes was indignant. 'I'll be giving her a piece of my mind!' he exclaimed, punctuating his words with hearty thumps.

'That I must see,' drawled the DI. 'Now let go of Julian before you karate-chop him to death!' A half-smile lurked at the corners of Julian's mouth, and the sombre mood temporarily lifted.

'How did you end up down in the undercroft?' Markham took over the questioning as Noakes resumed his seat.

'I remember looking round when it was teatime and Nat wasn't there. Someone said a runner – that's the fellow who takes messages round school – had come with a note telling Nat to get across to the cathedral sharpish cos Mr Woodcourt wanted him.'

So that's how the canon lured Julian there, thought Markham. Woodcourt had sensed his fear for the younger boy and exploited it for his own evil ends.

Julian's face was now flushed, and his voice throbbed with echoes of that earlier panic.

'But when I went, Nat wasn't there. I thought I heard noises in the undercroft. We'd had a History Soc meeting in the Bishops' Chapel – only the older boys. Nat was dead set on seeing the tombs,' he pulled a rueful face, 'so I wondered if Mr Woodcourt had promised to let him have a look.'

The climax of the story was approaching. Julian's flush deepened to a painful crimson as he stammered, 'Mr Woodcourt was in the chapel by himself. He just stood there smiling at me in a funny way. But it was funny peculiar, Mr Markham, not funny ha-ha.'

God, he was so young.

Markham's brain began to burn.

'I said, "Where's Nat?" but he didn't answer.' Julian wrinkled his nose. There was a sickly-sweet smell too. Not regular incense ... something else. It made me feel dizzy.'

Chloroform or whatever that sick bastard used to knock him out, thought Markham.

'Mr Woodcourt's eyes went all mean and nasty jus' like a snake. He c-c-called me—'

'Take your time,' Markham said gently, 'and remember, none of this was your fault.'

'—a detestable sneak,' Julian concluded miserably. 'But I'm not a sneak, Mr Markham. I never split.'

Markham fought for composure.

If Woodcourt ever gets out of the funny farm, he's a dead man.

When he found his voice, he spoke so tenderly that Noakes blinked in amazement at the transformation.

'We know you'd never do anything mean and underhand, never fear.'

Visibly heartened, Julian said, 'I didn't even tell Nat. He's so young and it would only have frightened him.'

Markham became aware of Sister Green hovering by the half-open door. They were running out of time.

'Can you remember anything else?'

'I must have passed out or something. When I woke up, the chapel looked different. There were candles everywhere, like on a feast day. And Mr Woodcourt was wearing purple vestments.'

Julian began tearing at his sodden handkerchief as though he would shred it.

'I wanted to run but my legs wouldn't move. Mr Woodcourt started chanting weird stuff about spotless victims, then he said some poetry...'

'*Poetry!*' Noakes was far out of his comfort zone.

Markham shot him a quelling look. 'Did you recognize it, Julian?' he asked.

'I think it was from the Bible. The choir sang it at a service last year.'

Julian thought for a moment then recited, '*Let him kiss me with the kisses of his mouth: for thy love is better than wine.*'

The 'Song of Solomon', the great love-song of the church. Invoked by Woodcourt to justify his perversion.

Despite the stuffiness of the room, Markham suddenly felt icy cold.

Noakes looked at his boss. The skin seemed stretched over the high cheekbones and his eyes had a tigerish intensity. Again, he wondered, *what's going on here? The guv's taking this very personal.*

'I don't remember anything after that, Mr Markham,' Julian concluded. Tears were not far away.

Christine Green bustled forward.

'Time's up for today, gentlemen. I think our young friend here needs to rest.'

Noakes heaved himself up with a grunt. 'Look after yourself, fella. The boss and I need all the help we can get. An' Nat'll be like a cat on hot bricks until you're back where you belong.'

Markham smiled, plumping up Julian's pillows as efficiently as any nurse.

'Mr Markham.' Julian's voice was tremulous. 'Were there other boys like me? Ones who d-d-didn't … didn't make it? Was that why I found the *Star Wars* toy in the grottoes – cos something bad happened down there?'

'Yes,' answered Markam quietly.

Noakes beamed at Julian. 'But one thing's for sure. The guv and me, we'll bust a gut to make sure no other lads get hurt. An' once you're well, your're gonna help us. Cos you know the case from the inside. Here, I've got Obi Wan Kenobi with me.' He produced the little plastic toy from a pocket and handed it over with a wink. 'You can look after him for us. Be our Exhibits Officer, like. P'raps we'll even get you on the payroll!'

Once again, Markham felt a great rush of gratitude towards the big ox-like subordinate for his sure and compassionate touch. Chain of evidence be damned. What mattered was closure for Julian.

With a last reassuring thumbs-up, they followed Sister Green from the room.

Outside in the corridor, the smiles faded.

Markham experienced once again the disorientation – that sense of the cosmic insignificance of humanity – into which he had been plunged when he attended the Advent service in the cathedral with Olivia. An abyss of meaninglessness seemed to yawn before him as he scrabbled to find some, *any*, redemptive spark in the ghastly story of child abuse, suffering and murder.

Woodcourt, that supposedly devout priest, was the Anti-Christ – absolute for Death, his true deity. Light on top, dark underneath.

Although he was a hardened police officer, inured to the worst depravities, somehow the canon's crimes struck an unprecedented chill to the DI's heart.

Suddenly, as he looked dazedly round the hospital corridor,

it seemed bathed in the lurid sea-green of Sir Philip's house. Green. The colour of Death, his mother always said.

Hell is above ground, Markham groaned to himself.

He felt an overmastering self-contempt, shrivelling inwardly at the thought of the invisible miasma that enveloped him – the ineradicable pollution of childhood abuse.

Then, in that moment of ultimate despair, like an electric shock, a memory came to Markham. Olivia's high sweet voice recounting the Arthurian myth of Sir Gawain, vanquisher of the Green Knight – Death incarnate. 'That's you, Gil,' said the clear tones in his ear. 'My knight in shining armour. Bringing good out of evil. Slaying the demon.'

It was as though Olivia's soul had wandered from its cell to comfort his.

He was himself again.

'Don't worry about Julian, Inspector. We'll take good care of him.'

Christine Green patted his arm and left Markham alone with Noakes.

Markham swayed slightly, light-headed with exhaustion but reinvigorated by the moment of psychic connection with Olivia.

'Well done in there, Noakesy.'

The DS was gratified but doing his best not to show it.

'What next, boss?'

'Back to St Mary's.' Markham straightened up. 'Preston's still at large. We need to bring him in. Fast.'

'He's one of 'em then.'

Not a question but a statement of fact.

'Yes, I believe he's *Ned*.' Markham's voice was hard.

'What do you reckon to Miss Gibson then, Guv? Aren't she and Preston meant to be a couple?'

Markham thought back to the unsettling conversation that Olivia had overheard. 'Cynthia could be in denial about Preston's interest in children. Or she could be an enabler – facilitating the abuse so as not to lose him.' Markham winced with atavistic anguish and a muscle leaped near his jaw. 'Worst case scenario, she could be an active paedophile. Whatever the set-up, we need to get to her. Even with the news blackout on developments with Woodcourt, that station's like a leaky sieve. And if Preston gets wind, then we've lost him.'

'How does O'Keefe fit in?'

'My gut instinct tells me he's with us, Noakes.' Markham strode purposefully towards the exit, the DS wheezing and puffing in his wake. *'C'mon. We're about to find out!'*

The final chapter was about to begin.

16

Slaying The Demon

The two policemen sat motionless in their squad car. Although early afternoon, the light was starting to fade and snow was falling thickly, muffling the comings and goings around them.

'*A fucking little molesting society!*'

Noakes slammed his fist down on the steering wheel.

'Sorry,' he muttered. 'It just really got to me … that poor kid imagining he was to blame and then asking about the ones who didn't make it.'

Markham thought of the boy they had just interviewed – how Julian would wonder as each birthday came around whether it was OK to celebrate being alive when others were not.

Come, the bright day is done, and we are for the dark.

The air in the car was thick with unspoken words. Markham held his breath, trying to keep what was inside him from igniting.

But suddenly, he understood there was no need to share his own sad story. Beneath what could be said beat the steady thrum of a world that belonged only to darkness. The world of Markham's childhood abuse and its roar on the other side of silence.

At that moment, in his mind's eye he saw all the lost boys in a tight glowing circle smiling and laughing. *No-one can hurt them anymore*, he thought. *They're safe now.*

'Right, Noakes, we've got a job to do. Are you ready?'

Noakes straightened his shoulders and started the engine.

* * *

When they drew up outside St Mary's, everything looked picture-postcard perfect, snow softening the building's angles and ornamenting its brackets with delicate fleecy ruffles.

The week before Christmas when children should be sleepless with excitement, thought Markham with a wrench. *Sleepless with dread, more like.*

Grim-faced, he and Noakes walked into the entrance hall where Desmond O'Keefe and a fresh-faced constable were waiting. Everywhere was hushed, almost bereft, the Christmas tree's silver bells chiming forlornly in the draught created by their arrival.

The impact of recent events was very apparent on the principal's face as he ushered them into the visitors' parlour. He looked haunted, with bags under his eyes and the strain of the police investigation reflected in the withered pallor of his face. Yet he spoke with his usual self-containment.

'The staff are all on site, Inspector. We haven't been able to locate Miss Mullen and Miss Gibson yet. They were with young Nat earlier, but no-one appears to have seen them after that.'

Markham's insides somersaulted. *Someone's slipped up*, he thought savagely. He didn't want Olivia anywhere on her own with Cynthia Gibson or, God forbid, Cynthia's boyfriend.

'I want these two women found *now*!' he barked at the young officer. 'Get all available uniforms on it.' With a meaningful glance at Noakes, he added, 'I want the cathedral architect located as well.'

His furious tone had the effect of a starting-pistol. Flushing an ugly brick-red, the constable headed for the door, almost colliding with a boiler-suited figure.

'Sir, we've found a hidden camera lens—' the SOCO announced without preamble.

'—in the basement shrine,' the DI finished the sentence, his voice flat.

Noakes noticed that his boss's gaze was fixed on 'The Forty Martyrs' painting which dominated the parlour, as though he was answering a challenge by the stiffly ruffed figures who stared intently from across the centuries. Suddenly, Noakes remembered Woodcourt talking about a 'master illusionist', the anomalous fustian-clad carpenter responsible for creating numberless hidey-holes. What was it the priest had said? Then he heard it quite clearly. The soft caressing voice which had disarmed them so completely. *'Rumour has it there may even be one here at St Mary's.'*

In that instant, Noakes knew the guvnor was right. The airless little museum with its collection of relics, shut off from the world above, would have been the paedophiles' 'special place' where they surreptitiously observed their prey and savoured the delights to come: the sick rituals which led to rape, strangulation and someone's flesh and blood being laid out on a slab.

The SOCO was speaking. He sounded disappointed, cheated of the big reveal.

'It's behind one of the reliquaries, sir. If you'd like to look.'

'Lead the way.'

The group adjourned to the plain little room which had more the feel of a modest archive than anything specifically religious. At least, that is, until one noticed the walls lined with mementoes of execution and suffering. The cornucopia of grisly exhibits lodged a shard of ice in Markham's chest.

At the far end was a hinged oak reredos stretching from floor to ceiling, with carvings of the twelve apostles two-by-two in three tiers on each of the side panels and Christ as the centrepiece. This was no 'gentle Jesus meek and mild', however, but rather the stern judge of men's souls.

It were better for him that a millstone were hanged about his neck, and he cast into the sea, than that he should offend one of these little ones.

Markham turned his attention from the hooded, reproach-ful eyes and magisterially uplifted a finger to scrutinize a set of red velvet curtains which flanked the screen on either side.

He lifted a fold of the rich fabric on the side nearest a mahogany credence table intricately decorated with wheatsheaves and grapevines. Behind the curtain was some simple panelling.

Delicately, as though by a reflex, the DI skimmed the tips of his fingers over its surface.

'Ah, there it is!' he exclaimed, beckoning Noakes closer to the small raised whorl like the knot he had uncovered in Irene Hummles's flat. The curlicue concealed a wicked little spy hole.

He tapped the panel, registering the soft thunk of hollow cladding.

'What've we got behind there, then?'

The SOCO consulted a sheaf of notes then fussily cleared his throat.

'Down here was part of a convent at one time apparently, sir. There were confessional boxes at this end, sealed up at the time of the Reformation.'

Markham's gaze dropped to the credence table.

'And underneath that?' he asked, gesturing at the chest.

The SOCO's thin lips compressed.

'Cement manhole cover. But we've checked it out. There's a stone stairway which leads to the confessionals.' In response to Markham's raised eyebrows, the other said wryly, 'Your guess is as good as mine, Guv. Priests and nuns up to all sorts, no doubt.'

O'Keefe stiffened.

'No offence, I'm sure,' came the hasty qualification.

Suddenly Markham badly wanted to breathe clean air, to get away from the chapel and the suffocating malevolence that he sensed all around him. From the queasy look on Noakes's face, the discomfort was mutual. O'Keefe, meanwhile, looked around the chapel with appalled fascination, vile images flashing before him like pictures from a nightmare magic-lantern show.

There was a sudden commotion. A distraught Alex Sharpe lurched down the narrow aisle towards them, closely followed by two uniforms.

'Is it true?' he burst out. 'About Woodcourt and Julian Forsythe – is it true?'

At a sign from Markham, the two policemen retreated to the chapel entrance.

'Julian's safe,' replied Markham quietly.

Sharpe collapsed into the nearest pew, his head bowed and his whole body shaking.

'Mr Sharpe, my—.' The DI recollected himself then continued, 'Ms Mullen and Miss Gibson are missing. Finding them is my priority. Whatever you know, *now* is the time to tell us.' His voice was low and level, the note of personal anguish audible only to Noakes.

'I was just a new teacher at Cedar Hill High School when it started.' Sharpe's eyes were beseeching.

'When *what* started?' Noakes's voice was harsh.

'I'd downloaded inappropriate pictures of children on my computer.'

'Kiddiporn,' amended Markham.

'Yes.' Sharpe's voice sank to a whisper. 'It was a bad time in my life. Kate and I were trying for a baby, but she couldn't… Work was a nightmare… I couldn't get a handle on the kids. We both started drinking a lot and our marriage seemed to go down the drain. I'd been surfing the net … it got out of hand.'

'Go on.' Markham's expression was inscrutable.

'Woodcourt found the images on my PC. He agreed not to turn me in. At first I thought it was because he really *cared* – didn't want to see my life go down the swanee.' Sharpe's left knee started juddering uncontrollably and his voice throbbed with bitterness. '*How wrong can a person be?* Once he had me where he wanted me, he dropped the saintly pretence and offered a quid pro quo – he'd keep shtum about my … lapse … provided I sent a steady flow of boys his way under cover of extra-curricular activities. God,' he exhaled in disgust, 'the music department at Cedar Hill was a perverts' carousel.'

'Blackmail.' At the DI's succinct verdict, Sharpe's shoulders drooped even lower.

'Yes, Inspector. You can guess the rest.'

'Why don't you fill us in?' Not by so much as a furrowing of his brow did Markham show how badly he wanted to choke the information out of the wretched specimen in front of them.

'Woodcourt was a millstone round my neck after that.' It was a self-pitying whine. 'Where he went, I went.'

Noakes took a step towards Sharpe. 'What about when kids went missing?' he challenged. 'Why didn't you say something then? How could you go on keeping Woodcourt's secrets for so long?'

Sharpe looked like a prisoner on the rack, white-faced, his weazened features twitching uncontrollably.

'You've got to understand, I didn't know anything for sure,' he said imploringly. 'I just oiled the wheels. Anyway, who'd have believed me?' His tone took on an edge of defiance. 'Woodcourt had friends in high places. Not just Sir Philip but a whole network... MPs and bishops ... maybe even royalty for all I knew.'

Markham remained impassive.

'Then later...' Sharpe's voice trembled. 'I was scared ... the two bodies in the grottoes....'

'Jacob Smith and Colin Saunders,' put in Noakes, kicking a nearby pew by way of relief to his feelings. 'They had names, you know.'

'I had nothing to do with that, *I swear!*' Despite the chill of the chapel, the Director of Music's forehead shone with perspiration. 'All I know is that one of them was going to blow the whistle, so the other got the job of ... sorting it.'

He ground to a halt, his gaze focusing fearfully on some remoteness beyond.

'But the second man was a liability too,' prompted Markham.

Sharpe grasped the lifeline.

'Yes. It was too great a risk to keep him in play. That's what Preston told me. He had to take care of it. Like the matron.'

The temperature seemed to drop by several degrees. Markham felt goose-pimples forming on his arms. That embarrassingly handsome young man with his easy, engaging manner and laid-back charm. A calculating, clinical murderer.

'You are saying Edward Preston murdered Colin Saunders and Irene Hummles?'

Sharpe blanched then nodded. Markham reflected that he was a living embodiment of the fear that Woodcourt and Preston inspired.

'Yes,' he said shuddering, as though something inside him had dissolved with the admission, 'Preston was one of them. But I didn't know for sure that he had ... done ... the workman and Irene until a few days ago.'

Noakes thrust his face towards the cringing figure.

'For God's sake, you must have suspected foul play when that poor woman disappeared!'

Sharpe recoiled.

'*See no evil, hear no evil,*' he replied desperately. 'I couldn't afford to rock the boat.'

As Noakes continued to glower, he explained, 'Look, Irene was a troubled woman and could well have done a bunk. At the time, it felt like a reasonable explanation.'

'Even though two lads went missing from St Mary's around the same time, and there was talk about a night-time prowler?' Noakes was scathing.

It was the last twist of the rack.

'What do you want me to say?' Sharpe cried despairingly. 'That I'm a miserable stinking coward? *All right, I admit it!* I looked the other way ... didn't want to believe it ... couldn't face the truth. You've got to understand, Kate was a nervous wreck and I was walking a precipice. One false step and my life would be over. And Woodcourt was always there...' His face contorted.

'Sir Philip is dead, Mr Sharpe,' Markham said quietly. 'Murdered.'

Sharpe closed his eyes and swayed slightly in his seat.

'*My fault,*' he breathed through cracked, desiccated lips.

Noakes stiffened to attention. Was this a confession? Markham stilled him with a gesture

'What do you mean, Mr Sharpe? How was it your fault?'

'I should have warned him. I could see Woodcourt was losing it. Something about his eyes...' He gave a strangled groan. 'I overheard Sir Philip arguing with Woodcourt and Preston. About the situation being out of control and things going too far. I didn't catch all of it, but Preston laughed and said something about expendable casualties.'

Georgina Hamilton, thought Markham, his iron self-control on the point of exploding into fragments.

Then his policeman's mask was back in place.

'We are almost out of time, Mr Sharpe,' he said in a voice whose calmness surprised him. 'Other lives are at stake.' Ruthlessly, he fought back tears. 'Olivia Mullen and Cynthia Gibson. Where would Preston have taken them?'

'*The grottoes!*' Sharpe and a uniform at the chapel entrance burst out in unison.

It was the response which, Markham realized with sudden sickening clarity, he had both expected and dreaded to hear.

Later, Markham could remember little of their route. Only an endless stretch of white shrouded tumuli and tussocks, like little bedsteads each with its quiet sleeper. The winter sun was already in retreat, streaking the sky with strips of flame as louring clouds mottled the skyline. At first, only the crunch of their feet across the snow and the mournful song of a scavenging thrush broke the silence. Ahead, police arc lights illumined the crenelated rock face of the caves, their spectral nimbus adding to the surreal atmosphere.

It was a desolate place, albeit the jagged caverns from which the site took its name were softened by their ghostly white drapery. At the lowest level the terrain appeared to dip into a hollow, presumably the gully which led underground, surrounded by police officers huddled amidst scaffolding, light stands and all the paraphernalia of a stakeout. The cold struck through to Markham's very bones, but far more chilling was the sense of an invisible enemy softly stalking him, swirling up towards him like some noxious charnel vapour, steam rising from the arc lights as though in sinister confirmation of hellish secrets. In an instant, he understood what was beneath him.

The DI turned to Sharpe. 'This is where they originally stashed the remains, isn't it? In the grottoes and the little cemetery?' Suddenly, he remembered Georgina Hamilton's report of nocturnal digging. 'But that became too risky when the renovations started up again. The gang had to find another hiding place, and where better than the cathedral graveyard.'

The Director of Music looked like a soul in torment.

'I never knew for certain,' he whimpered. 'Look, Inspector, if I ever said anything, I'd have ended up there as well.'

'*You bastard*,' Noakes rumbled. 'Those perverts dumped the bodies here and you knew it! Then, later, they grubbed about and shoved what was left down a hole ... all jumbled together, no respect ... skulls, ribs, shoulder blades... Gloat over it, did they?' He scuffed the ground viciously, sending up a flurry of snowflakes. 'Keep trophies, did they? *Scum!*'

It was the final insult, thought Markham. Leaving those desperate families with nothing to bury. Leaving them hoping and praying that the police would one day find all the bones and put their children back together again. As though those poor victims could be tidily rearranged like skeletons in science classrooms. God!

'That's enough, Noakes,' he said urgently. 'Our priority is to get Olivia and Cynthia out of there in one piece. By now, Preston will know the game is up. The women are his insurance, so he won't surrender them without a fight.' Fear gripped the DI's heart and lengthened his strides. 'A cornered animal is dangerous,' he added sombrely. 'And this one's got nothing to lose.' Markham guessed that Woodcourt's headlong descent into full-fledged insanity had overturned the architect's plans, sending him scuttling back to the catacombs like a rat to its hole.

'There's a negotiating team in place, sir.'

Markham recognized a sergeant from CID.

'Fine, but keep them well back will you, Sarge. We're going in with this gentleman.' Alex Sharpe shuffled his feet in an agony of wretchedness. Markham turned to the DS. 'Same pack drill as before, Noakes, so let's have a torch and some rope.'

It was the work of minutes to equip themselves.

'Firearms, sir?' the sergeant quietly enquired.

Markham met his eyes steadily. 'Can't chance a gunfight in such a confined space.'

'Sir, I really think—'

Markham cut in, his voice suddenly raw with emotion. 'Look, man, that's my *girlfriend* down there.'

A ripple ran through the ranks. *That's got their attention*, he thought with a queer sense of exultation. The encircling band that had bound his heart through all those months of subterfuge and concealment snapped suddenly. For a moment, he felt almost giddy with joy before churning dread surged up to grapple him by the throat.

'Olivia's down there,' he muttered hoarsely, 'and we've got to get her out.'

He felt a hand on his shoulder. Noakes has my back, the DI told himself. Gulping a lungful of frosty air and ignoring the buzz amongst the assembled personnel, he gingerly descended the flank of the gully, his feet sinking into the thickly blanketed steps which led to the tunnels.

Once at the bottom, the three men looked up to see the wraith-like faces of the police team peering anxiously down at them. As if, thought Markham with a shudder, they were now dead to the world, covered by a pall.

De profundis.

Again, he felt the reassuring solidity of Noakes behind him and pressed forward into the mephitic space.

Markham saw a pinprick of light ahead. Gradually it resolved itself into the steady glow of candles. And then, without warning, they were in the clammy chamber of Noakes's recollection. The vault with its dreadful shelves glistening blankly. The niches where children's bodies decomposed in the dark, alone and unmourned.

Edward Preston stood waiting at the rear of the vault.

Markham wondered how he could ever have thought him handsome. The merry companion of Nat and Julian was gone as though he had never been, his features twisted into an ugly sneer, his lip curling at the sight of Alex Sharpe.

This, then, was the face the lost boys saw in their final moments: the implacable countenance of a killer.

Clamped to Preston's side was Olivia, chalk-white and blue to the lips. They stood entwined in some horrible parody of a lovers' embrace while Cynthia Gibson cowered a few feet to the side. The expression of naked longing on the teacher's avid face as she gazed at Preston plainly showed that this was the god of her idolatry. The DI's heart lurched as, with a lightning flash of insight, he saw Olivia's safe dependable friend – 'so devoted to the boys' – stripped bare.

Preston followed Markham's glance. The cruel mouth curved up like a razor blade.

'Yes, Inspector. Cynthia understands me. We're soul mates.'

Noakes made a disgusted sound.

'What, so she's up for torturing young lads and bumping folk off when they get in the way?'

'*It's a lie!*' cried Preston's lover, her voice shrill, her eyes feverishly bright. 'You could *never* understand. Never!'

Preston held up his index finger. As though hypnotized, she fell silent.

The next moment, there was a knife at Olivia's throat. A wicked little blade pressed to the porcelain-white skin.

Time stood still. The heavy cloying scent of tallow was thick in Markham's nostrils, and diabolic shadows danced across the roof of the cavern in the guttering candle-light.

Olivia's hair had come loose from its messy chignon and rippled over her shoulders like a russet waterfall. Despite the pallor, when she looked at him her face was full of love.

She had never looked more beautiful.

A wave of vertigo hit Markham, but he forced himself to stay upright.

'The ladies and I are going to leave together,' Preston announced with a ghastly show of courtliness which turned Markham's blood to ice water. 'You will instruct your colleagues to let us leave unmolested.'

There was a restless movement from Noakes.

A crimson bead blossomed where the tip of Preston's knife flicked the delicate skin of Olivia's throat.

'We will leave together,' the architect repeated with no variation of tone. '*And you will let us.*'

Markham raised his hands palm upwards in a gesture of surrender. Looking at Noakes, he gave the silent command, stand down. The two policemen pressed themselves acquiescently against the right-hand wall of the vault. Alex Sharpe moaned and sobbed incoherently, oblivious to what was passing around him.

The architect nodded to Cynthia. Mutely, she edged towards the entrance to the vault. Tossing an auburn lock out of his eyes in a boyish gesture so horribly at variance with his true nature, Preston advanced with Olivia clasped tight. Watching his elegant white hands, with the long tapering fingers, Markham had a sudden shocking vision of them snaking like talons around a child's throat, squeezing and squeezing...

Wait for us! We're all here! Don't leave us in the dark!

It was the piercing scream of a child.

The colour drained from Preston's face. He jerked backwards as if he had been shot, dropping the knife with a clatter.

Markham sprang like a tiger, catching the architect off balance and sending him crashing to the ground. Dimly he was aware of Noakes joining the fray.

'Cuff him with the rope, for God's sake, Noakesy!'

'On it, sir!' wheezed the DC, looking down at the writhing figure on the ground with an expression of grim satisfaction.

Markham spun round and caught a fainting Olivia in his arms. 'It's all right, I've got you now,' he murmured tenderly, turning her away from the spectacle of Preston trussed like a turkey but still spitting defiance at Noakes amidst fierce kicks and struggles. Cynthia, meanwhile, stood rooted to the spot as though turned to stone.

It was over.

Falling snow swirled round the convoy parked in front of St Mary's, thick flakes slapping against windscreens and clinging to the tops of vehicles. Uniforms, paramedics and SOCOs stood in a gaggle, stamping feet and clapping hands together, their tracks criss-crossing the white tablecloth which covered the school forecourt.

The DI and Noakes sat quietly in the squad car against a background of wailing sirens and the screech of tyres, shut off from the hubbub as though in an airlock.

Markham had no clear recollection of making it back to the car. He looked around him in bewilderment, vision blurring at the edges, as Noakes thumped and cursed the refractory heater.

'*Olivia,*' he said groggily, '*don't leave me.*'

Noakes spoke gently as though to a child. 'No need to worry, Guv, Olivia's in safe hands. The medics are checking her over. We'll have to see, but she looked OK to me, so maybe it's just shock.' He looked at Markham with an expression of concern and put a hand on his arm. 'You could do with a once-over as well. You took quite a knock back there when Preston lashed out. Might be concussion.'

Markham shook his head. The wooziness was subsiding, though his whole body was tingling as though he was on fire. With shaking hands, he wound down the window and stuck his head out, holding his face up gratefully to the frosty air.

'I'm OK, Noakesy,' he said, eventually retreating to the steamy fug of the interior.

Mercifully, the world seemed to have stopped tilting and the roaring in his head had subsided to a dull throb. 'C'mon,' he prompted, gesturing at the walkie-talkie in the DS's hand, 'what gives?'

'Well, if you're sure, sir,' replied Noakes doubtfully. 'HQ wants Woodcourt interviewed as soon as possible.' He pulled a sour face. 'Nothing we can use at a trial, obviously, but gives us a chance of smashing the paedophile ring.'

'Where've they got him?' Markham asked wearily.

'The Newman,' was the glum response.

'Right, let's get over there. You can drive.'

The drive to the Newman Hospital, a high-security facility situated behind Bromgrove General, later seemed to Markham to possess the quality of a prolonged fugue. Neither man spoke, although Noakes shot furtive glances at his boss from time to time as though Markham was a casualty in triage.

The dream-like feeling of being in an airlock persisted as they passed though the booking procedures at reception before traversing endless sliding doors and corridors fitted with cameras. In this hermetically-sealed, rubber-soled universe, the DI felt mysteriously detached from his surroundings, as though insulated from reality by an invisible wall of plexiglass. He also felt a paralyzing sense of misery; despite the acres of glass and glimpses of brightly-coloured day rooms, there was no disguising the rancid whiff of fear and suspicion which – to his overwrought imagination – seemed to hang in the air like a deadly gas. The further they penetrated into this wracked world with its swivelling lenses, that had to have wide awake eyes upon it twenty-four hours round the clock, the stronger his wish to breathe fresh air. Beneath the pervading scent of pine disinfectant, it was all hopelessness and sweat. Crossing into the section marked *Forensic*, lined on both sides with heavy locked doors bisected by louvered panels, he felt needle-sharp prickles all over his skin as though caught in the crosshairs of a thousand malignant gazes. Judging by Noakes's unusually alert bearing, it was clear the DS shared his discomfort.

At last they arrived at what appeared to be a heavily fortified nursing station. A lean sandy-haired man whose badge proclaimed him to be Dr McGrath shook hands.

'You'll not get much sense out of the patient, gentlemen,' he said resignedly.

'You don't think he could be shamming?' demanded Noakes bluntly.

'If it's an act, then he's the best I've ever seen.' The psychiatrist smiled wanly. 'No, I would say acute paranoia and possibly schizophrenia. At a guess, he's been suffering delusions and hallucinations for some time.'

'Did a bloody good job of fooling us,' growled Noakes.

Dr McGrath sighed. 'It's likely he set up mental blocks to protect himself from the memory of what he did to those poor children.'

The terrified stares. The screams.

'I would imagine the dissociation enabled him to go on functioning as a priest, but gradually the parameters of his personality came apart.'

Behold, Myself and Heaven, And Hell.

Markham became aware that Dr McGrath was examining him narrowly.

'I gather you've just come from a major incident, Inspector. Can I arrange some refreshment?'

'Thank you, sir, but we'd better see Woodcourt straight away.'

'As you wish. Mike,' the doctor turned to a brawny orderly, 'can you please take the officers to the interview room?'

'Where'll you be?' Noakes asked suspiciously.

'Behind the two-way mirror, Detective, following the interview from next door.'

When they entered the interview room, Woodcourt was

slumped at a formica table rocking backwards and forwards and muttering to himself, his hands handcuffed and attached to a belly chain. Another warder, a giant of a man, sat impassively next to him.

Markham and Noakes slipped into chairs on the other side of the table.

Gradually, Woodcourt became sensible of their presence and the facile, running babble ceased.

He looked up at Markham and a secretive, sly expression stole over the ravaged features.

'They've got me in a living grave now ... but I spit on them and always will.'

It was the face of a snared animal with no resemblance to the suave cleric of their previous encounters. The contrast was shocking. Even Noakes was at a loss, the furious accusations dying on his lips as Woodcourt, with a look of low cunning, alternately wheedled and cursed. As he listened, Markham felt perspiration pooling in the small of his back and noticed that Noakes's face was as bleached as his shirt. The warder, meanwhile, did not move a muscle.

There was evil squatting there in the room with them like a toad, thought Markham. Like something foul and misshapen. All his senses screamed at him to get out.

He met Noakes's eye. *Nothing for us here.*

Suddenly, Woodcourt lunged. Steel fingers closed around Markham's wrist and yanked him across the table. For a moment, the maniac's breath was hot and fetid on his face. Then the attendant was on his feet, forcing Woodcourt back into his chair.

'*Mors janua vitae... Fiat voluntas tua, sicut in caelo et in terra.*' His mind was evidently wandering to his old life, for he continued to jabber in Latin, without appearing conscious of their presence otherwise than as a part of his vision, beckoning to Markham as to an altar boy. Tears stung Markham's eyes at the thought of all those innocents who had proudly served the canon's Mass, unconscious that the paths of glory led but to the grave.

Blindly, the DI rose to his feet and jerked his head at Noakes. *We're leaving.*

At that moment, the door of the interview room crashed open and, before anyone had time to react, a tall, bronzed man hurled himself at Woodcourt. It was all over so quickly, that Markham did not realize Woodcourt had been stabbed until he saw blood pumping from his chest.

'That's for Jonny, you fucking child killer!'

Two attendants appeared in the doorway, but Markham shouted, 'Get back, he has a weapon!'

Woodcourt looked steadily at his attacker with an expression which Markham later identified as gratitude. Then, to the horror of all who witnessed it, he emitted a high, snickering laugh which shook him like a paroxysm, making the tears roll down his cheeks and shaking his mortally wounded body with its mirthful abandon. Just as suddenly as the laughter had started, it stopped. The hair on the back of Markham's neck stood up as Woodcourt gasped in horror, gesticulating wildly with his bound hands at someone only he could see.

'So, you've come for me! Don't let me burn … anything but that!' The despair in his voice was so powerful, that no-one moved or spoke. Then his eyes rolled back in his head, his body spasmed, and he fell to the floor.

Markham looked across Woodcourt's corpse at the father of Jonny Warr.

Justice had been done.

'It was surely the best outcome, Inspector.'

Markham and Noakes sat drinking coffee at the conference table in Dr McGrath's well-appointed office. To Markham's relief, it was well away from the wards and looked onto a large open area free of buildings. Screams of demented fury, wild lamentations and howls of rage had pursued them down the corridors in the aftermath of Woodcourt's death, as though a legion of deranged souls – though unable to see what had transpired – somehow knew that one of their number was gone. The comparative silence of the office made his ears ring.

'What was all that stuff about someone coming for him?' asked Noakes. 'Gave me a right turn that did.'

'Ah, that was part of his psychosis, Detective,' answered the psychiatrist. 'He continually behaved as though speaking to an invisible presence or answering hallucinatory voices. Sometimes he punched the wall as though in a rage with these imaginary characters. Most of what he said was incomprehensible gibberish, but latterly he kept shielding his eyes from some unbearable sight—'

'One of his victims, perhaps,' interjected Markham quietly.

'Quite possibly he was haunted by the remembrance of his crimes. When your colleagues first brought him in, he was ranting at someone he called Master. Of course, such behaviour is typical of a psychotic in florid mode and he decompensated very quickly, but I had the feeling this was a real person.' Dr McGrath appeared to weigh his words. 'Someone whose death triggered overwhelming feelings of guilt and abandonment.'

Markham thought back to Steve Sinnott's revelations. Sir Philip Soames had *stuck to Woodcourt through thick and thin otherwise he'd have been out on his ear.* They shared an unbreakable bond. A bond forged in blood. But later, according to Alex Sharpe, the conspirators had argued and the bond was torn asunder.

'He kept screaming the same words over and over. "Why did you fall away from the true path? Why did you force me to give you up?"' The psychiatrist observed Markham closely. 'I can see by your expression that these words mean something to you, Inspector.'

'They do indeed, Dr McGrath,' replied Markham gravely.

Sir Philip Soames was another victim to add to Preston's tally. Presumably Woodcourt had agreed that he would have to be sacrificed. In all likelihood, the loss of his long-time friend and fellow occultist tipped him into madness.

'At the end, the patient's mania centred on an angel hauling a millstone attached to a chain.'

There was a prolonged silence eventually broken by Noakes.

'He should have been dragged to court to face the families,' he said flatly.

'Edward Preston faces a whole life sentence and Cynthia Gibson will at the very least go down as an accessory. There will be some closure.' Markham's tone was mild as if he too felt cheated. He turned to Dr McGrath. 'We'll be requesting a clinical assessment of Woodcourt's killer.'

'I'd like to shake his hand,' muttered Noakes.

'Then there's the chain of events which enabled him to breach hospital security,' continued Markham, ignoring the interruption.

'An investigation is already underway, Inspector. I suspect we'll find he had help from someone on the inside ... a relative of one of the victims...'

Markham nodded, his thoughts resting compassionately on Jonny Warr's avenging father.

Whoever kills a human being, it is as though he has destroyed the world.

If only the worlds of Dick Woodcourt and the lost boys had never met.

'C'mon, Noakes.' Markham signalled to the DC. 'Time to head back to base.'

Bromgrove Police Station resembled an anthill, with uniforms scurrying in all directions like demented termites. Clearly a full-scale operation was now underway to amalgamate cold cases involving missing children and the St Mary's murders.

Markham spotted Barry Lynch, the slab-faced PLO, preening on the sidelines.

'Oh God, that's all I need,' he groaned to Noakes. 'That self-important twerp muscling in for a few soundbites.'

'Bandits at six o'clock,' was the DS's muttered rejoinder.

'*Markham, Noakes!* Excellent work!'

DCI Sidney bore down on them in full dress uniform, beaming from ear to ear.

'The DCC will be along shortly to congratulate us in person.'

Markham noted the DCI's use of the first-person plural. Smashing a paedophile ring while delivering a massive boost to Bromgrove's clear-up statistics was PR nirvana. Natural enough, he supposed, for his superiors to want a slice of the action. Evidently, Sidney's previous instructions to jettison Woodcourt as a suspect clashed with his cherished persona of all-wise commander and could therefore be conveniently expunged from the record.

Markham decided he was more than happy to play second fiddle. All that mattered was justice for the victims of Woodcourt, Preston and Soames.

Sidney was pontificating as though addressing a police conference. Dimly, Markham registered the usual tropes: '…tragedy of mental illness … abuse of digital technology … distortion of personality … social breakdown…'

So, Sidney was going to spin this decades-old cover-up as some kind of collective psychosexual aberration. *Good luck with that!*

Suddenly, Markham realized he didn't care. The great and the powerful always had their partisans. He and Noakes would do their job regardless, without fear or favour.

Whoever saves a man, it is as though he has saved the world.

Lynch was hovering with various underlings.

'If I could just have a line for the journos, sir,' he said obsequiously to the DCI.

Sidney clapped Lynch on the shoulder in an unprecedented display of bonhomie. 'Just tell them we are *delighted* with developments at this stage, Barry. Absolutely *delighted*.' He turned to Markham, all solicitude, and enquired. 'Do you feel up to fielding questions from the press, Inspector?'

Markham recognized his cue.

'If it's all right, I'd far rather leave that to you, sir,' he murmured. 'I'm still a bit off balance, to tell the truth... I'd prefer to get off to the hospital ... check on Olivia.'

'*Naturally, naturally.*' The DCI was positively effusive, his earlier invective against ill-advised liaisons quite forgotten.

An attractive young woman from the media office sashayed towards them, holding a stack of glossy press releases. Sidney's eyes gleamed.

'Right, Markham, you and Noakes,' he inclined graciously in the DS's direction, 'can get off now.' He stroked his pips before adding, in an ebullition of goodwill, 'The gentlemen of the press must wait a bit longer for their exclusive.' The entourage tittered dutifully as he swept out of the station foyer, bobbing in his wake like a flotilla.

'Think we got off lightly there, Noakes.' Markham sagged with relief.

The DS made a sound that was somewhere between a guffaw and a growl.

Markham hesitated, but Noakes got there first.

'Of course I'm coming to the hospital with you, Guv. But perhaps we should have a wash and brush-up first.' He gestured theatrically at their dishevelled appearance. 'Don't want your girlfriend keeling over again at the sight of us!'

The casual words held a world of understanding. No need for anything more. Without a backward look at the excited bustle around them, the two men headed for the locker room.

Epilogue

New Year's Eve. The Sweepstakes.

Markham sprawled lazily in his favourite overstuffed armchair, savouring the comforting warmth of a log fire crackling in the hearth.

It doesn't get much better than this, he thought, watching Olivia who sat cross-legged at his feet perusing a heavily blotted letter.

'What news of your little scallywags?' he enquired.

'Having a wonderful time by all accounts.' She grinned. 'There's a postscript from Julian – by way of corrective to Nat's more colourful assertions!'

Markham gazed at the fire ruminatively. 'Extraordinary that O'Keefe came up trumps like that.'

'Well, those two desperately needed a happy family atmosphere and that's what they'll get on his sister's farm. Lots of fresh air and fun ... and four other rascals to play with over the holidays.'

'O'Keefe was a suspect at one point, you know.' Markham laughed at the expression on Olivia's face. 'Don't look like that, sweetheart, virtually everyone was.'

'Not Cynthia, though.' Olivia's voice was full of pain. Her naturally open and trusting disposition had taken a terrible blow when the full extent of Cynthia Gibson's involvement finally became clear.

Markham ached to comfort her. 'Cynthia was delusional, totally in thrall to Preston. That's how it started.'

'But she became an abuser, Gil. *My old friend an abuser!*'

It was a whisper.

'Yes, dearest.' There was no point sugar-coating it. 'Female paedophiles are rare, but Cynthia was more than a spectator. As she said in her confession, "Wherever he has gone, I have gone."'

'D'you think she was planning to draw me into it, Gil? To *turn* me?'

Markham put his hands on her shoulders, kneading them in a soothing rhythm.

'"When you look into an abyss, the abyss also looks into you." That might have been her plan, yes, but I don't think we'll ever know for sure. Maybe, at some subconscious level, she wanted to bring it to an end ... needed your strength to help her break free.'

Olivia gave him a look of gratitude. 'She didn't know about you being a policeman, though. That was a real shock.'

'Certainly the timing of your arrival couldn't have been worse from Preston's point of view,' Markham observed.

'At least she had no part in the killings. That's some comfort.'

Gesturing at another letter lying on the hearth rug, Olivia added in more cheerful tones, 'That was a lovely letter from your old mentor.'

'Yes. I reckon Mike Bamber thought about those boys every day, and the terrible way they had to go. As he says, at least they're free now and the parents have some sort of closure.'

'What will happen to Jonny Warr's dad?' Olivia asked anxiously. 'When Noakes said he'd done us all a favour, I couldn't help agreeing.'

'It'll probably be manslaughter on the grounds of diminished responsibility and a probation order. I can't imagine any judge sending the poor man to prison.'

Suddenly, Olivia gave a convulsive shudder and seemed to shrink into herself.

'What is it, my love?' Markham asked gently.

His girlfriend had turned very pale.

'I still can't forget how he looked when he grabbed me in the corridor at St Mary's,' she said faintly.

No need to ask who *he* was.

'One minute all normal and smiling.... The next, it was like a wolf's face ... the mouth all stretched ... like he was going to bite me... *The hatred...*'

Markham took both Olivia's hands in his.

'Leave him to rot in his little room. He'll never breathe free air again.' Looking deep into his lover's eyes, he added, 'The conspirators marched hand in hand to hell, but we must hope for better things.'

The shadow cleared. '"This truth within thy mind rehearse, That in a boundless universe, Is boundless better, boundless worse,"' Olivia quoted dreamily.

Markham chuckled. 'Trust an English teacher to cap my eloquence with Tennyson!'

Nestling closer to him, Olivia looked up at the chiselled profile of this most unlikely policeman as he gazed thoughtfully into the flames.

'I've felt Georgina Hamilton quite close to me in the last few days,' he said eventually. 'Her friend Joan – you remember, the cook from St Mary's – said the same after the funeral. Like a cloud had lifted from her shoulders and she knew Georgina was at peace.'

'Was Georgina murdered, then, Gil?' Olivia asked softly.

'Oh yes, not a doubt of it now. She had cancer, but I never believed the theory that she'd decided to end it all. Turns out Alex Sharpe had poured out his soul in a diary which must somehow have come into Woodcourt's possession, because Nat came across him burning documents one night. I think Georgina stumbled across something incriminating – a scrap of paper with names – and was planning to get in touch with me when she was silenced by Woodcourt after he had followed her home... It struck me at the time that the way the body was positioned suggested some lingering regard for the victim.'

A tremor rippled across Markham's face, but his voice was

steady. 'What exactly happened will likely never be known. Georgina was such a *decent* woman – that British sense of fair play. I think she let Woodcourt into the apartment hoping he could explain everything. By the time she realized the danger, it was too late.'

'What about the Diazepam? Weren't there tablets next to her when you found her?'

Markham's face was sombre. 'All part of Woodcourt's 'killing kit' according to Alex Sharpe. He always had a supply on him. Chloral hydrate too.'

'How *horrible*! Masquerading as a holy man when all the time...'

There was a long silence. Markham recalled the great copper basin he and Noakes had found in the undercroft when Woodcourt was finally trapped, presumably designed to catch Julian's blood as his throat was cut. He knew this was one detail he would never share with Olivia.

'Well, we must leave him to a greater power!' exclaimed Markham at last. 'The avenging angel came for him in the end. Perhaps now Irene Hummles and all the other poor innocents can rest in peace.'

'That cry we heard in the grottoes, Gil...' Olivia said tentatively, 'the child's scream...We all heard it.' Her face was pensive. 'D'you think it was a ghost ... one of the murdered children?'

Markham chose his words carefully. 'It certainly felt like someone was there with us,' he answered. 'I think it must have been a benign presence trying to shine a light in the darkness. It stopped a killer in his tracks, so you could say love had the last word. If the souls of those poor waifs were wandering abroad, somehow they've come home now.'

Olivia shivered. 'All the time I was at St Mary's, it felt as though I was being watched and followed. As though the grounds were haunted.'

Markham forbore to comment that the shadowy presences Olivia had sensed flitting about were not necessarily spectral.

The work of dismantling the paedophile network had just begun, but the conspirators no doubt had eyes and ears everywhere. It was a sobering thought.

Olivia's voice caught on a sob. 'I can't erase that image of Woodcourt digging in the little school cemetery. *Reburying the victims.* As if those poor children were being killed again. As if they would never stop being killed. In my mind, I'm there, shouting at him to stop, to let them go.'

'We'll lay flowers, my love,' said Markham's quiet voice, 'and say goodbye properly.'

Olivia's face brightened at the thought of a memorial, her thoughts diverted from darker channels.

'Poetic justice that Sir Philip Soames met his end at Preston's hands, wasn't it?' she said musingly.

'It was indeed,' replied Markham with grim satisfaction.

'What about Alex Sharpe?'

Markham sighed. 'He'll be tried as an accessory, the snivelling wretch. The wife's a basket case. She almost certainly suspected what had happened to Irene Hummles, but anaesthetized herself with drink and prescription medication.'

There was another silence. How damnably clever Preston had been, planting the idea that his deputy had seen the matron leave St Mary's on the day she had vanished. Taking that witness statement at face value had cost lives. Privately, Markham cursed the incompetence and vital missed opportunities. At least lessons had been learned, so *Operation Acacia* stood some chance of excising the evil which had hidden deeply in the recesses of the school organism like a rogue synapse of cells that cried out to be cauterized.

'Enough of this!' Olivia jumped to her feet and disappeared into Markham's galley kitchen, returning with a bottle and two glasses. 'We're going to banish all the horrors for tonight and look to the future,' she said lovingly.

'I'll drink to that!'

The little fire sputtered and crackled in the hearth.

Clinking glasses, the lovers looked into the flames and traced their castles in the air.

The shadows of the past receded and the pilot light of their love burned strong and steady. Whatever the next day brought, they would face it together.